ABOUT THE AUTHOR

Janet Gover grew up in outback Australia, surrounded by wide open spaces, horses ... and many, many books.

When her cat lets her actually sit in her chair, she writes stories of strong women, rural communities and falling in love. Her novel *Little Girl Lost* won the Epic Romantic Novel of the Year Award presented by the Romantic Novelists' Association in the UK, and she has won or been shortlisted for awards in Australia and the USA.

As Juliet Bell, in collaboration with Alison May, she rewrites misunderstood classic fiction, with an emphasis on heroes who are not so heroic.

Her favourite food is tomato. She spends too much time playing silly computer games, and is an enthusiastic, if not always successful, cook.

Janet loves to hear from readers—so do drop her a line.

janetgover.com

facebook.com/janetgoverbooks

Twitter: @janet_gover

JANET GOVER

The Library at WAGTAIL RIDGE

FICTION
HQ

First Published 2022
First Australian Paperback Edition 2022
ISBN 9781867230052

Published by
HQ Fiction
An imprint of Harlequin Enterprises (Australia) Pty Limited (ABN 47 001 180 918), a subsidiary of HarperCollins Publishers Australia Pty Limited (ABN 36 009 913 517)
Level 13, 201 Elizabeth St
SYDNEY NSW 2000
AUSTRALIA

A catalogue record for this book is available from the National Library of Australia
www.librariesaustralia.nla.gov.au

Printed and bound in Australia by McPherson's Printing Group

MIX
Paper | Supporting responsible forestry
FSC® C001695

This book is for all the lonely children who found friends and adventure and wonder between the pages of a book, and for all the librarians who helped them do it.

PROLOGUE

Luca's hand looked incredibly frail as she reached for the door handle. Her fingers wrapped around the frosty metal, but she felt nothing. She gripped as tightly as she was able, twisted and pulled. The newly constructed door opened smoothly and she silently blessed her small town. She hadn't been able to open the big front doors of her shed for some time now. Her friends had spent an entire day installing this smaller door so she could return to the place that was the whole world to her.

Inside the shed it was quite cold, but Luca was well rugged up. It was dark too, despite the beams of winter sunlight spearing through the cracks and holes in the timber walls. Luca didn't need much light. She knew every inch of the shed and the vehicle stored in it as well as she knew her own kitchen. Until recent weeks, she had spent far more time here, sorting the contents not only of the truck, but of the boxes stored on the shelves that lined the back wall of the shed. She couldn't read the labels in the darkness, but she didn't need to. The lower shelves were all boxes of school textbooks, maths and English and history ready for the next intake of students who needed them. The boxes on the second shelf held musical instruments and sports equipment. Close to the door were a couple of boxes of fabric and yarn. The art materials box was empty, but it always was. Paper and paint and crayons were always in high demand.

She crossed to the truck and laid her fragile hand against its familiar and comforting shape. Her bones were as brittle as birds' wings. Her skin was almost translucent, exposing a network of blue veins. Luca wasn't as old as her hands looked, but that was what illness did to a body. There was nothing she could do to stop the tremor in the hands that had once driven this truck through the bush or repaired a delicate book … or held a child.

She gently caressed the letters painted on the side of the truck. They had faded a little and the layer of red dust made them dull, but Luca felt the same passion she had always felt for this wonderland that had given her so much joy. She felt a welcome sense of familiarity, almost like coming home, as she opened the door set in the side of the truck. The stairs were folded safely away and she opened the panels below the door and took hold of the metal frame. Her strength was barely up to it but finally the steps slid into place with a familiar and satisfying click. That sound had always heralded the start of a new and exciting journey, and not just for her.

Luca gripped the rail firmly as she climbed into the interior of the truck. The lights came on at the touch of a switch. She had known they would. One of her friends would have made sure everything was ready for her to make this last visit to the library. She was exhausted by the time she slid into the chair behind the small desk bolted to the wall. Walking from the house to the shed had sapped what little energy she was still able to muster. She would have to rest a few minutes before she could do what she had come to do.

Closing her eyes, Luca took a deep breath. Despite all these weeks left idle in the shed, the mobile library had retained all its magic. That magic came from the books that lined the walls. Even with her eyes closed, she could see each one of them in its proper place on the metal shelves. She loved them all, but some were special.

The rear wall was given over to the children's collection, from books with colourful numbers and letters to learn, to Dr Seuss and *Little Grey Rabbit*. Luca could once have recited the words of all her favourites. The books for the older kids resided in the higher shelves. Pride of place in the middle went to the brumbies—white horses roughly sketched against a mountain backdrop. She must have read them all a dozen times over the years, and had always planned to read them again. She probably didn't have enough time now.

On the left wall of the library, the top three shelves held a well-worn cluster of romance novels. She always smiled when she saw a male reader surreptitiously slide one of those from the shelves when he thought no-one was watching. She always kept the book between two meaty crime novels as she checked it out. She'd often wondered what the slightly embarrassed romance fans would have said if they knew how many other hatted and booted stockmen and farmers had a soft spot for a happy ever after.

The single poetry shelf had attracted fewer visitors, but her bush poets had been eager, and the turnover had always been high.

She could still hear the voices. And see the eager faces. *Have you got any more books by this author? Thank you for suggesting this; it was great. I cried as I read the last chapter … Fascinating … Interesting … Wonderful.*

Yes—full of wonder. Those were the words she used when she talked about her little mobile library. A magical place of dreams and wonder for young and old alike. Even after both she and the library were no longer 'official' she had kept those dreams alive for herself and for readers in the small towns that had been forgotten or left behind. So many books. So many readers. So many memories. But not one of them as important as what she was about to do.

Luca picked up the tote bag she'd brought from the house. She carefully laid the writing paper, pen and envelopes on the desk. Then she pulled a photograph in a silver frame from the bag and placed it where she could see it. She looked at it for a long time. Her own face was much changed from that of the young woman in the photograph. She barely recognised herself now. The child would be a young woman today, but Luca would still know her. She was the reason Luca had made the effort to come all the way to the library today. She could have done this in the house and saved herself both the physical and emotional journey, but so much of her life had been lived within these walls that she couldn't imagine being anywhere else.

The first letter was easy to write, despite the tremor in her hand. The recipient had received detailed instructions months ago. He knew what she wanted and he would do it.

But the second one …

Her hand hovered over the white sheet. She had written this letter in her mind so many times over the past couple of years, and while the words had been different each time, every one of them had said the same thing—words that were so important they might begin a journey of discovery, or lay waste to her best hope. She would never know which.

Luca took a deep breath and looked once more at the photograph. She didn't need the doctors to tell her she had very little time left. She could only hope that when she was gone, her words would be read by that little girl.

She picked up a pen.

My Darling Daughter …

CHAPTER 1

Lou unchained her bike from the stand and wheeled it to the cycle path. A few seconds later she was moving swiftly away from the university, her tiny office and the stack of marked essays ready to go back to their writers. The cycleway curved down towards the Lane Cove River and her heart lifted as she was surrounded by trees. She loved these few minutes without brick walls or fences. She loved the feeling of openness, the towering gums and the air that was a little less polluted by car exhaust and big city smog.

She was sweating in the midsummer heat and moving fast as she dropped down onto Riverside Drive. At this time of day there weren't many cars and she could almost convince herself that she was already on holiday. Just two weeks to the end of the term, and then she was taking a well-earned break. No classrooms, no students, no lectures and no walls. Just hiking boots, a tent and the mountains. With a loud whoop, she steered her bike around the next corner, the river glinting through the trees below her. She wasn't entirely sure what a master's degree in environmental science was going to do for her job prospects. When she'd chosen the course, it seemed to suggest travel, the possibility of mixing city excitement with her love of the bush. So far, beyond the tutoring work she'd been doing, she hadn't thought too hard about it. There was still plenty of time for her to make that decision.

Lou loved Sydney. She liked the energy and the excitement. She loved the way the harbour and the Opera House looked at sunrise and the fireworks on the bridge at New Year's Eve. But still there were times when all she wanted was to get away from the noise and the people. Between school and uni, she'd taken a year off to go fruit picking in Victoria. It was back-breaking work, but she'd never been happier than labouring under the open skies and getting dirt under her fingernails. She was a city girl, born and raised—well, raised at least. She'd never really understood why the bush called to her like it did, but there was something to be said for feeling comfortable in both worlds.

The boathouse came into view ahead of her. She lifted herself off the seat and pushed hard, feeling the bite in her leg muscles as she built up more speed for the sweep around the big curve in the river then up past the picnic area and across Delhi Road. She was in suburbia now, but it was the best suburbia she could imagine. She knew how lucky she was to have been brought up here, where the homes overlooked the river. There were ample trees and while the city was all around them, it didn't intrude too much.

Lou turned up the sloping driveway of her parents' home, a big white house half hidden among the trees. She braked and stored the bike in the open garage next to her father's car. It seemed early for him to be home, but she wasn't sure. She'd only recently moved from uni accommodation back to her parents' house, gladly accepting their offer of help. She didn't make a lot of money from her few hours tutoring and marking essays each week, and was saving for her escape to the bush.

'I'm home,' she called as she walked through the front door, wiping the sweat from her face. 'I'll just have a quick shower.' She didn't wait for an answer as she headed upstairs.

The house was unusually quiet when she came back down ten minutes later, her short blonde hair still damp. According to her watch, it was time for the ABC news. Her parents always watched the news. She put her head through into the living room, but the TV was off and her parents weren't there. She found them sitting at the oak kitchen table, staring at a white envelope that lay between them. They had been talking softly but stopped as she walked into the room.

Her mother's brown eyes were troubled. Deep lines surrounded them, and Lou was struck for the first time by the knowledge that her parents were no longer young. They'd never been as young as her schoolfriends' parents, but now both her mother and her father suddenly looked old.

'Mum? Dad? What is it?'

'This came for you today,' her father said, pushing the envelope towards her.

Lou sat down and picked it up. In the top corner, the return address was a lawyer's office in the city. Lou had no idea what it might be, but her parents' faces told her they knew only too well.

'What is it?'

'That law office,' her father said with a voice devoid of all expression. 'It's the one that handled your adoption.'

'Oh.' Lou dropped the envelope back onto the table as if it was burning her fingers. She'd always known she was adopted. Her parents, for that's what they were regardless of biology, had told her as soon as she was old enough to understand. She'd never really thought much about it. She had parents who loved her. Wasn't that what family was supposed to be? And if kids at school had been mean and teased her when she was younger—well, kids could be cruel. It didn't matter to her.

'What could they be writing to me about?'

'Maybe …' Her mother's lips trembled. 'Maybe it's your birth parents trying to find you.'

'No. It was a closed adoption. That can't happen. Can it?' She looked to her father for reassurance.

'It could. We always made it clear we were happy to have your birth parents in your life. It was their decision to remain anonymous.' His voice was odd. Not exactly angry. He sounded almost afraid. That wasn't right. Her father was the strongest man she knew. He had protected her smaller self from spiders and bullies and dark nights. Also dragons, ghosts and boogie men hiding under her bed. He was fearless about such matters. But this … this was obviously different.

'You know that whatever is in that envelope, it's not going to change anything. You are my mum and my dad and I love you. Whoever it was that gave birth to me and gave me away, they are not my parents and they never will be.'

Lou was a little afraid she was protesting too much. But it was true. She really didn't care about her biological parents. Why should she? She didn't know them. And she probably didn't want to; especially if they were going to disturb her comfortable and happy life and upset the parents she loved. She picked up the envelope. Part of her was tempted to just throw it in the bin. She didn't have to read it. But if she threw it away, there'd probably be another one next week. Whatever it contained, she had to deal with it. She wasn't a kid any more. Her father couldn't scare this monster away.

She turned the envelope over and opened it.

The letter was only a few paragraphs. She read it, then read it again. Ought she feel something? Because she didn't.

'She's dead.'

'Your birth mother?' Her father's voice was gentle.

'Yes.'

'Oh, Lou, I'm sorry.' A familiar comforting hand was laid over hers.

'Why, Mum? I never knew her. Why should you be sorry? I'm not.'

'But you did know her. You lived with her for more than two years. You were nearly three when you came to us.'

'But I don't remember her. Nothing at all. I can't picture her face or the sound of her voice. This letter is about someone I don't know.'

Her father, as always, was the practical one. 'What are you going to do?'

'The letter asks me to go and meet the lawyers. Apparently there's some sort of legacy for me.'

'What?'

'They don't say. I guess I'll go. If there's a bit of money, it can go towards my holiday. Or help me get set up when I find a job. I may as well take it. She's never done anything else for me.'

'She gave birth to you.' The sadness in her mum's voice was heartbreaking.

Lou stood up and walked around the table to hug the woman who had raised her. 'Maybe, but the best thing she ever did for me was to give me to you.'

The office of Curtis and Moore Lawyers was on the seventh floor of a glass office tower a few minutes' walk from Chatswood station. Lou told herself that the unease she felt as she rode the lift was simply because she didn't like the busy shopping district or tall buildings. Or lifts. Or lawyers. It had nothing to do with the contents of the letter that lay in the bottom of her bag.

Mr Ashley Curtis, the man who had signed the letter, rose to greet her as the receptionist showed her into his office.

'Please sit down, Miss Taylor. Would you like some coffee?'

'No.' She hadn't meant that to sound as abrupt as it had, but she was holding on to her composure pretty tightly and didn't have the emotional strength for pleasantries. She shouldn't feel like this. The death of a woman she didn't know should mean nothing to her, but it did. She'd stayed awake late into the night, trying hard to remember something, anything, of the first three years of her life. Before the Taylors adopted her. There were no memories to haunt her, but this was still proving a lot harder than she had thought.

'Of course. Shall I get straight to business?'

'Did you know my—my biological mother?'

'No. We never met. This firm acted on her behalf during your adoption. That was before my time, of course. The firm has held her instructions for some years. We received news of her death several months ago and opened those instructions.'

'Months ago …'

'Her instructions were to have the will clear probate before we contacted you. This we have done. Her estate is now yours. It includes a cottage in a town called Wagtail Ridge in the Upper Hunter Valley, household fittings, a vehicle and personal possessions. There is a small amount of money in the bank.'

Lou held a hand up, shaking her head. 'Stop. I don't want to know about … this … person. She deserted me when I was a child. I have no memories of her. I want nothing from her.'

'Be that as it may, you are her beneficiary and you are now the owner of her property.'

'Can you get rid of it for me?'

'Of course. I can sell it and, if you don't want the money, it can be donated to charity in your mother's name if you like.'

'My mother is Fiona Taylor.'

The lawyer nodded slowly and looked at the file on his desk. 'Miss Bonnet's instructions …'

'Miss …'

'Luca Bonnet. Our client.'

Luca Bonnet? It was the first time Lou had heard that name and the shock of it made her breath catch in her throat. Luca was her name too. Her middle name. She was Susan Luca Taylor, but she'd always been called Lou. She could never remember being called anything else. She'd never wanted to be called anything else.

Had her birth mother called her that?

She rose to her feet. She had to get away from this tiny office and this horrible building, and those files and the terrible threat in them. 'I'll be in touch when I've had some time to think.'

'Of course.' He rose to his feet to escort her from the office. 'But please do take these.' He held out a set of keys. 'They're for the property in Wagtail Ridge. The address is on the tag.'

Lou took them because arguing was suddenly too hard. She looked at the four keys attached to a slightly rusty keyring featuring what looked like a cheap souvenir. For the first time, she felt a spark of curiosity.

'How did she die?'

Mr Curtis looked uncomfortable. 'I'm sorry. I don't know. I'm sure I can find out. We must have the death certificate …' He turned as if to look for it, but Lou shook her head.

'It doesn't matter.'

'I am sorry for your loss.'

His words followed her as she walked towards the lift, hands deep in the pockets of her jacket where she could pretend they weren't shaking.

Sorry for your loss …

What loss? She hadn't lost a mother; her mother was at work as always.

But perhaps she had lost something else.

The house was silent when Lou got home. Her parents had offered to go with her to the lawyer's office or be there for her when she returned but she'd sent them to work as normal, assuring them there was nothing to be worried about. There was nothing difficult about this day, or this meeting or this news.

She dropped her bag in its usual spot on the table just inside the door, then walked through to the kitchen to get a bottle of water from the fridge. She was very conscious of the feel of the keyring in the pocket of her jeans as she walked out the back door and across the lawn. This block of land sloped quite steeply at the back, and long ago her father had installed a wooden bench there. As the vegetation around it had grown, the seat had become hidden from the view of anyone in the house. That same vegetation had also hidden the city. This had always been the spot where Lou came to think. And today she had a lot of thinking to do.

She leaned back, taking comfort from the familiar feel of the weathered wood against her back. This was her place. Her home. Her family. She had hopes and dreams and plans, none of which included a long-lost birth mother, a house in some small town or any other part of this legacy. That was just an annoyance she'd have to deal with. She could simply instruct the lawyer to get rid of everything. She'd take the money and that would be that.

Or would it? This wasn't just about the past—it was about the future too. Lou wondered how old her birth mother had been. It seemed likely that she had died young. And why? Was there something Lou needed to know about for her own future health? And what if she decided to have kids herself? She would need to know then.

A momentary and uncharacteristic anger flashed through her. Why did this have to happen now, just when she was getting ready for the next phase of her life? She didn't need this.

She closed her eyes and tried to calm her thoughts.

She was still there and still thinking more than an hour later, when her mother joined her.

'How did it go?'

Lou told her.

'So what are you going to do?'

'I don't know.'

Fiona was silent for a few moments. 'Yes, you do. You always know. Ever since you were a little girl, you have always known what you wanted.'

'But it's not just about me, Mum. There's you and Dad to think about too. I don't want any of this to worry either of you. Nothing is going to change our relationship.'

'I know that.'

'I was going to tell them to just sell everything, but I keep looking at this.' She pulled the keyring out of her pocket and handed it to Fiona.

'That's the Big Pineapple. I saw souvenirs like this when we went to Queensland on holidays. It was years ago. You must have been seven or eight.'

'I remember that trip. Maybe Luca Bonnet went there too. These are the keys to her house.'

'And?'

Just like that, she knew what she had to do. 'I need to go there. Just once. I'm not sure why or what I will do, but I have to. I can't have this hanging over me.'

'I think you're right. Do you want me or your father to come with you?'

'No. It'll be fine.' Lou said the words firmly, but she wasn't sure she'd convinced her mother. She certainly hadn't convinced herself. It probably wouldn't be fine, but this was something she had to do.

She'd always been happy being Lou Taylor. Now she had to decide what to do about being the daughter of Luca Bonnet.

CHAPTER 2

Keith Urban serenaded Lou as she drove into the small town of Wagtail Ridge. Country music for a country trip, although she'd always been a fan. She didn't look too closely at the town as she drove. She wasn't staying here. She'd make this one visit to satisfy her curiosity while uni was in recess for a month, and then she'd tell the lawyers to sell everything and she'd use the money to maybe take some more time off and travel to some of the wild places she'd always dreamed of visiting. Maybe Kakadu. Or even Antarctica, if there was enough money. That would be the best thing the woman called Luca would ever have done for her.

The GPS told her to turn left just past the war memorial, and then right again to reach the address she'd been given by the lawyers.

'You are now at your destination.'

She turned off both the annoying voice and the engine and stared at the house she apparently now owned. The small cottage sat on low wooden stumps and differed little from similar cottages in rural towns everywhere. The weatherboard walls were painted pale yellow, or at least a yellow made pale by years of exposure to the sun. The corrugated iron roof was a similarly faded red. The front of the cottage boasted a covered veranda, the curved timber at the roof line the only attempt to make the building in any way attractive or stylish.

A gravel drive ran down the side of the building to the back of the block, where a large wooden shed looked very much the worse for wear. This wasn't the sort of shed that people in Sydney brought home from the garden centre and erected in their backyards. This shed looked a hundred years old and as if it could hold a tonne of horse feed or a truck. Or both.

The house was slightly unkempt, but not as bad as she had expected. If Luca Bonnet had been dead for several months, someone must have been looking after it. The grass—it wasn't really lawn—had been cut and the mailbox wasn't overflowing with junk mail. The metal gate leading to the driveway was closed. She got out of the car to open it. Then stopped, as if hit by an electric shock.

She knew this place!

Something about the pattern of the cheap metal gate was familiar. She ran her fingers over the curved decorations on the top of the gate, trying to ignore the flaking paint and the rust. Trying to see it as it had once been—clean and newly painted white. She had always reached up to stroke that curve as she walked through the gate, as if it was some sort of magical portal.

Reached up? The gate was not even a metre high. But she knew she'd walked through this gate before, as a child who thought those cheap metal curves were beautiful.

That couldn't be right. She had no memories from before her adoption. She'd been two and a half years old when she went to live with her mum and dad. She remembered nothing before that. She'd read a paper that suggested people who claimed memories from their first three to five years were wrong. They were remembering the stories told by people who really did have memories of that time; older siblings, parents. Family. Her family—her real family—didn't know anything about those first two and a half years. No more than she did. There were no memories to share.

She glanced at the cottage again. It was the sort of house that had been built in the tens of thousands in rural towns throughout the country back in the day. It looked familiar because it was. She'd seen it in every small town she'd ever driven through. On every TV show or movie set in a small town. There were no memories here. Likewise that gate. It could have been in *Neighbours* or *McLeod's Daughters*. She really didn't remember it—she couldn't.

Lou pushed the gate open and marched up the stairs to the veranda. She pulled the keys from her bag, opened the door and stepped over the threshold without giving herself time to think about what she was doing.

After the brightness outside, it was very dark inside the cottage. Lou braced herself as she pulled back the curtains, but as the afternoon sun streamed through and the room slowly came into focus, nothing looked familiar. The living room was unremarkable. The walls were painted a plain cream and the furniture was well worn and perhaps a bit dusty. A thin layer of dust also covered the coffee table and the big television set that looked so old it might possibly be black and white. Lou tried not to look too closely at the personal items on the table and the sideboard. Instead she allowed herself to study the one truly remarkable thing about the room. The books.

Bookshelves lined every wall. There were books stacked on top of a wooden toy box under the window. More books sat on the coffee table. She looked into the hallway. It was also lined with overflowing bookshelves. So, she and her birth mother had at least one thing in common.

Lou peeped through another doorway and found the kitchen. She didn't go in. She might legally own this cottage, but she couldn't shake the feeling of being an intruder in someone else's home.

A noise in the back garden was the excuse she needed to leave. She backtracked, locking the front door behind her, and walked down the side of the house. The big old shed loomed in front of her, but as she reached the corner of the house, movement caught her eye. A half-grown black Labrador flung itself at her, tongue lolling from its mouth, tail wagging furiously.

'Ollie! Get down. Come here.'

The pup ignored the command and jumped up to put his extra large paws on Lou's skirt. She should have been annoyed, but the dog was so cute she couldn't be angry.

'I am so sorry. He's just a pup.' The man who hurried across the yard was almost as cute as his dog. He was average height and build, with sort of middling brown hair with a bit of wave. But there was nothing at all middling or average about his sky blue eyes and the cheeky grin that twisted the corner of his mouth.

He took Ollie by the collar and pulled him away from Lou. 'Ollie, sit down. That's better. Good boy.' He ruffled the pup's ears as the dog placed his rear end almost, but not quite, on the ground. The dog's eyes darted from Lou to his owner and back again and his tail didn't stop wagging. Clearly it wasn't going to take much to set him jumping again.

'I really am sorry.' The man looked to be a couple of years older than Lou, no more than twenty-five. His skin was tanned from outdoor work. 'He doesn't mean any harm. He'd possibly lick you to death, but that's about it.'

'He's very cute.'

'Yeah. He is. He's going to be a guide dog one day, aren't you, mate? But first you need to learn some manners.' The dog's pink tongue flashed as he licked his master's hand, leaving it wet and slobbery.

'I should introduce myself—but perhaps a handshake isn't what we're looking for now. I'm Jake Barnes.'

'I'm Lou Taylor.'

'I thought you might be. I'm so very sorry about Luca. She was a wonderful person. We all miss her very much.' His voice wavered as he spoke.

Lou wasn't sure what to say to that. She could hardly tell Jake that she didn't miss Luca at all, not when his own grief was so clear. 'Thank you.' It seemed the correct thing to say. 'Are you the one who's been looking after the place?'

'Yes. I should have said. I've been keeping the yard tidy. Checking in to see everything is all right with the house.'

'Thank you.' The puppy wandered off to sniff something interesting near the shed, and Lou absently watched him.

'Here.' Jake held out some keys. 'I guess you want these back.'

'Can you keep them a little longer? I've only just arrived and I'm not sure how long I'll be here. If I needed you to keep looking after the place, would you be able to do that?' She saw his eyes dart to the keys in his hand. 'I'll pay you, of course.'

'I can, and there's no need to pay me. Luca asked me to keep an eye on the place and I'm happy to do it.'

Did she ask you to keep an eye on me too? The thought leaped uninvited into Lou's head and she blinked twice in surprise. Where had that come from? She had barely met this man, and already she was suspecting him of something nefarious. Lou decided it was because the whole situation had her rattled. She kept the thought inside her head. She had no reason to vent her tension on Jake.

'Well. Thank you. I'm really not sure what I am going to do. All I know is that I have inherited a house which seems to be full of books.'

A slow smile spread over Jake's face. 'That's the overflow.'

'Overflow? What do you mean?'

'Take a look in the shed. You'll understand then. Come on, Ollie, time we left Miss Taylor to look around. If you need to find me, check the pub. I'm there most evenings.' He didn't tip his hat as he left, but Lou felt as if he had.

She half turned to watch Jake and Ollie leave. Their brief encounter hadn't made things any clearer for her, but that didn't stop her noticing that the joyful bounce and energy in Jake's walk very nearly matched that of his dog.

She fished the keys out of the pocket of her jeans, and found the one that fitted the padlock holding the big front doors of the shed closed. It wasn't a very strong lock. Perhaps people didn't need strong padlocks in Wagtail Ridge. The wooden doors were old, the timber weather-beaten, and there were a few cracks here and there in the walls. As well as a small, new-looking side door, other new timber showed where someone, Jake perhaps, had done some repairs. Whatever was in the shed, it had been looked after.

The double doors opened outward and needed a couple of hefty tugs to get them moving. Lou pulled one open, then went back for the other. As she grabbed it, she saw the vehicle. A truck? What had that to do with books?

When the second door was wide open, and even more light was pouring into the shed, she saw the words written in faded colours along the side of the truck body.

Mobile Library.

Luca Bonnet had kept a library in her shed? Or, more accurately, Lou Taylor now had a library in her shed?

It seemed very big. Lou walked slowly around it. Perhaps by other standards it wasn't that big. It only had four—no, six—wheels. Lou, however, drove a small city car, and to her the truck looked enormous. It certainly took up most of the space in the shed. Apart from the truck, there were a few shelves holding cardboard boxes of various sizes. Lou imagined they were filled with the kind of almost-rubbish that filled sheds and garages everywhere. She would look at them later, maybe. Or maybe not. Right now, the library was far more intriguing.

The truck cab seemed a long way off the ground to someone who only managed 165 centimetres on a good day, but there was a step so Lou managed to drag herself awkwardly into the cab. She sat in the driver's seat with both hands on the wheel. It was a bit dusty, but otherwise looked much as she imagined any such truck would look. There were two seats which were—she bounced a little—really quite comfortable. The centre console had a small compartment, but it was empty, as was the shelf behind the seats. In the glove box she found a small fake leather folder. Inside, the truck registration and insurance documents were up to date. The owner's name leaped off the page at her. Luca Bonnet. She quickly refolded the documents and put them away.

She got out again and tried the side door leading into the truck body. It was locked but, not surprisingly, she found the correct key on the pineapple keyring. She could barely reach the lock, but when she did, the door swung open to reveal the dimly lit interior. The floor of the truck was about waist height. She couldn't see any stairs. There must be some, or else how would library patrons, particularly elderly ones, come on board? That was a question for another time. She turned her back to the truck and placed her hands on the metal floor. With a jump and a kick, she slid on her backside into the library.

She stood up and looked around. She'd thought there were a lot of books in the house, but that was nothing compared to what was here. It was, as it said on the outside, a library. Every spare centimetre of wall was covered in bookshelves crammed with books of all types—kids' books, fiction, non-fiction. So many books ... paperback and hardback, picture books and thick tomes that looked to be very heavy going. Could any reader even step inside these four walls and not find something to captivate them?

Lou had heard of mobile libraries, of course, but never been inside one. It was much as she might have expected, but there were a few surprises. A sign on the wall gave a wi-fi password. A truck with wi-fi? The desk might once have held a computer, but now all that sat on it was a slightly battered metal tin, the sort used to hold file cards.

It seemed hard to imagine her birth mother driving the roads in a library truck with wi-fi.

She caught herself. Why did she think that? It was hard to imagine her birth mother full stop. She knew nothing about her. For all she knew, Luca Bonnet might have been a technical wizard.

To distract herself from that train of thought, Lou ran her hands over the spines of a row of children's books. She recognised so many of the titles. She selected one at random and pulled it down. *Possum Magic.* Her mouth twisted in a smile. Her mother, Fiona, had read this to her a thousand times when she was small. She turned the pages slowly, falling back in love with the illustrations of the star-studded world of Hush and Grandma Poss. She probably still had her old copy on a bookshelf back home in Sydney. She hadn't thought about it for years. Maybe she should indulge herself and reread it again while she was here.

She pushed the book back into its place on the crowded shelf.

Lou slipped into the chair behind the desk bolted to one wall of the truck. She slid open the top drawer. She couldn't see the contents clearly in the poor light, so she lifted them out and placed them on the desk.

An envelope was addressed in an unsteady hand. *To my daughter, Luca Taylor.*

Luca! Very few people knew that Lou's name was really Luca. She'd never used it, and most people had assumed Lou was short for Louise. She'd never disabused anyone of that notion. But this woman had known. That made it real. The handwriting on the envelope did seem, if not familiar, then not exactly unfamiliar either. Lou had a feeling she'd seen it somewhere before, but that was nonsense. Where would she have seen Luca Bonnet's handwriting? The photograph with it, however, was a different matter. The woman's face sparked no memories, but the child in her arms … the child who was laughing and gazing up at her mother with such love on her face, that little girl, Lou recognised. She had seen that face, a few months older perhaps, every day in a wooden frame on the mantle of her home in Sydney. It was unmistakably her face.

Lou's hand clenched the photo's silver frame so hard that it hurt. She forced her fingers to relax and dropped it back onto the desk as if it was burning her. She left the letter lying there and fled, locking both the truck and the shed behind her, as if metal locks could somehow keep the truth imprisoned.

CHAPTER 3

'Are you sure you're all right, Lou?' Even over the bad connection, Lou could hear the concern in her mother's voice. She also heard the love, and that was exactly what she needed.

'Sure, Mum, I'm fine.' It wasn't a very big lie. She was close to fine, now that she was talking to Fiona. 'I've got a room at the pub. It's clean and safe and I'm fine.'

'It's not your sleeping arrangements I was asking about, and that's twice you've said you're fine.' Her mother had always been able to read her every mood.

'All right. I confess I do feel a bit strange. I met someone today who knew her … Luca. He seemed really fond of her. Like she was a nice person or something.'

'She probably was a nice person. I was always sorry that your father and I didn't ever get to meet her. We wanted to, but her lawyers said no, just as they said she would stay out of your life. We never wanted that.'

On the rare occasions Lou had thought about her birth mother when she was growing up, 'nice' was not the word she would have used to describe her. Callous, perhaps. Disloyal. Uncaring. Those would seem better words for someone who could send their child away. Although, the only times she had ever thought about being adopted was when she was teased or bullied at school because of it, and at those times, she wasn't exactly in the mood to think nice things about the woman who gave her away. The woman who had now upset her happy life.

'How long are you planning to stay up there?'

'I don't know. Not long. I didn't spend much time at the house. I'll have another look tomorrow then go and talk to a real estate agent about getting it sold.'

'You don't have to rush that, you know. Take all the time you need.'

'I don't need any more time. There's nothing in that house that means anything to me.'

'You don't know that.'

'Yes. Yes, I do.' If she kept saying that in a firm voice, she would continue to believe it. 'Although, there was one thing that was strange.'

'What was that?'

'In the shed behind the house there was a library. A mobile library. In a truck.'

'How unusual.'

'Yeah, it is. I would have thought the council that owned it would have taken it away, but the paperwork is in her name. I'm sure the lawyers can figure that out. The house is full of books too. They're everywhere. Luca liked to read.'

'If she lived there by herself for all those years, perhaps she was lonely. Or maybe she simply liked to read. That's not so strange. Right from the day we got you, you always loved books and reading and you have never changed.'

'Reading is not genetic, Mum. I didn't inherit it from her. I got it from you, and all those books you and Dad read to me when I was little.'

'Maybe …'

'Anyway, I might be home tomorrow. Or the day after. No more than that, I think. There's nothing here for me.'

'Are you sure? Like it or not, you do have a connection to this woman. I just don't want you to walk away then regret it later.'

'I won't do that.'

'Your father and I are here if you need us. We love you very much.'

'I know. And I love you too.'

She ended the call and remained on the bed, which seemed comfortable enough. The door might not have had one of those fancy keycard locks you got in the city, but the old-fashioned brass lock seemed more than sturdy enough. She'd be fine here for as long as it took to do what she needed to do. A night or two—three at the most. In the meantime, she was hungry and feeling a bit drained. The drive from Sydney had been pretty tiring. She would get something to eat and then hit the sack. With luck, she'd get everything she needed done in a few hours, and tomorrow night would be back in her own bed, planning her real life again.

It seemed at least half the town's population was in the downstairs bar. There wasn't exactly a sudden silence when she walked in, but she did feel more than a few heads turn in her direction. Well, that was only reasonable. Every strange face probably turned heads here. No-one knew who she was, or what she was doing in this tiny town that was tucked in the Hunter Valley hills and that was the way she'd like to keep it. Her brief conversation with Jake hadn't been too bad, but it was highly likely that some, if not most, of the people in the pub, had also known Luca. And Lou wasn't ready to spend her whole evening talking about the woman who had given her up for adoption. Particularly not with people who might have been her friends.

'How's the room?' The woman behind the bar was also the owner of the pub and had signed Lou in earlier. 'Got everything you need?'

'Yes, thank you, Mrs Fraser.'

'Please, call me Deb. What can I get you to drink?'

'Lemonade, lime and bitters, please.'

'Sure, grab that table over there if you like and I'll bring it over.'

The drink was cold and the blackboard menu was surprisingly extensive. Lou was still studying it when a mass of wriggling black fur flung itself at her.

'Ollie. Get down.' Jake hurried over and pulled the excited Labrador away.

Lou laughed, scratching the dog's head and getting an enthusiastic and somewhat sloppy lick in return. 'Don't worry. He's fine.'

Jake smiled. 'He's pleased to see you again.'

'It is nice to see a friendly face.'

'His or mine?' Jake shrugged. 'Sorry. It was too good an opportunity to miss. Are you staying here overnight?'

Lou nodded.

'If there's anything you need when you go back to the house tomorrow …'

'Thanks, but I'm sure it'll be okay.'

'Well, the offer is there. In the meantime, if you can't decide, I can recommend the shepherd's pie. It's left over from last night, but it's good.'

'You've tried it?'

'No. I cooked it. I work here.'

'You're a chef and a gardener?'

'And plumber and general odd-job man. I can turn my hand to most things in a pinch.'

Of course he could. Lou studied him more closely while patting his dog. He was cute with a kind face and he did fill out a T-shirt very nicely. Not that it mattered—she'd be gone from here in a day. Besides, she had a whole life to plan. The tutoring job was only a stop-gap while she worked out a long-term plan. That plan certainly did not involve a cute man and a relationship that would never go anywhere.

'Here's your drink.' Deb appeared from the direction of the bar. 'Are you looking for something to eat? I imagine Jake has already recommended his shepherd's pie.'

'He has and it sounds good. I'll have that. Thank you.'

'Salad or veg?'

'Salad.'

'Coming right up.'

'I'll leave you to your dinner. Nice to see you again.' Jake turned away, leaving Lou once more with the feeling that he had courteously tipped a non-existent hat in her direction.

Lou pulled her phone out of her pocket to check her mail as she waited for her meal, but before she even had time to unlock it, a middle-aged woman with hair dyed an astonishing orange approached. Her clothes were no less bright than her hair, but the really unsettling part was the eagerness on her face.

'Hello. I don't mean to be rude, but are you Luca's daughter?'

'I'm sorry?'

'Are you Luca's daughter? You look a lot like her, you know.'

'I … Well. Yes.'

'I miss her so much. I'm Val. Val Colvin. My husband Peter and I run the post office.' The woman perched herself on the empty chair opposite Lou. 'I knew you'd be coming soon. I said to Peter that the will must have cleared probate by now, so you'd be here. We've all missed the library so much. Having you here is just the thing to buck us all up.'

Lou wasn't sure how to answer that.

'Of course,' Val continued, 'I imagine you want to know more about your mother. Well, she and I were friends for more than twenty years. She was such a wonderful person. We all still feel her loss, as do you too, I'm sure.' A hand sporting bright green nails reached out to pat her arm.

'Thank you.' Lou moved slightly so she was out of the woman's reach. 'I don't mean … but I'm just …'

The woman paid no heed to Lou's discomfort. 'And I remember you too. When you were little I used to bounce you on my knee while your mother restocked the library shelves.'

The words crashed into Lou's mind like thunder. This woman had played with her as a baby? She looked at Val's badly made-up face, but nothing about it was familiar. Lou was struggling to breathe as this stranger kept talking … and talking … and talking.

'Back when the council still ran the library. Before it was closed. That broke your mother's heart, you know. If it hadn't been for—'

'Val? I've been looking for you.' Jake had returned. 'We need to set a time for me to come by the post office and set up that new shelving for you.'

'Well, of course, Jake. Can you give me a few minutes? I was just saying to Lou here … Have you met her? She's our Luca's daughter.'

Jake cast a careful smile and a nod at Lou. 'Sorry, Val, but I have to get back into the kitchen in a few minutes. If we don't fix a time now, I'm not sure when I'll be able to get it done. I'm a bit busy at the moment.'

'Oh. Well, of course. Excuse me, my dear. Don't go away. I'll be back in a tick and we can talk some more about your poor mother.'

As Jake led the woman away, Lou got to her feet and darted out of the bar, almost running up the stairs and back into her room. She slammed the door behind her and leaned against it for a couple of minutes until her head stopped spinning and her heart stopped pounding. Then she crossed the room to drop into the armchair near the curtained window that overlooked the town's main street. This was going to be so much harder than she expected. In Sydney, her birth mother was some distant figure, but here, everything was different. Every person Lou saw had probably met Luca. Some would have been her friends. Lou should have expected that, and been prepared to deal with it. Now that she was here, she would have to find a way to cope, at least for a day or two.

The one thing she had not anticipated was that some of these people would have known her when she was a baby. Before Luca sent her away. When apparently she had already been known as Lou. She had no idea how to deal with that … or with them. How did you talk to someone who could tell you things about yourself—things you never knew?

She needed to get away from here. Get on with her life. As soon as she could.

There was a light tap on the door and her heart sank. She didn't want to see anybody right now. And if it was that dreadful woman with the orange hair again …

'I've brought your dinner.'

Lou opened the door to find Deb Fraser standing there, a tray in her hands.

'Sorry about Val. She's a dreadful busybody, but she means no harm. She is a kind and generous soul. Really,' Deb said gently. 'Anyway, I thought you'd be hungry so I brought your dinner up for you. Not that we usually do room service.'

Lou took the tray. 'Thank you. That's very kind of you.'

'It's no bother.' Deb turned to go.

'Did you know Luca?' Lou asked before the courage deserted her.

'Of course.' Deb turned back to face Lou. Her grey eyes were soft with sadness. 'Luca was my friend.' Then she smiled. 'I don't do room service for just anyone, you know.'

Lou wasn't sure what to say.

'If you want to talk about Luca, I'm here and would be very happy to share stories about her. But I won't intrude. Goodnight.' Deb turned back towards the stairs.

Jake was filling in behind the bar when Deb returned.

'Is she all right?'

'I think so. There are times I want to throttle Val. She has no tact.'

'Not her strong suit, no.'

'Have you talked to her? Little Lou? Luca's daughter, I mean. I can't keep calling her that. She's not little any more.'

'No, she's not little.' The edges of Jake's mouth began to twitch, before he pulled himself back into line. 'I saw her at the house. Ollie likes her a lot.'

'Ollie has exceptionally good taste.'

From the blanket on the floor at the far end of the bar came the sound of a tail thumping.

'So, how much have you told her?' Deb started polishing glasses, keeping her voice low so no-one nearby could hear.

'Nothing. Luca wanted to tell her in her own way.'

'You know I loved Luca, but in this I think she was wrong.'

'Maybe, but as her friends, we have to respect her wishes.'

'I know.'

'Don't worry. I'm here if she needs me. As are you. But we have to let her find her mother at her own speed. We don't want to be like Val, do we?' Jake grinned and winked. 'Red hair wouldn't suit you.'

'Get out of here.' Deb flicked the end of her cloth at him.

'Okay. Come on, Ollie. Time we were gone.' The dog left his bed and joined his master, his tail wagging as always. 'See you round.'

'You'll be right for doing dinners tomorrow?'

Jake flicked a glance at the stairs that led to the guest rooms. 'I hope so. I'll see how things go.'

CHAPTER 4

Wagtail Ridge was dark and still as Lou stood on the upstairs veranda of the pub just past two in the morning. She looked out over the main street towards the western end of town where the little wooden cottage would be in darkness, as would the shed behind it and the mobile library truck. She'd been struggling to sleep, tossing and turning between the crisp sheets. In her restless dreams, she had seen that truck, but not quite as it was now. She'd woken with the image of the truck moving down the highway, music playing. Try as she might, she couldn't remember the music, only that it had seemed familiar. The person driving the truck had seemed familiar too, in the way that people do in dreams, when you can't see their faces.

But it was only a dream, driven by tiredness and the emotional impact of yesterday's visit to the house where she had lived when she was very small with a woman she didn't remember. Being unsettled was only natural. But there was more to it than that. Lou could remember—even still feel—the grief that had engulfed her family when Fiona's father died. She had held her mother closely as they'd cried and told stories of his place in their lives until the pain was easier to bear. There was no grief for Lou in this moment. Instead she felt … what? Any chance she might have had to know her birth mother was now gone. Perhaps one day she might have wanted to do that. Her life was being disrupted, but only for a short time. Her birth mother's death was no more than an inconvenience, and that seemed terribly wrong. Shouldn't she be feeling something more? Or maybe she was and that was causing her disrupted sleep. Maybe Luca's death was stirring something deep inside her that she had yet to find or understand.

Lou inhaled a deep breath of the night air, taking in the smell of the gum trees and dust, and the quiet of a small town. Sydney was never this quiet. Even when she sought out her favourite spots by the river, there was always a distant hum of city noise. Always the smell of cars and city and the knowledge that she was surrounded by people; strangers all.

This was different. After just a few hours in this town, she already knew three people. Well, perhaps 'knew' was the wrong word, but she'd formed a connection—of sorts—and they had shown her nothing but kindness. Even Val had not had any malicious intent behind her intrusion.

The tension in Lou's shoulders began to loosen and the unsettling dream seemed to wash away on the night air. Everything was fine. She'd go back to that cottage to see if there was anything there she wanted or needed to see, and then go home to Sydney where she could think more clearly. As for that letter, she probably should take it back to Sydney with her. Once she was home and everything felt normal again, she could read it when, or rather if, she felt the need. There was no rush. The woman who'd given birth to her was gone now. It wasn't as if there was anything more for Lou to see or do out here, pleasant as this little town might be.

She yawned. Maybe she could sleep now she'd made some decisions. She slid back into the comfortable bed. As wakefulness turned to sleep, she dreamed she heard a woman's gentle voice reading stories about white horses to a little girl who looked up into a face that was blurred and unclear.

The bar was empty when Lou came down next morning, rucksack flung over her shoulder.

Deb appeared from the kitchen. 'Hi, Lou. I hope you slept well.'

'Not too badly, thank you.'

'Breakfast?'

'Just some tea. Toast, if you have it.'

'Eggs on that toast?'

'No. I'm a Vegemite-on-toast girl.'

'That I can do. Take a seat anywhere.'

Deb was soon back with her breakfast. 'There you go. Are you staying with us again tonight?'

'I don't think so.'

'That's fine. We're all square for last night. It's not busy, so if you decide you want to stay, there are available rooms.'

'Thank you.'

Deb smiled and returned to the kitchen.

As she ate, Lou debated asking Deb to tell her something about Luca. Some small, unimportant thing that would simply prove the woman was a stranger to her and shouldn't cause her sleepless nights. Then she decided against it. It didn't matter what Deb said. Nothing could change the past, and it wasn't as if Lou was curious. Well, maybe she was a little, but not enough to matter. She drank the last of her tea and left.

Back at the cottage, Lou walked in the door without hesitating. She moved through the rooms, trying to cast a businesslike eye over what was now her property. The living room was filled with small personal items, and much as she tried to ignore them, she found herself wondering about them. The souvenirs hinted at a lot of travel: Queensland, the Northern Territory, Tasmania. Luca seemed to have shared Lou's love of wild places, because there were very few things that had come from cities. A carved wooden lizard, a miniature of the Dog on the Tucker Box and a framed and faded photograph of the Victorian coast suggested Luca had cared more about the bush than the bright lights. Lou picked up a small bowl made, surprisingly, of some kind of soft polished stone. It was very pretty. She stared at it for a few moments, wondering where Luca had found it. Then she shook her head and put it back on its shelf. She would think of the house in terms of sale value and what that money could do for her future. There was no point wondering about the past.

As she went through the rooms, Lou realised someone must have been looking after the house. While Jake had been mowing the lawn, someone had been cleaning and vacuuming. There was a little bit of dust, but not enough for a house that had been empty for months. The fridge had been cleaned out and when Lou opened the pantry, she saw the perishables had been cleared away, leaving just a few cans and jars. Apparently her biological mother had liked spaghetti hoops, canned peaches and Vegemite, although presumably not together. Lou liked Vegemite, and in her weaker moments, she had been known to eat spaghetti hoops on toast for breakfast. It was a habit from her childhood, but that was purely coincidence. She very much doubted she'd learned to like either of those things in the time she'd spent in this house. As for canned peaches … Lou hated them almost as much as she loved the fresh ones.

Deb at the pub may have been the one responsible for the care given to the cottage. Lou should thank her. Perhaps she would drop by the pub on her way out of town this afternoon. If she didn't do it then, she would never do it, because she certainly wasn't coming back.

She stood in the middle of the living room, her gaze wandering over the crammed bookshelves, and finally stopping at a familiar hardcover book. She took it off the shelf and ran her hand affectionately over the brilliantly coloured cover, where a young koala in red shorts and yellow shoes was clutching a slingshot as he ran away from his mother. Blinky Bill. How often had her father read this book to her while she was in bed, trying not to fall asleep during her favourite bits? How often had Fiona read it to her when she was in bed coughing and sneezing, and once nursing a broken arm? When she was little, the book had been so wrapped up in the love and security she felt with her parents, how could she not have loved every word of it?

But when she closed her eyes for a moment of homesickness, the voice she heard reading those words was not Fiona's. It was the voice that had haunted her sleep last night.

She slammed the book shut and forced the dream voice away. She had no memories of this place or the woman who had given her life then sent her away. She was not going to let that woman intrude on her life. The voice she heard in her dreams was her mother's—the woman who had raised her.

She let the book fall onto the table and left the house, locking the door behind her. She had lived without whatever was within those walls her whole life, and she didn't need it now.

She was so lost in her thoughts that she almost tripped over the puppy sitting at the bottom of the stairs, grinning up at her with a lolling tongue.

'Well, hello, you.' She sat on the stairs and scratched the dog's head. Her reward was an enthusiastic bark.

'Ollie? Here boy!'

The pup turned his head in the direction of the voice but showed no sign of moving.

'Come on.' Lou stood up. 'We'll both get in trouble if you ignore that. We'd better go and find him.'

Lou and the dog walked around the side of the house. The main doors to the shed were open, revealing the library truck parked inside, the front body panel lifted up to expose the engine. Jake was standing beside it, wiping his hands on an oily rag.

Ollie gave a happy yap and bounded over to him.

Jake patted him. 'Now, Ollie. Sit down.'

The dog cocked his head to one side and kept wagging his tail.

'Sit down.'

Still no response from the dog. Jake placed his hand on the dog's hindquarters and pushed gently but firmly. 'Sit.'

This time, the pup obeyed.

'Good dog!' Ollie's reward was a scruffing of his head and ears. 'Now stay.' Jake held his hand up in front of the dog. Ollie stayed.

'You're very patient with him.'

'I try, although at times it's hard work.' His smile took the sting out of the words. 'I hope he wasn't bothering you.'

'No bother at all,' Lou said. 'He's sweet.'

'I'm sorry about Val last night. She has a good heart, but she's not strong on tact.'

'It's fine. I understand. Thank you for stepping in, though. I had a feeling I was going to be trapped there all night, and I have a long drive this morning.'

'You're going back to Sydney?'

'Yes … but how did you know I live in Sydney?'

'Luca told me.'

'How did she—wait. Forget it. It doesn't matter.' Lou took a steadying breath. 'I was hoping I could ask you to continue keeping an eye on the place until I make arrangements to sell everything. As I said yesterday, I'm happy to pay you.'

Jake dismissed the offer of payment with a wave of his hand. 'Of course I'll keep an eye on the place. Anything you need. I've been doing some work on the library engine. It could go back on the road any time if you wanted it to.'

She glanced over his shoulder at the gaily painted truck. 'It will be easier to sell if it's going, I guess.'

'If that's what you want. It will be missed though. A lot of people relied on it. And not just here in the Ridge. It was … well, I guess it was like the old Cobb and Co coaches. It did more than just deliver books. It helped hold these communities together.'

Lou felt a flash of annoyance. Of course she wanted to sell the library truck. She had a newly inked degree under her belt and a life ahead of her, which she hoped would be filled with travel and excitement, friends and her family. What would she want with an old mobile library? And no-one, especially a dead woman, had any right to pressure her into changing her mind.

'Maybe whoever buys it will start it up again.'

'Maybe.' He sounded disappointed.

'Thanks. I should go now. Bye, Ollie. It was nice to meet you.' She bent to ruffle the Labrador's fur. 'Oh—and you too of course, Jake.'

'That's all right. I'm becoming used to playing second fiddle to him.' The smile reached all the way to his blue eyes. It was a very nice smile.

Lou hesitated for a second, then walked back towards the drive, where she had left her car. She had just opened her door when she heard running footsteps behind her.

'I think you might have missed this.' Jake held out an envelope. It was the one she had left in the library truck yesterday. The one she had chosen not to read. She didn't want to read it. Not now. Not ever.

'How did you find this?'

'I was checking the electrics inside the library and saw it on the desk.'

'I left it there because I don't want it.'

'That's your moth— That's Luca's handwriting.'

'I guessed that.'

'You should take it. In case you change your mind.' He offered it again. The smile was gone from his eyes, which now seemed to look right into her heart. He seemed disappointed by what he saw there.

'Did she put you up to this? Tell you to make sure I read that letter?'

'I know it was important to her that you did read it. I know it's really none of my business, but I honestly think she deserves that much of your time. And you might regret it later if you don't.'

That flash of anger returned. She wanted to tell him that she wouldn't read the letter and he was right: it was none of his business. Instead she snatched the envelope out of his hand. She tossed it onto the passenger seat next to her phone and rucksack and, without another word, got behind the wheel and started the car. As she turned into the street, she saw him in the rear-view mirror watching her drive away. She felt a bit like a petulant child. Not that it mattered. She was done with Wagtail Ridge and that included Jake, his cute dog and the woman whose handwriting glared at her from the passenger seat.

CHAPTER 5

My Darling Daughter,

If you have found this letter, it means you have come home to Wagtail Ridge. I've hoped for so long that you would do that. Of course, it's too late for me, but I honestly believe there is good to come from this for you, if only you'll give me a chance to tell my story. To explain. Please.

I knew the letters would be hard to write. Not as hard as giving you up all those years ago. Not by a long shot. But still so very hard. I have accepted that I am dying. But now my last days are here, I find it far harder to accept that I will never see you again. That might seem strange, after all, I gave you up a long time ago. But I guess deep down I always thought that some day—somehow—we would meet up and talk again. As adults, not as we talked when you were small. I guess I did most of the talking then. And I have never stopped talking to you, even though you weren't here to listen.

There's so much I want to say. I want to explain the things I couldn't tell a toddler. There is so much I want you to know about me. And there is so much I wanted to know about you and your life. How I wish there was still time.

All these years, I've talked to you as I drove this library truck, as if you were really there sitting beside me. You were there, you know. When you were a baby. Do you remember any of those times? It was just us and the books and the road. At night, when you were sleeping, I would read books out loud and record myself. Then I could play it back as we drove. The sound of my voice, even in the recordings, seemed to make you happy.

Sometimes we played music. I always loved country music and you seemed to as well. You'd burble along with Kasey Chambers, and bang your fists to Keith Urban. I hope you still like music. Especially country music. It would be nice to know we share that.

I miss being on the road. When I started to get sick, I kept driving as long as I could. When it became too much, Jake started driving for me, so I could stay on the road. It wasn't just because I loved it. The library is so important to these small towns and the people who live in them. I didn't want to let them down. But it's beyond me now.

Sometimes, when Jake was driving, I think I talked to him as if he was you. I must have seemed crazy to him, but I guess he knew it was the medication. I hope you meet Jake. He's a good man. Like your father was.

I want to hear your voice now more than anything. I want to meet the young woman you have become. You were such a wonderful child, smart and happy. Your smile could chase away the darkest clouds. You are my daughter, so I guess it's natural I'd think those things of you, but they are true. Other people felt them as well.

Is this letter making sense? I have trouble keeping things straight in my mind. The doctors told me to expect this to happen. But it's all right, everything is organised. I made sure of that. The same way I made sure you would have a good life. A better life than I could have given you.

But now, at the end of mine, I wish … I wish I could tell you this in person. I have always been so afraid you would hate me. Please don't. I hope as you read the letters you will come to understand … and to forgive me.

I love you. I always have.

Your mother,

Luca.

Lou slumped against the familiar wooden bench and raised her eyes to the blue sky above her. It occurred to her that the sky here in Sydney was marginally less clear, less brilliant than in Wagtail Ridge. But she was home and it felt good.

As she folded the letter carefully, she heard the kitchen door open as Fiona made her way across the back garden to this secluded spot.

'I thought I'd find you here. Are you all right?' Her mother sat on the bench next to her.

'I'm not sure.'

'I'm glad you finally read that.'

The letter had remained unopened for two days after Lou's return from Wagtail Ridge. She'd pretended she was busy checking the online job sites, or catching up with friends, but she wasn't fooling anyone. Least of all herself.

Lou unfolded the letter and glanced again at the words she already knew by heart. She offered it to Fiona. 'I had to read it, but I don't know what to do or think now that I have.'

'Are you sure you want me to read it?'

'Yes. Whatever that letter or anyone else says, you are my mother and I want your advice.' Fiona had sat in this spot with Lou when she'd cried over her first real crush at age twelve. She had offered sympathy and words of wisdom when Lou had fought with her best friend or struggled over university exams and career paths. Her mother had always been there when Lou needed her.

Silence settled over them, broken only by the distant hum of the city traffic and the occasional hoot of a car horn. Lou watched her mother's face as she read the letter, surprised to see her brown eyes well up and a tear stream down her cheek.

'Oh, that poor woman!'

'You feel sorry for her?'

'Of course I do. To lose a child is every mother's worst nightmare.'

'She didn't lose me, she gave me away! She didn't want me.'

'Of course she wanted you. No mother would let go of a child unless she had no other option. The thought of losing you breaks my heart.' A second tear followed the first.

'Oh, Mum, you will never lose me.' Lou hugged Fiona and each clung to the other as if something was trying to tear them apart.

'I'm afraid that as you learn more about Luca, you'll stop seeing me as your mother. Because I'm not. Not in that sense.'

'You are my mother in every way that matters. You always will be. I promise.' Lou believed that with every fibre of her being.

Fiona folded the letter and handed it back. Lou ran her fingers over the paper. 'Mum, what did you mean, as I learn more about Luca? I'm done. I'll sell the house and that stupid mobile library and then it's over and I can get on with my life.'

'What about the other letters?'

'What other letters?'

'She said the letters were hard to write. That means there have to be more.'

Lou looked at the words on the page again. 'I guess you're right. Did she ever write to me? Or to you?'

'No. If she had, your father and I would have given the letters to you.'

'I wonder what letters she's talking about?'

'You didn't see any in the house?'

'No. Not that I looked very hard—she left this where it would be easy to find. I'm not sure I want to go digging through the house looking for more.' Lou couldn't keep her hands still. She unfolded the letter again. 'You know. This handwriting looks almost familiar.'

'That's because it is.'

'What?'

'We never told you, but when you came to us, some things came with you. Clothes and so forth that are long gone. But also some books.'

'Which books?'

'I'm thinking of *The Magic Pudding* in particular.'

Now she remembered. The book she had loved so much as a child had been signed with love from her mother. 'I thought that inscription was from you.'

'No. In those first weeks when you were still settling in, I used to read it to you and it seemed to calm you down. I guess she used to read it to you as well. The message in the front, it's from her. Luca.'

Lou could remember her mother reading the books to her, but try as she might, there were no memories before that. No memories of another voice reading those same stories. 'You've never told me that before.'

'No. Perhaps we should have. But by the time you were old enough to understand about the adoption, you weren't reading those books any more, so it never really came up. I'm sorry.'

'No! Mum, never say that. You and Dad took me in when this Luca didn't want me. You loved me and raised me. You are my mother—not her.'

Fiona sniffed and hugged Lou tightly again. When she let her go, she spoke very softly. 'When are you going back?'

'I'm not going back.'

Fiona smiled as she got to her feet. 'Yes, you are. After all these years, do you think I don't know the daughter I raised? You'll go back and look for those letters. Because if you don't, you'll always wonder.' She set off down the narrow path back to the house.

As she went to bed that night, Lou hunted through her bookshelves and, among the classic novels and bestsellers and uni reference books that were stacked two volumes deep, she found her old copy of *The Magic Pudding.* She smiled at the drawing of Sam Sawnoff, the penguin. She'd loved him so much when she was a child. She'd also wished she'd had a pudding that magically re-formed, no matter how many times you ate it.

She opened the cover and there it was: *To my darling daughter. I hope you find as much magic in life as you do on these pages.*

The handwriting was not Fiona's. It was clearly the same hand that had written the letter that now lay on her bedside table. She took the book to bed with her and flicked through the pages, loving the familiar images and words. Her lips started moving as she read the poetry of Egbert Rumpus Bumpus. Her voice changed as she whispered, 'It's a magic pudding,' in the penguin's voice. She chuckled, recognising Fiona's tones in the words as she spoke them. A different voice appeared when she spoke the words of the pudding and startled Lou. It was not a voice of Fiona's making. She stopped and read the words again and there it was—the same pitch and tone and the same humour. Someone had taken great care to create the voice of the pudding, and must have read it to Lou so many times that, even after all these years, her mind found the character again.

Whoever had created that voice had spent a lot of time reading to Lou. If it wasn't Fiona, there was only one person it could be.

Lou closed the book and turned off her reading light. She should sleep now. She had a long drive ahead of her in the morning.

Leaving the city and driving into the bush, Lou's heart lifted a little. It wasn't that she was looking forward to what lay head, it was just the release of tension she always felt whenever she left the city. Much as she loved her life in Sydney, she loved the bush as well. She had always felt at home in both worlds. Perhaps the letter that lay tucked away in the bottom of her rucksack explained why. She must have been very young when she travelled with Luca in the library, because she remembered nothing. But maybe those trips had imprinted something into her memory or her heart or maybe even her soul: a love of the wide open spaces that could not be ignored. She turned on her radio. The country beat that issued did nothing to shake the feeling that was almost like coming home.

This time, as she drove through the town, Wagtail Ridge looked familiar. The pub, of course, and the real estate office. She even saw a face or two she recognised, though she did not see a tall man with a black Labrador.

The small weatherboard cottage and the iron gate looked even more familiar this time. She pulled her car all the way into the driveway and parked beside the house. A mid-sized suitcase sat on the rear seat. Fiona, as always, had been right. Lou did need to clear her head of the swirling questions and as for her emotions—they too were proving unruly in this matter. She didn't know how long it would take, so she'd come prepared to stay a few days.

She left the bag in the car as she made her way to the front door. Staying at the pub seemed a terrible waste of money. Not to mention that she'd have to face a bunch of people who had known Luca. But neither was she sure that she wanted to sleep in this house that had been Luca's home.

The key slipped easily into the lock. The house was less strange to her this time. She wouldn't go so far as to say it was welcoming. This wasn't her home, so why should it feel welcoming? She stood in the middle of the living room and looked around. In this cluttered room with its overflowing bookshelves, it was going to take her some time to search for the letters. Where would they be? Perhaps a box or a drawer somewhere. Maybe a cup of tea would help her think.

She checked the kitchen. It didn't take her long to find the electric kettle and an unopened box of herbal teas in the pantry. The use-by date on the tea was only a few months past, not enough to matter. She filled the kettle with water and turned it on.

The smell of the sweet tea filled the living room as Lou mapped out a plan of action. The bookshelves first. Then the cupboards below them. Then the drawers. Starting with the bookshelves seemed the right thing to do, given Luca's love for books. In truth, it was probably some form of procrastination to give her time to overcome the feeling that she was searching some other person's home.

Starting with the shelves closest to the window, she ran her hand along the top of the books, looking for anything that might have been slipped between them. So many of the names on the spines were familiar, books Lou had read and loved as she grew from a child into an adult. Adventure stories, classic literature and bestsellers. There were fabulous romances, biographies and history books. Luca had obviously shared Lou's wide taste in reading. Or was it the other way around? Lou even discovered a shelf of fantasy books, including some by her favourite authors. There was a title she had never read. She pulled it off the shelf and leafed through the pages. It looked interesting; she must buy a copy. Her hands stilled. Why? She already owned a copy. This one. She could take this home to Sydney with her. It wasn't as if she would be stealing.

She ran her fingers over the cover, then opened the book, flipping through the pages and skimming the words. The book looked well read. Had this been one of Luca's favourites? Lou had a few books she read again and again. Had Luca been the same? Had she also been able to recite passages from books that had moved her?

Lou put the book to one side. She might start reading it tonight.

The shelves done with, Lou settled herself cross-legged on the carpet and began to explore the cupboards below them. There were no books but, in a few minutes, the floor around her was littered with oddments collected throughout a lifetime. Lou picked up a rounded piece of quartz, polished by nature or perhaps by being held in someone's hand. She turned it over, enjoying the feel of its smooth surface, before placing it gently on the coffee table. Another box contained a tangle of blue wool. A part-finished garment hung from some needles. The pattern for an infant's cardigan that lay in the box looked old. Had Luca been knitting this for her child, and abandoned the project when she gave birth to a girl?

Lou dropped it back into the box.

This was hard, much harder than she had expected. She hadn't known this woman. Luca Bonnet had given away her child, so Lou shouldn't feel anything for her. Pushing the box of knitting back into the cupboard, she shut the door firmly. She stood up and shook herself, shaking away memories as much as the stiffness. The afternoon was passing quickly, so she made a decision. She paused long enough to add the cottage keys to her keyring before setting out in the direction of the main street.

Lou parked outside the rather grandly named Wagtail Ridge Supermarket. A fat white cat sleeping on the bonnet of the next car opened one eye to glare at her as she walked into the wooden building. The store didn't quite deserve the title it gave itself. The shelves were not very well stocked, although the basics were there.

She made a mental note that she'd have to drive into Scone if she stayed in the cottage more than a couple of days, and wanted anything even slightly above basics. For now, though, this was good enough.

She had her arms full when a woman appeared at the counter. She looked quite sad and world-weary, although her face brightened when she saw her customer.

'Oh. Hello, Lou. Let me help you with those things.'

'Um. Hello. Have we met?'

'Not recently.' The woman smiled broadly as she began stacking Lou's items next to the cash register. 'But I knew you were back. That's the thing about small towns. News travels fast.'

As she'd only been back in town a couple of hours, Lou had to agree.

'And I knew you as a baby, of course.'

'Oh.' Lou's grip on the items in her arms tightened involuntarily.

'You look so much like your mother. But I guess everyone's said the same thing.'

Lou fumbled with her shopping and dropped some of it. The woman swept it all back onto the counter while Lou struggled to regain her composure.

The woman bustled behind the counter and started ringing up Lou's purchases. 'Of course, I've been in town longer than some. I remember when you were about two years old, you were so like your mother we started calling you Little Lou … for little Luca. I guess the Lou part of that stuck.'

Lou looked away and dug in her shoulder bag for her wallet and a tote bag. She started shoving her purchases into the bag while the woman kept talking. Lou didn't hear a word of what she said. Her head was spinning so much she wasn't entirely sure she could drive.

She completed her purchase without another word and dashed out of the store. The cat glared at her again as she got in her car, where she paused for a few seconds to gather herself. The last thing she wanted now was an accident. Then she took a deep breath and started the engine. As she pulled away, her focus was on getting back to the cottage and slamming the door behind her, to put a barrier between herself and the woman who used to call her Little Lou.

CHAPTER 6

'I wonder what that was about.' Jake walked up to the white cat and scratched its head as he watched Lou drive away. Ollie was bouncing eagerly around his feet, keen for his share of the patting, or possibly to get closer to the cat, who was studiously ignoring him.

'I think it was my fault.' The unexpected answer came from the shop behind him.

'Hi, Kelly. What do you mean, your fault?' The shop owner, Kelly Bridge, was a kind woman, verging on motherly. She worked hard to keep the store going, and he suspected she might not be succeeding. But even in these hard times, Jake couldn't imagine her doing anything to upset anyone.

'I talked about how we gave her the nickname Little Lou. I guess that was thoughtless of me. I didn't want to upset her. I was just startled by how much she looks like her mother at that age.'

Jake was a relative newcomer to the town—he'd only lived there for five years—so most of his memories of Luca were recent, when she was already aged by her illness. Though he'd seen a hint of the pretty young woman she must have once been. A pretty young woman a lot like Lou.

'And she left some of her stuff behind,' Kelly said.

'I'll take it to her. I'm going that way.' He wasn't, but he would now.

'Thanks, Jake.' Kelly vanished inside the shop and emerged with a small cardboard box with a bottle of milk and some fruit in it. 'When you see her, please apologise for me. Tell her I didn't mean to upset her.'

'I'm sure she knows that.'

'I hope so. Poor thing. It must be so hard for a young woman to lose her mother like that.'

As he loaded the box into his car, Jake wondered if the thing upsetting Lou wasn't so much losing a mother as it was suddenly gaining one she would never know. He wasn't sure which would be harder.

'I think maybe we can help a bit,' he told Ollie, who waited patiently by the passenger door to be invited into the car. 'What do you think?'

The pup gave a small whine and wagged his tail.

'Yeah. I agree.' Jake didn't bother locking the car as he walked across the street to the pub.

Deb Fraser was behind the bar. 'I hear Luca's daughter is back in town.'

'Yep.'

'She can have the same room if she needs it. It's pretty quiet.'

'I think she's planning to stay in Luca's cottage.'

'That's going to be tough for her.'

'Yeah. I guess money's got something to do with it.'

Deb snorted softly. 'We all know that feeling. If you see her, tell her she can have mate's rates for the room, if it helps.'

'Are you sure?' Jake knew the pub, like the store, wasn't doing as well as it once had.

Deb nodded.

'Thanks. I'll do that. She left some stuff at the shop. I was going to run it over to her and wondered if I could take that leftover pasta bake from last night. She might not feel too much like cooking.'

'Good idea. I'll toss in some wine as well. As a welcome for her.'

'Thanks.'

As he drove to Luca's—Lou's—house, Jake's mind wandered back to the friend he had lost. Luca had been of another generation, but they had become friends almost as soon as he'd arrived in town. As her illness progressed, she'd relied on him for many things—not just driving the library. He'd been glad to help. He'd tried to lighten her load all through that devastating final year and had made a promise to her before she died. He'd cried at her funeral, as had so many of the townspeople, and ever since, he'd been living up to that promise. That was why he'd made sure Lou took Luca's letter back to Sydney with her. But there was more he had to do.

As he pulled up outside the cottage, his determination to keep the promise was still strong, but he hadn't counted on one major problem: the pleasure he felt at seeing Lou back in the Ridge. He was pleased in a way that had nothing to do with his promise to her mother and everything to do with the way she smiled, the sound of her voice and the bounce in her walk. He needed to figure out some way to keep the promise, while giving himself a chance …

A chance at what, exactly? In one moment, Lou had both discovered and lost the mother she had never known. The confusion and pain that he'd seen on her face as she'd fled the supermarket told him how fragile she was. She didn't need any pressure, and certainly not from a man she'd met only twice. Not even one who had been thinking a lot about her.

He parked his car in front of the cottage and ruffled the top of Ollie's head. 'Come on, Ollie. We made a promise.' Keeping that promise meant keeping secrets from Lou. It might even mean lying to her. Jake didn't like it, but he had to do it.

Lou was slow answering his knock on the door. When she finally did, her face was rigid with bottled-up emotions. Jake's heart clenched. It wasn't fair that Lou had to go through this because of something that had happened so long ago.

He saw the beginnings of a smile start to tweak the corners of her mouth. Despite the sadness writ large on her face, her messy hair and her rumpled clothes, Jake was absurdly pleased that he was responsible for that half-smile.

'Hello, Ollie.' Lou knelt to pat the ecstatic pup.

'I see. I come bearing gifts, but you only have eyes for the dog. I guess I'll have to contain my heartbreak.'

As she looked up, the smile on her face became a tiny bit brighter. 'Hi, Jake. Sorry, but Ollie is much more demanding.'

'I might have to work on that. When you left the shop, you forgot some of the things you'd bought. I told Kelly I'd drop them off for you.'

'That's kind of you. Kelly is?'

'The owner of the Wagtail Ridge Supermarket. Otherwise known as the shop.'

'Of course she is. I suppose she told you I left a bit abruptly.'

Jake nodded. He wasn't going to tell her he'd been there, just a few steps away, and she had been too upset to notice him.

'I'll apologise to her tomorrow.'

'I'm sure there's no need to.'

'Thanks.' Lou held out her hands as if to relieve him of his load.

'How about I take it through to the kitchen? Deb at the pub threw in a couple of extras for you.'

She hesitated before she nodded and stepped back. 'How much do I owe you—or Kelly or Deb?'

'Nothing.' He carried the box into the kitchen.

'Are you sure?'

He saw a lot of Luca in those brilliant eyes, her spirit and her independence. 'I'm sure. We thought you might not be up to cooking tonight.'

She took a slow breath and he could almost see the tension draining out of her. 'Thank you. What I need most of all is the milk. Luca liked herbal tea, it seems. The pantry was full of it, but I prefer good old-fashioned tea with milk.'

'She did like her herbals. They always smelled too sweet to me. I like a good strong cup of Bushells too.'

'Would you like one now? I mean, if you don't have to be somewhere.'

If he did, he would happily have cancelled. 'I'd love one. Thank you. And could I get some water for Ollie?'

'Of course.'

'There's a bowl just inside the back door. I use it when I come to mow the lawn.'

'Oh.'

He suddenly felt like an idiot. 'I'm sorry. I didn't mean—'

'No. No. It's fine. Of course you know your way around. I've only been here a few hours, but you've been looking after the place for months. Or even longer, I guess.' She scurried away to find the dog bowl and filled it with water for a grateful Ollie.

Once the tea was made, Jake followed Lou through to the living room. He moved a bundle of books so he could sit down on the sofa.

'Sorry. I've been trying to sort through a few things.' Lou fussed with the books then stopped.

'It's fine. I'm used to it looking like this.'

Lou avoided his eyes as she knelt down to pick up more books. 'Did you spend a lot of time here with her?'

'Some. Especially near the end. She needed more help then. Either Deb or I used to come over most days. Other times … well, Luca had a lot of friends to help her.'

'You must have cared for her a lot.'

'We all did.' He stopped, waiting for Lou to take the lead. If she really wanted to talk about Luca, he would do that. But it was her call.

'What was she like?'

Jake thought for a moment. 'Kind. Smart. Funny. I see a lot of her in you.'

'You've barely met me. How can you say that?'

'Because she used to kneel there like that fiddling with the overflowing books too.'

Lou scrambled to her feet and went to sit in the armchair by the window. 'Tell me about Ollie and the guide dog thing.'

At the sound of his name, the dog padded over and laid his head on Lou's knee. She started patting him, her gaze fixed on his big brown eyes and happy grin. Jake got the message. If she didn't want to talk about Luca, he was fine with that. In fact, sitting here drinking tea with Lou and talking about anything at all was fine—maybe more than simply fine.

'Ollie?'

The Lab pricked his ears in Jake's direction, but stayed by Lou's side. Traitorous beast. Jake relaxed back into the sofa. 'I've had him since he was about two months old. The guide dogs have people like me to raise the pups and socialise them.'

'What do you mean, socialise?'

'I keep him with me all the time. He meets lots of people. When I work at someone's home, he comes with me. Or if I'm cooking at the pub, he sits behind the bar. Don't tell the health inspector. The idea is to teach him basic manners and get him used to lots of people and situations.'

'Then?'

'Then I give him back. He gets trained as a guide dog and assigned to someone who needs his help.'

Lou bent down and kissed the dog on the top of his head. She was rewarded with a sloppy kiss to her cheek. She laughed. Jake liked that laugh a lot. It was almost musical.

'It's going to be hard for you to give him up.'

'It always is. But I know he'll have a good home. And he'll be helping someone.'

'So he's not your first?'

'No. My parents have been raising puppies for years. When I moved here, I started doing it too. The guide dog centre is in the northwest of Sydney. Normally you have to be closer to the centre to go to puppy classes and so forth, but they're happy to have me because they know I've done it before. And I do get to classes fairly often. Ollie's something of a star at puppy school, aren't you, Ol?'

Ollie responded with a short bark.

'Tell me about your family?'

He shouldn't have been surprised by the question. Family must be at the forefront of Lou's mind right now. 'Teachers all. Not just my parents, also my older brother and sister. My brother's in Sydney. My sister moved to Queensland with her husband. Also a teacher.'

'So what happened to you?'

'I like teaching—ask Ollie.' The pup who had settled at Lou's feet lifted his head at the sound of his name and was rewarded with a pat. 'I also like working with my hands, so I do a lot of odd jobs around the place. Helping people with home maintenance. Building things. And I like to cook. I'm not ever going to be the chef at some fancy city restaurant, but then, I wouldn't like living in the city.'

'Cooking at the pub suits you?'

'Yes, it does. I like living in the Ridge. I originally came here as part of a team working on new stockyards just out of town. We all stayed at the pub and I liked it here so much that when the job was over, I didn't leave with the rest of the crew. I feel like part of a community. And I enjoy cooking for people I know and like.'

'It's good to enjoy what you do.'

'What about you?'

'Brand new degree says environmental science. When I was a kid, I saw myself as some sort of superhero, out to save the planet. I really had no idea what that took. I still don't, but understanding the environment and the crisis we're facing seems a good start. I don't like being indoors. I like wide open spaces and the bush. Which is strange, because both my parents are city people. I don't know where I got it from …'

Her voice trailed off. The silence that settled was awkward. Jake didn't dare speak the thought that was in his mind, but he didn't have to. It was obviously in hers as well.

Then Ollie stood up and shook himself. He trotted to the front door, turned back to look at Jake and whined.

'That's my call. It's time for his afternoon walk.' Jake stood up. 'You're very welcome to join us if you want to.'

He was disappointed when she shook her head. 'I've got a lot to do here, but thanks.'

They went to the door together. Ollie raced onto the veranda and looked back at Jake expectantly. But before he could go, there was one more thing Jake had to do.

'You know, I was thinking.' He turned to Lou, hating himself as he saw the honest question on her face. 'The mobile library used to belong to the council library in Scone. If you're not sure what to do with it, you could go and talk to them.'

'I really haven't thought much about it. Well, to be totally honest, I have. But I don't know what I want to do yet.'

'There's no rush. It was just a thought. I'll see you around.'

'Yeah. Bye. Bye, Ollie.'

As he made his way to his ute, Jake was so very tempted to turn around and tell Lou everything, but he didn't. He let Ollie into the front of the ute, then got behind the wheel.

'I hope you're up for some real exercise,' he told the dog. He was feeling a twinge of guilt over what he'd just done. He hadn't exactly lied to Lou, but he hadn't been entirely honest either, and there was likely to be more of that ahead.

Much as he'd cared for Luca, he was beginning to wish he'd said no when she'd made her last request of him.

CHAPTER 7

Next morning, Lou was woken by the sound of a book hitting the floor. She leaned over and picked it up, slowly focussing on the drawing of the koala in the red shorts. The light beside the couch was still on, but daylight was streaming into the room. As the fog of sleep cleared, she stretched, remembering settling on the couch to read the book. She hadn't wanted to go into the bedroom that still seemed to belong to someone else and had obviously fallen asleep while reading.

'Sorry, Blinky Bill.' She closed the book gently and put it on the table. 'I wasn't bored by you. Honestly. I was very tired.' She sat up, rubbing her eyes. She had a big day ahead of her and it probably wasn't going to be easy. Jake's suggestion about visiting the Scone Library had preyed on her mind while she'd continued her fruitless search of the bookshelves and cupboards for any other letters from Luca. Later, as she ate Jake's pasta and treated herself to a glass of wine, she'd decided he was right. The main library was a good place to go next. In fact, it was the only place to go next.

A shower and a light breakfast energised her and she was on the road to Scone shortly after nine. The library opened its doors at ten o'clock and she was one of the first through them. It wasn't a huge library, but the shelves were well stocked and some computers sat to one side. The staff were still getting organised for the day, and it occurred to Lou that she should have rung ahead. It was too late for that now.

She approached the librarian standing at the main desk. 'Excuse me, is it possible to talk to the … I guess the head librarian? It's about your mobile library?'

The woman frowned. 'Could you wait a moment, please?' She disappeared through a door marked STAFF ONLY.

A couple of minutes later, a smartly dressed woman appeared.

'Hello. I'm the senior librarian today. My name is Jan Hudson. Can I help you?'

'Hello. I'm Lou Taylor. I seem to have your mobile library in my shed.'

'I'm sorry. You must be mistaken. We don't have a mobile library.'

'It's a white truck, with "mobile library" in big red and blue letters along the side. It's full of books, and I saw your library stamp inside most of them.'

'I believe we did have a mobile library some years ago, but it was discontinued. Funding cuts and our online book program made it redundant. But that was before my time. I'm sorry. I don't think I can help you.'

'Is there someone here who could?'

'Perhaps the council records office? They would know about it. When it was discontinued. If the truck was sold. That sort of thing.'

Lou's heart sank. That wasn't what she was looking for. She nodded her thanks to the librarian.

As she turned to go, an older woman approached. She was tall and thin, with a tight grey perm, but her gentle eyes and the soft smile on her face belied the severity of her appearance. She laid a hand gently on Lou's arm.

'I think I might be able to help.'

Lou followed the older woman to an unoccupied reading table where they sat down.

'Do you remember the mobile library?' Lou kept her voice low, not wishing to disturb readers at nearby tables.

'I certainly do. I'm Mary Woods. I helped Luca start it up. At first, we went out on runs together, but the council didn't have the funding for two of us, so Luca took it on while I stayed here. But we still worked together when it came to picking the books for the mobile.'

'You were friends?'

'Yes. After they closed the mobile and she left, we'd meet up whenever she was in town.'

Lou kept her hands tightly clasped on top of the desk, hoping Mary wouldn't see how strangely nervous she felt about talking about Luca. 'When did they close the library?'

'About five years ago.'

This woman didn't meet Luca until after she had given Lou away. She would know nothing about those early years. Lou wasn't sure if she was pleased about that. 'How did she end up with the mobile library at her home? Did she buy it?'

'That's a long story, but basically, the communities it served weren't ready to let it go. Or to let Luca go either. It was far too important to them all. They kept it alive with fundraisers and donations.'

'They must have been very successful fundraisers.'

'There were a lot of towns involved. And it wasn't just that they loved the library, they needed it. They needed your mother too.'

It took a moment for the meaning of those words to register. 'How … how did you know?'

'I heard you say you had the library truck in your shed. I assumed you meant Luca's shed. We all knew she was leaving the library to her daughter to take over. And besides—' Mary patted her hand, '—you look a lot like her. I am so sorry for your loss.'

'I'm not taking …' Lou paused. The grief on the woman's face told her this was not the right time for that discussion. 'I'm sorry. I think it was your loss more than mine. I never knew her.'

Lines formed around Mary's eyes as she closed them for a second, as if to hold back the memories both good and bad. 'I'm sorry you never knew her. They say only the good die young, and in this case it was so very true.'

'I don't even know how old she was when she died. I know nothing at all about her.'

'I can help with that. Wait here a minute.' Mary got up from the table and vanished behind the staff only door.

Lou looked around the library, wondering how much time Luca had spent here. Had she searched these shelves for requested books to take on her mobile runs? Had she stood behind that desk advising readers on books they might like? She probably could have given good advice, judging by the number of books in her house.

Could a love of books be inherited? Lou knew full well that such a thing wasn't genetic, but it could be passed from parent to child. From mother to daughter. Had her love of books come from Luca or from Fiona, whose bookshelves were tidier but no less laden?

Her thoughts were interrupted by the librarian's return. As Mary resumed her seat, Lou became aware that a couple of other library employees were glancing her way. Had they too known her mother?

It was time she left. She gathered herself to stand, but the woman sitting opposite her put out a hand to stop her.

'Before you leave, Luca asked me to give you this.' She slid a book across the table. 'She said it was possible you would come here, asking questions. At least she hoped you would. I guess there may be some answers in there.'

Lou stared at the book. It was old, with a slightly battered cover that showed a drawing of a man walking through the outback, a small girl at his side. She knew this book. *The Shiralee*. Her mother—her real mother, Fiona—had read it to her many times. She didn't remember much about it, except that it was a story about a father and child who began as strangers, but finally came to know and love and need each other. There was something inside the book. Lou opened the cover to find an envelope with her name written in a now familiar handwriting. It was exactly what she had come here hoping to find, but now it was there in front of her, she was afraid to take it. She was afraid that the words inside would further shake up the world she had already felt slipping away from her control.

Mary smiled gently. 'Your mother told me how people used to call you Little Lou. She often wondered if you had kept that name. She would be so glad that you did.'

This was getting too hard for Lou. 'Mary, thank you for your help. I should be going now.'

'You are most welcome, my dear. If you want to come back at any time to talk about Luca, I'm here three days a week. And I'm always happy to talk.'

Lou closed the book, the envelope still inside. She put it into her shoulder bag and shut the flap firmly, as if that would put some barrier between her and whatever it contained.

She stood up and turned to leave, but then changed her mind. 'Mary. I do have one question.'

'Of course.'

'How old was Luca when she died?'

'You don't know?'

'I guess it's in the paperwork from the lawyer somewhere, but no, I don't know.'

'She was forty-five.'

As Lou walked out through the glass doors, her throat tightened. It didn't matter how much resentment she carried against the woman who gave her away, that was far too young for anyone to die.

CHAPTER 8

My Darling Daughter,

I hope I'm not writing this in vain. I want to believe that one day you will read my letters. I have to believe that you haven't just shrugged me off as a part of a past that you forgot long ago and have no desire to revisit.

I can understand why you might feel that way. It might seem to you that's what I did to you. But it's not. Far from it. I hope you'll come to understand that, if you decide to give me a chance to talk to you. I hope you have found your way to my home and my little library.

You must have, if it led you here.

Do you read? Do you love books still? If you do, I'll allow myself to take just a tiny bit of the credit for that. Books have always been important to me. When I was small, they were my escape from the unhappiness around me. Then when you came, they were my joy to share with you. After you were gone, they were the only thing left in my life. I could no longer share my love of books with you, but I could share it with others and hope that, in some way, I might brighten their lives.

But listen to me—rambling on about books. That's not what you want to hear, is it?

There's so much to say. I'm not sure where to start. Do you remember me singing the Julie Andrews song to you when you were small? You used to smile and laugh and sing the ABC bits. Even after all this time, I can still hear your voice. I hope you still sing sometimes.

It's all very well to say start at the beginning, but where does the story of a family really begin?

Perhaps I should start this story with my mother. Your grandmother Christina.

My mother was Swedish, so I guess that makes you one quarter Swede. Anyway, she was beautiful. Quite tall and blonde. People always told me I looked like her, but where she was tall and curved, I was short and skinny. When you were small, you looked a lot like her. And a lot like me too, I was told. She came to Australia on holiday when she was nineteen and she never left. That was because she met my father. What should I tell you about your grandfather? He was handsome. And charming. He must have been charming. My mother would not have fallen for him if he wasn't. But he was … feckless.

Isn't that a nice word? Feckless. It seems so right for your grandfather. He wasn't a bad man. He just seemed incapable of staying in one place. Or with one job. Or with one family. He left and never came back when I was about ten, so I do have memories of him. I used to think that maybe he was in a car accident and lost his memory. Or maybe he died rescuing someone from a flooded river. I didn't want to believe he would run away from my mother and me. There had to be some reason, I thought. But there probably wasn't. He just left us.

So we were alone, your grandmother and I. It wasn't a bad life. We had each other. We were very, very close. She used to read to me. The Shiralee *was one of my favourite books. I used to imagine my father coming back and taking me with him on his travels through the bush. And my mother waiting at the house for us when we came back. It never happened of course.*

My mother taught me to cook, to drive a car and patch up all sorts of scrapes and bruises. They were my scrapes and bruises, but she was always there to make them better. The most important thing she taught me was how to love.

We lived in that same cottage that I have given to you and we were happy. I went to school in Wagtail Ridge, but there wasn't a high school in those days like there is now, so I had to take a bus to Scone every day. There were times I so desperately wanted that bus to keep going. Maybe that's when I started to realise that I took after my father. Whatever was over the next ridge, whatever was further down the road … it called to me. When I finished school, all I wanted to do was travel. My mother understood. I think she knew I was going to leave one day, with or without her agreement, so she gave it in the hope that I would come back.

I went all over the place. Fruit picking in Victoria. I was a nanny for a while in the Northern Territory. I went to Tasmania to make chocolates. That was a good job. We ate so many of them—all for free. Until I got so sick of them I thought I would never eat chocolates again. Then I worked my way up to Queensland. I did all sorts of strange jobs so I could lie on the beach and swim in the ocean. The best job in the world was using a whipped cream gun to swirl cream over fruit desserts at the Big Pineapple. We got into a fight with those one night, after the tourists had gone. The best food fight ever.

I was able to do all these things because I always knew that cottage was here—and my mother with her overflowing bookshelves, her home-cooked meals and her open arms, waiting to welcome me home.

I wanted that for you too, my darling daughter. I wanted to BE that for you. But when I understood I couldn't, I had to find someone who could. Can you understand that? I hope you can. I need you to know that saying goodbye to you was the strongest show of my love I could ever give you.

I love you, my darling daughter—more than I have ever loved anyone or anything in my life.

Please believe that.

Your mother,

Luca.

The letter ended there—halfway down the page, the last few words written in a hand that was a little less sure. Underneath was a small smudge, as if the reader had wiped away something that had stained the page. A glass of water spilt by a shaking hand. Or maybe a tear.

All around Lou, people were chatting and drinking coffee and the coffee shop staff darted between tables with plates of cake and sandwiches. She barely heard anything as she stared at the letter and the door into her past that was starting to open. It was just a tiny crack, but faint shapes and colours—and people—were beginning to appear.

In the bottom corner of the letter, someone had been doodling with the same black pen used to write the letter. It took a moment for Lou to realise that the doodle was the letters A, B and C with a woman between them, her arms wide open, just like Julie Andrews in the movie poster.

Lou started to sing 'Do-Re-Mi' very softly then realised what she was doing and stopped. That wasn't a memory. She knew the words but everyone knew the words of that song. Everyone.

She folded the letter and shoved it back into her handbag. When she reached for the cup in front of her, the tea was cold. The slice of carrot cake remained untouched. She stood up and left the coffee shop, feeling restless. She could tell herself it was simply that she was missing the exercise of her daily bike rides to and from the university in Sydney, but she knew it was more than that.

She walked down the main street, gazing without interest into the shopfronts. Scone wasn't a big town, but it was a lot bigger than Wagtail Ridge and the street was fairly busy. She was very aware of the people around her. A lot of them exchanged greetings as they passed each other. In that the two towns were alike. But no-one knew her here. No-one called her Little Lou or said she looked like Luca. No-one said they were sorry for her loss—a loss that she was only now beginning to feel as the words of the letter swirled through her mind.

She now knew she had a Swedish grandmother called Christina. Someone else she looked like but had not known existed until just a few minutes ago. There had been no hint in the letter as to whether this grandmother was still alive. Given that Luca had been so young when she died, it was highly possible. Lou had two grandmothers she loved very much and her mum's and dad's mothers lived close enough that visits had been regular all through her childhood. They were at every family Christmas. And Grandpa Taylor was still alive too.

Did she have a third grandmother?

What about her other grandfather? The feckless man. Was he still alive?

She turned away from the shop windows and glanced at the people walking past. There were men and women all around her of the right age. Grey-haired men with weather-beaten faces. Women with silver perms and a dash of lipstick. Some of them smiled or touched the brim of their hats as they walked past. She found herself searching for some resemblance in their faces.

A middle-aged man with fair hair cast a curious glance at her as he walked past, and the ground seemed to vanish from underneath her feet. She staggered a step or two and dropped onto a bench seat set against the wall of a shop, struggling to even draw breath.

What about her father?

She had been so caught up with the death of Luca and learning about her birth mother that she hadn't given a thought to her birth father. Was Luca ever married or had Lou's father been a short-term relationship? A fling? A one-night stand? Who was he and where was he? He would likely be in his mid-forties, so there was every reason to believe he was still … somewhere. Maybe here. Or in Wagtail Ridge. Had he abandoned Lou too? Had he even known she existed? And if he didn't … maybe she should—

'Excuse me. Are you all right?'

She looked up to see a stranger leaning over her, his forehead wrinkled with concern.

'Are you ill?'

'Um. No. Thank you. I'm …' She struggled to finish the sentence.

The stranger reached into a bag he was carrying and pulled out a bottle of water. 'Here. Take this. It's all right. It's unopened.'

She twisted the top off the bottle and took a long, steadying drink. A couple of deep breaths later, she felt able to talk. 'Thank you. I guess I got a bit too much sun.'

The man nodded wisely. 'It's easy to do this time of year.'

'Let me pay you for the water. How much?'

'No. Think nothing of it. You should get out of the sun and take it easy for a while.'

'Yes. Thank you. I'll do that.'

'Well, if you're sure you're all right …'

'Yes. I'm fine. Thank you again.'

The stranger tipped his hat at her and walked on.

Lou watched him walk away, uncertain of whether she felt embarrassed or angry. Not at him; that stranger had treated her far more kindly than the stranger who had given birth to her.

She would sort out her conflicting emotions later. But first, it was time to find out more about who she really was. She drank the rest of the stranger's water as she drove back to Wagtail Ridge.

At the edge of the town, she saw a white-painted weatherboard church she'd paid no attention on her previous visit. And right next to it … She braked sharply and pulled over to the side of the road. With a shaking hand, she turned off the engine and stared at the neat white fence and the mowed lawns beyond. It wasn't a big cemetery, but then Wagtail Ridge wasn't a big town. It was like a dozen other cemeteries she'd seen in small towns. There were one or two carved white angel headstones. Most were simply engraved slabs of black or white marble. She imagined there were other graves marked only with plaques.

But this cemetery was different, because she might have family buried here. No. Not family. Relatives. Being a relative did not make you family, just as giving birth did not make you a mother. Did it? Luca Bonnet must be buried here. There was no reason to believe she would be buried anywhere else.

It hadn't mattered before. For as far back as she had memories, Lou had always felt secure and loved and happy with her mum and dad. How she wished she'd never received that solicitor's letter. Never heard the name Luca Bonnet. But now she had, she couldn't stop the questions that were swirling through her mind. Damn Luca. Lou pounded her fist on the steering wheel, her earlier turmoil returning. Hadn't she done enough when she rejected her daughter because a toddler was getting in the way of her lifestyle? Now she had to torment her as well. Lou had about had enough. She would go back to the cottage and look for any more important papers and then she was out of here.

She started the engine again and drove the rest of the way to the cottage a little faster than was strictly necessary. Once there, she stood in the middle of the living room and looked around again. She'd already searched some of the rooms, the more obvious places. But there were still plenty of drawers and shelves and cupboards. Anger fuelled her as she pulled papers out of drawers and spread them around, looking for anything that might give her the information that suddenly seemed so desperately important to her. She emptied the toy box that served as a coffee table and found some old games, another unfinished knitting project and a box of papers.

She opened the box eagerly, but all it contained was a bundle of receipts and some old newspaper clippings. Lou took a closer look, but they all seemed to be about the mobile library.

That bloody library had meant more than her daughter.

Lou got to her feet. The only room left to try was Luca's bedroom.

She stomped into the hallway and got as far as the door before a sob caught in her throat. What was she doing? This was too hard and it was nothing to do with her real life. This wasn't doing her any good at all. It was time to go home.

She threw everything she'd brought with her into a bag and locked the door behind her, telling herself that this was over and she would never return. There was nothing here she wanted. Then she got into her car and pulled onto the road that would take her through the centre of Wagtail Ridge and on to Sydney. She would make one stop, and then she'd be gone from here for good.

CHAPTER 9

The minute he saw her, Jake knew that Lou was at the end of her tether. Her eyes sought him out in the sparsely populated bar and she came directly to where he was standing in front of the blackboard, writing the daily specials.

'Lou?'

Ollie lifted his head from his blanket in the corner and instead of leaping up to greet her, tapped the tip of his tail tentatively on the floor.

'Here.' Lou thrust a set of keys at Jake. 'Take these back. Can you keep looking after the place for me for a bit? Please. I'm going back to Sydney.'

'What's wrong?' He didn't bother mentioning that he still had his own set of keys to the cottage and shed. That didn't seem very important right now.

'I'm sorry to spring this on you, but I thought, as you'd done it before you wouldn't mind. But if you can't ...'

'No. Of course I can.' He reached out to take the hand that was almost shaking with tension, but before he could touch her, Lou dropped the keys into his open palm and snatched her hand away.

'Good. Thanks.' She glanced around the room and almost winced as she noticed the other people in the bar looking her way. 'I'll be in touch … somehow. I'm going now.' She turned.

'Wait.'

She didn't.

Jake untied the towel that was wrapped around his waist as an apron and dropped it on the bar then stuck his head through the entrance to the kitchen. Deb was there, unpacking a box of new glasses for the bar.

'Deb. I gotta go. It's Lou.'

Deb must have seen the urgency in his face. 'Go. And if you can't come back, don't worry. I've got it.'

'Thanks.'

Ollie leaped to his paws to follow Jake as he hurried through the door of the pub. Lou was sitting in the seat of her small white Honda, forehead resting on her hands, which clenched the wheel so tightly he could see the whiteness of her knuckles.

'Lou? Are you all right?'

She shook her head without looking up at him.

'Okay. Well, you're certainly in no fit state to drive. Come on, get out of the car.'

He heard her take a breath. It was very shaky. 'Go away. I only need a minute to get myself together. I just want everyone to leave me alone.'

'When I'm sure you're all right, I'll leave you alone if that's what you want. But right now, I'm pretty sure you don't have any idea what you really want. Let me help. Please.'

He decided to take the muffled noise she made as agreement and reached for the door handle. As soon as the door opened, Ollie stepped forward and pushed his nose under Lou's arm, whining softly. Jake heard a sniff as she patted the dog. Ollie placed his front paws on her lap and both her arms went around him. She laid her face against his warm fur and then she looked up. Her eyes were the saddest thing Jake had ever seen in his life. More than anything, he wanted to wipe that sadness away and see her smile again. He gave Ollie a couple of moments to work his magic, then he opened the door all the way and stepped back to let Lou get out. When she turned back and locked the car, he was half tempted to tease her about her city girl habits. But then he saw the jumble of bags and oddments on the rear seat and knew she was planning to leave. His heart sank, and not just at the thought that he had failed Luca's last request.

'You need a bit of space to get your head together, I think. Somewhere with no people and no memories. Come on. I know just the spot.'

She mumbled something that, again, he took for assent.

'My car's right here. It smells a little bit doggy. I hope that's okay.'

She didn't answer, but reluctantly followed him across the parking area.

Once the three of them were in his car, Jake started the engine and drove out of town.

They'd been driving in silence for a few minutes when Lou finally spoke. 'Where are we going? Your place? You live a long way out of town.'

'Actually, I don't. I live not far from you. But I thought you probably needed a break away from everyone and everything to do with the Ridge, so we're taking the scenic route.'

'Oh.'

Lou squealed and Jake laughed. 'Sorry. I shouldn't laugh, but I did warn you. Ollie, you have no manners at all.' He ruffled the dog's head.

Ollie barked happily and wagged his way backwards, looking from Jake to Lou to the stick.

The stick-throwing game that ensued was as energetic as it was fun. Jake and Lou played with the dog, joked with each other and got splattered with water by Ollie more than once. When even Ollie's energy started to wane, the three of them set out for a walk along the river bank. For a while they walked in silence, enjoying the sounds and smells of the bush, and the undemanding company.

Lou was the first to speak. 'Thank you.'

He didn't need to ask what she was talking about. 'You're welcome. Ollie and I have had a good afternoon.'

'I would offer to cook you dinner to say thank you, but you are probably a far better cook than I am. And besides …' Her voice trailed off.

Jake understood that she didn't want to go back to the cottage and all the memories—or lack of memories—waiting for her there. 'Why don't I cook dinner for you instead?'

She remained silent but he felt her break stride.

'It would be nice to have someone other than Ollie to talk to over dinner.'

The smile was back on her face. 'Thank you. I'd love it.'

It was just starting to get dark when they paused at the pub to pick up Lou's car. Jake parked beside his house and the little white Honda pulled up behind him. He waited for Lou to get out.

'I'm afraid I'm a bit muddy, thanks to Ollie,' she said. 'Maybe I should go back to the cottage and get changed.'

Not home—the cottage. He couldn't blame her for that. She owned it now, but that cottage wasn't her home and it might never be. She wasn't going to end her day by going back there and sitting alone in a place where she didn't feel welcome. Not if he had anything to do with it.

'Ollie is a lot muddier than you, and he's allowed, so I think you'll be all right.'

She turned back and locked the car.

'We don't do much of that here, you know.'

'Much of what?'

'Locking cars.'

'In Sydney, leaving a car unlocked is almost asking for it to be stolen.'

'Tell me again why you live there?' He kept his voice light and smiled to show he was joking.

The dog led the way up the stairs. Jake put his key in the lock but hesitated. He hadn't planned on bringing home someone he wanted to impress. He glanced sideways at Lou and decided she wasn't going to judge him over a pair of used socks on the floor. 'The place is likely to be a bit messy. If it is, I'm going to blame Ollie. There's just the two of us living here.'

The dog answered with a shake of his head and Lou's laughter wound its way around Jake like a spring breeze through the standing gums. They went inside and he watched Lou look around the room, relieved that she didn't seem to find it messy.

'Wow.' She stepped closer to the shelves that lined two walls of the room and began to walk along, her head tilted to one side to better read the titles of the books. Every now and then she would nod her approval. 'Some of these are first editions?'

'Yes. I still read them. Carefully, of course, but I don't think a book is really appreciated if it's not being read.'

'Not one for ebooks?' She was still making her way along the shelves.

'No. You?'

She gently stroked the row of book spines. 'I like the feel of paper. I guess it's something I learned when I was small and never got over it.'

He was absurdly pleased to hear her speak so freely of her past. It was a step in the right direction. 'If we're talking about old habits, how do you feel about vinyl?' He opened the doors of another cabinet to reveal several shelves full of records.

'What sort of music?'

'A bit of everything really. A lot of blues. Some rock and roll. Even the odd classical piece that took my fancy.'

'That's quite a collection. Both of them.'

'It's a small town. I live alone. Well, me and a dog, so I have lots of time. There's a pretty broad DVD collection too. We could always watch one after dinner, if you wanted to relax.' Now that the words were out, he wanted nothing more than to do just that. He almost held his breath as he waited for an answer.

'That sounds good. I need to be distracted. I don't want to think about ... anything.'

'I know,' he jumped in as her voice trailed off. 'And there's no reason to. For a start, Ollie is looking for his dinner.' At the sound of his name, the pup reappeared from the hallway where he had vanished when they first arrived. 'Let's do that then. I wasn't really planning on much tonight, but let's see if I can rustle up something a bit better than baked beans on toast.'

He did. His fridge was always well stocked and it wasn't long before they were enjoying grilled chicken with a mushroom sauce and a glass of wine. Ollie, fed and exhausted after his day out, was curled up on his mat, asleep, as the conversation above him ranged through books, music and movies, never once straying to anything particularly personal. Later in the evening, Jake and Lou moved into the living room and opened a second bottle of wine. It didn't take long to find some light-hearted entertainment in Jake's DVD collection and they settled down to watch the movie, with Ollie snoring softly by the couch.

After a time, Jake felt Lou move slowly and the weight of her head settled gently on his shoulder. When he looked down, her eyes were closed and her breathing slow and deep. He was content to let her sleep there as the movie played.

As the closing credits rolled, Jake eased himself away from Lou. She'd had too much to drink to drive home, and besides, he still thought she was better off not being alone. At some point, she was going to have to face whatever had upset her that day, and tomorrow would be a far better time.

He found a pillow and a light blanket. She stirred slightly as he tucked her in, but she didn't wake. He crouched next to her, looking down at her face. Asleep, she looked so young and fragile.

Luca had been his friend and he had cared for her. He had helped her through her illness, looked after her home and driven her mobile library for her when she couldn't. But at this moment, he was almost angry at her. Luca might have meant well, but in doing what she'd planned so carefully, she was causing her daughter pain. And Jake was as guilty as she was, because he was the one who had put this plan into action. Lou should not have to face this sort of heartache.

CHAPTER 10

Lou was wakened by a rough wet tongue running over her face and warm panting in her ear. She shuddered and forced her eyes open.

'Ollie. Stop it.' She groaned as she pushed the dog away and blinked in the morning light. Her head hurt. Her mouth felt as rough as Ollie's tongue and she ached all over. Slowly, she brought her mind and the room into focus. This wasn't her house. She was sleeping on a large and not altogether comfortable couch. She was still wearing her filthy jeans and rumpled top, but someone had placed a pillow under her head and a light blanket over her. She wiggled her toes inside her favourite Wonder Woman socks, remembering that her muddy shoes had been left by the door. As she forced herself into a sitting position, she became aware of the smell of coffee wafting from the kitchen.

Everything came flooding back and she groaned again, this time from embarrassment. She had drunk too much wine and fallen asleep in the living room of a man she barely knew. She started to shake her head, then decided against it. She contemplated lying down again and pulling the blanket over her head to delay facing the day.

Jake appeared in the kitchen doorway. 'The bathroom is that way. There's a towel and a clean T-shirt if you want a shower. The coffee will be ready by the time you get back.'

Before she could reply, he had vanished back into the kitchen. She took the chance and bolted to the sanctuary of the bathroom. She found some toothpaste and rinsed her mouth before diving under the steaming shower. The water pummelled her body, clearing away the last of the fog of alcohol and sleepiness. The embarrassment, however, remained. The towel Jake had left for her was unexpectedly soft. The plain white T-shirt was far too big for her but had been ironed and neatly folded. She wondered if he did that to all his T-shirts, or if he'd done this one especially for her while she was sleeping on his couch, possibly snoring or even worse—dribbling. She shuddered again. She took a bit of time to brush some of the dried mud off her jeans, but she couldn't hide in Jake's bathroom forever. She ran her fingers through her hair, bringing it into some semblance of order. Then she took a deep breath and headed to the kitchen.

'Good morning.' Jake smiled broadly as he lifted a pot of coffee. 'Want some? Or I can do tea, if you prefer.'

'Coffee. Please.' The corners of his mouth twitched as he handed it to her. 'And don't you laugh at me. If you do, I'll either cry or throw this at you.'

'That would be a terrible waste of coffee.' Jake's mouth was still twitching. And to make matters worse, his eyes were laughing at her too.

Trying to hide her confusion, she took a mouthful of coffee. It was good. She drank some more and suddenly she was laughing. 'I can't believe that happened. I am so, so sorry. I blame Ollie.' She waved in the direction of the door where the pup sat, his tail wagging furiously at the mention of his name.

'That probably didn't help.' Jake pointed at the kitchen bench where one empty and one almost empty bottle of wine sat. 'Breakfast is on its way. Scrambled eggs on toast sound all right? I can do some bacon too if it would help.'

'Eggs on toast is fine. Thank you.'

While Jake made the toast, Lou checked her phone. There was a missed call from her mother in Sydney. She'd call back later.

They ate sitting at the breakfast bar.

'This is good,' Lou said. 'I'm feeling better already.'

'Cereal is no good when you've got a hangover—a cooked breakfast works every time.'

'I haven't got …' She stopped as he raised an eyebrow at her, in that way that was both charming and infuriating. 'All right. I may have a suggestion of a hangover. I'm really sorry. I don't know what happened. I never drink that much. And to pass out on your couch, that's …'

'Let's say you fell asleep and leave it at that. I've got a feeling you had a rough day yesterday.'

'I went into Scone. To the library. I wanted to ask about the truck in the shed. Instead I got another letter from her.'

'Luca?'

'Yes. One of the staff gave it to me.'

Jake picked up their empty plates and took them to the sink. 'I guess it was hard to read.'

She liked that he hadn't asked what the letter contained, and the way he kept his back to the table as he stacked dishes, giving her some space.

'The staff member … she knew Luca. It's so hard to meet people who knew her. They liked her and they tell me they're sorry she died. They expect me to feel something, but I don't. I don't know who that woman is. I can't act like a grieving daughter when my mother is still alive in Sydney. I can't be what everyone seems to expect me to be. It makes me feel as if there's something wrong with me.'

'I didn't think that when I met you.'

But you're different. She didn't say the words out loud. 'Thank you for that.'

'They don't know you or the circumstances. I imagine some people feel a bit uncomfortable around you for the very same reasons.'

He was probably right. Except for him. He obviously didn't feel uncomfortable around her. In fact, yesterday he'd made a point of being with her, even though she'd been upset and pretty much ready to murder the next person who mentioned Luca. Perhaps that was why he'd wanted to be with her—so she didn't do grievous bodily harm to any of the townspeople. Otherwise why would he have spent the whole afternoon and evening with her, watching old movies and talking about anything except the thing that was weighing so heavily on her mind?

Lou carried her empty coffee cup to the sink. She put the cup on the bench and her hand on his arm. He turned the tap off and looked down at her with amber eyes that were full of compassion.

'Thank you. I needed last night.' She stood on tiptoes and kissed him gently on the cheek.

'You are most welcome. Any time.'

Lou wasn't sure how long they would have stood there like that, looking at each other in the light of an afternoon and a night spent together, if Ollie hadn't come running in to tell them he wanted a walk. After that, it was easy to finish clearing up and head outdoors without any uncomfortable silences. Jake walked her to her car.

Lou paused before she opened the door. 'Thank you.'

'It was my pleasure. Honestly, it was.' He spoke softly and Lou felt he was speaking the truth. Her insides did a little skip and before she could stop herself, she was offering to return the favour. Dinner at 'her' house.

'I'd like that very much. But first, you're going to need these.' He held out the keys she'd given him yesterday.

'Yes, I will. Thanks.' As she took them, she realised that she had changed her mind about going back to Sydney.

'What time do you want us for dinner? I'm assuming Ollie is invited too.'

She stumbled some words out and hopped into her car before she could do anything else foolish.

The drive home was filled with self-recrimination. What was she thinking? Just because he'd been kind to her when she was feeling vulnerable …

As soon as she got back to the cottage, she changed into fresh clothes and poured a large glass of orange juice. She went outside to sit at a little metal table under the tree behind the house, and pulled out her phone.

'Hello, Mum.'

'Lou, honey. Is everything all right? I called last night but you didn't answer.'

'Sorry. I didn't hear the phone. I was … with a friend. Well, not really a friend. But …'

There was silence and she could almost hear her mother's frown turn to a smile.

'A friend? Tell me all about this friend.'

So she did. It was a relief to be able to talk to her mother. To someone who knew her but did not know Luca. Definitely didn't know Luca.

'It sounds to me like you needed some time to relax and be yourself yesterday. If Jake saw that, then he really is a friend.'

As always, her mother was right.

'I'm not sure what to do, Mum. Part of me wants to come home and forget about all of this, but a part of me wants to follow through. There are more letters somewhere. And now it's not just a matter of finding out about Luca—I'm starting to wonder who my biological father is too.'

'Of course you are.'

'And I might have relatives here somewhere.'

'Yes, you might.'

'Mum, stop agreeing with me.'

'Why? You've obviously been thinking about this a lot. It's preying on your mind. You are twenty-three years old with your whole life ahead of you. Do you really want to go through it with those questions unanswered?'

'But I might not find the answers.'

'No. You might not, but at least you'll know you tried.'

Her mother's words echoed around her mind as she unloaded her things from the car then spent the morning pottering around the cottage. She had yet to actually cook a meal in that kitchen and she was about to make dinner for someone who cooked for a living, even if he didn't call himself a chef. The cottage was reasonably well stocked with cooking implements and the crockery, although not fancy, was fine. It looked a bit as if Luca had liked to cook. Maybe she could ask Jake tonight, if the conversation happened to veer in that direction.

It took her a while to figure out what to cook, but she googled on her phone until she came up with a couple of ideas. It would all depend on what she could get in the store. She wasn't looking forward to facing—what had Jake said her name was? Kerry? Kelly? But when she got there, a teenage boy was serving. Some of the things on her list weren't on the shelves, and Lou revised her menu ideas for the evening to fit. A simple dinner it would have to be. The boy helped Lou find most of what she was looking for and passed it all through the till, pretty much without lifting his nose from his mobile phone.

After that, the day passed slowly. Lou pulled out her laptop. The cottage didn't have wi-fi, but she'd long since learned how to tether her laptop to her phone. She looked at some job sites. When she'd taken the tutoring job at uni, it was only supposed to be for one term. Now that was done, she should be looking for a job. She could go back for another year of tutoring, but what she really wanted was to leave uni behind and get on with her life. Her searches found very few jobs for a newly graduated environmentalist and none of them seemed particularly pleasing. This might simply be because her mind wasn't on it, so she put the laptop away. Job hunting could wait for another time.

Instead she settled on the couch to read and, as she felt herself nodding off, she realised that she hadn't actually slept in a bed since her return to Wagtail Ridge.

The sun was low in the sky when Jake pulled up outside Luca's cottage. Lou hadn't said what time she expected him and he hoped this would be all right. He suspected she would be pretty relaxed about time anyway—she had other things to be tense about.

When she answered his knock on the door, he held out a bottle of wine. 'I wasn't sure if you would want any of this after last night, but I thought I'd be polite.'

She pulled a face. 'Not for me tonight. Do you want some? Or I have beer.'

'Beer sounds fine.'

He followed her through to the kitchen, noting with appreciation the smells emanating from the oven. Ollie padded gently behind. He took a lap of water from the bowl near the back door and almost immediately curled up and went to sleep.

'He looks tired,' Lou remarked.

'I took him into Sydney today for his guide dog lessons.'

'How did he do?'

'Not too bad. He's got a bit to learn yet, but he's coming along.'

They talked about the dog and his future as Lou poured the beer and checked the meal. 'It'll be a little while yet.' She led him through to the living room. When they were settled, him on the sofa and her in the armchair, her face became serious.

'Jake, can I ask you something?'

'Of course.'

'You knew Luca quite well, didn't you?'

'Yes.'

'You spent a lot of time together when you drove the library truck. Did she … did she ever talk about me?'

He smiled. 'Of course she did. Especially towards the end. I can share some of what she said if you want me to.'

'I'm not sure I'm ready for that yet. Maybe one day. But there is one thing I need to know … did she ever tell you who my biological father was?'

'No.' He spoke with absolute honesty and her face fell a little. 'As far as I know, there's no-one in town who knew. If anyone does, it will be Deb at the pub. She and Luca were close. You could ask her.'

Lou nodded, but he suspected it was still too soon for that conversation. He wanted to put his arms around her and hug her. She looked so lost and alone. He couldn't do that, of course. She didn't need any more complications in her life. But he could be her friend. He could distract her or help her in whatever way she needed. He'd promised his friend Luca he'd do that. But the promise wasn't what was driving him. It was his desire to lift that haunted look from her big brown eyes, and to hear her laugh.

'That letter I got when I was in Scone yesterday, it was inside this.' She retrieved a book from a pile on a chair by the window and handed it to him.

'*The Shiralee*. That's a classic. We studied it when I was at school.'

'We did too. I have a copy at home.' She took the book back and returned it to its place on the pile.

Jake kept his face immobile as he waited for her to go on. She didn't offer to show either letter to him, for which he was glad. He was already trapped in a difficult place: between a promise to a dying friend and his feelings for Lou—feelings that were becoming more personal and less like just a friend every time she smiled at him with her head tilted in that cute way she had.

'I wondered if sending it with that particular book was some sort of hint that she wanted me to find my biological father. She says there are more letters. I've looked just about everywhere in the house but I can't find any more. I don't know what to do next.'

'The library was her great love.' He wanted to add *after you*, but it didn't feel right. Not yet. 'If there are any clues, they're likely to be associated with the library.'

Before Lou could answer, a timer went off in the kitchen. 'That's dinner. Would you help me look through the library afterwards?'

'Of course.'

They studiously avoided the topics of the library or Luca while they ate spiced chicken and roasted vegetables. Jake had a beer, but noticed that Lou stuck with soda water. She declined his offer to do the dishes and instead opened the back door and led the way to the shed. They went in through the side door and then opened up the back of the truck. Jake showed her a small compartment under the library door. It contained a set of metal stairs which he effortlessly slid into place.

Once they were inside the library, Lou turned slowly and looked around at the small space. 'If you wanted to hide something where you were sure it would be found, where would you put it?'

He wasn't sure if the question was rhetorical. 'The desk?'

'That's where I found the first letter. And this.'

She handed Jake a battered grey tin, the type used to hold file cards. He opened it and lifted out a couple of the bits of cardboard. 'Those are the book sleeves Luca used to check books in and out. She'd attach the borrower's library card.'

'There are no cards attached to these book sleeves. What are the titles? Let's see if they're back on the shelves.' Lou began flicking through the cards. There weren't many and it didn't take long to realise that none of the books were in their proper place in the shelves.

Lou flicked through the sleeves again. 'One of these is for *The Shiralee*, the book the librarian in Scone gave me.'

Jake already knew that. 'And there was a letter in that book.' He made a pretence of pausing. 'Maybe whoever has those books has the letters.' It wasn't the most logical conclusion to draw, and he could only hope she didn't notice his not-so-subtle push.

Lou sat down and flipped through the cards. 'Maybe. But how am I going to find them?'

Now was the time to fulfil his promise. He fought down the feeling that he was manipulating Lou. 'You could take the library out again.'

Lou looked up. 'You're kidding?'

'No. Seriously. If you want to find out more about Luca, that would be the best way. And you might get those books back from whoever has them. Then, if there is some sort of message for you …'

Lou tilted her head slightly, deep in thought as she leafed through the cards, then dropped them back in the tin. 'But I don't know where the library went. I don't even know how many places there are to visit.'

'I do. I drove for her, remember. I could help you, if you want me to. I could drive the truck again.'

'Maybe, but I'd only planned to stay a couple of days. This is going to take longer than that.'

'It is. We'd only be able to do one or maybe two trips per week, because I do have to work. That means it'll take a few weeks. But you don't have to visit all the towns. If we don't find anything, you can stop whenever you want to.'

'You'd be willing to spend that much time helping me?'

'Of course I would. It'd be fun doing the library run again. I always enjoyed it. The towns will certainly welcome you back. The library was more important to them than you might think. For some, it was the town's only regular social event.'

'I never thought of a library visit as a social event.'

'You've never lived in a small town—at least, until now.'

'I don't live here now. I'm just passing through.'

He was hoping that might change. 'If you did the library run, you'd learn a lot about your m— about Luca.'

'Maybe.' She nodded slowly and he felt as if a weight had been lifted from his shoulders.

He'd done what he'd promised.

CHAPTER 11

Val hovered behind Jake as he tried to work. 'So, have you spent any more time with our lovely Little Lou? She has grown into a very pretty girl, hasn't she?'

Jake was glad his face was hidden by the new shelving he was screwing into the post office wall. 'I'll be with you in a second, Val. I need to get this right.' He doubted the woman could be diverted, but it was worth a try.

'Of course, silly me. Sorry to interrupt. I'll go and put the kettle on.'

And that would lead to biscuits and what Val called a 'chat'. Her chats were more like interrogations if she thought the tea drinker had any sort of gossip to share.

'Not for me thanks, Val. I have a shift at the pub, so I need to get this done and get over there.'

'What would we all do without you? You're such a help to everyone in town. Why, I remember how much time you spent driving the library truck for dear Luca when she wasn't well. Have you told Little Lou that? I'm sure she'd appreciate it.'

Jake made a non-committal grunt, but Val didn't even hesitate.

'I should try to talk to her. I'm sure she'd love to hear more about what a wonderful person her mother was.'

Jake emerged from underneath the shelves, screwdriver in hand. 'I guess there's a lot for her to absorb right now,' he said, reaching deep inside himself to find the tactfulness he needed. 'It might be better to let her settle in and learn about Luca at her own speed.'

For a moment he thought he'd won. Then Val frowned and shook her head. 'That's a kind thought, Jake, but the poor girl is probably lonely. And she'll still be grieving for her mother, if she's only just found out. I think I'll bake a cake when the post office closes at lunchtime, then I can take it over to her and keep her company as she goes through her mother's things.'

'She might not want company,' he said, trying one more time. He knew Val meant well, but she had no tact, no boundaries and absolutely no empathy.

'Rubbish. Of course she does. My, those shelves do look good. Thank you, Jake. Get your invoice to me as soon as you can. You know those accounts people take forever to pay.'

He did and he would. He wondered if he should warn Lou of the storm that was about to descend on her. But it was also possible she did want to hear more about Luca, and Val would be glad to oblige.

He was loading the last of his tools back into his car when the phone in his pocket beeped. He and Lou had shared numbers yesterday, and he wasn't surprised to see the message was from her.

Have you got some time today?

He certainly did. *I'm cooking at the pub. Going there now. Come over?*

Sure. See you soon.

That solved the problem of Val very nicely. He went to the backyard of the post office to reclaim Ollie, who was visiting Val's chubby spaniel Victor.

Jake was peeling potatoes while Ollie slept on his mat in the bar when Lou finally put a tentative head through the doorway.

'Hi. Come on in. Pull up a stool if you like.'

'Thanks. Are you sure I'm not disturbing you?'

'I think I can peel potatoes and talk at the same time.'

'I always thought pubs and the like used powdered mash. Or bought it in bulk or some such.'

'Not in my kitchen. I may not be a proper chef, but I do make fine mash. You should try it sometime.'

'I will. Val from the post office dropped by. I hope you don't mind, but I used coming here to see you as a reason to escape. She can be a bit … intense.'

'That's a very kind way of putting it. I'm sorry, I should have warned you. I was putting up some shelving for her this morning and she said she might drop by.'

'That's fine. She seems harmless, but …'

'I know. Use me as an excuse any time.'

'Thanks. I went back into the library today. I'm not sure why. Maybe just for a last look before I left.'

He didn't say anything, simply waited for her to continue.

'But then I started thinking about that tin of book sleeves. If the missing books really do lead to more messages from Luca, how would I even find them? Do you know who has the books?'

'No, I don't. I usually went for a walk or ate sandwiches while Luca sorted out the books. I would help you find them if I could, but I don't know where they are.'

'Then I have to take the library out again.'

'I guess that could do it.'

'So, can you teach me the route, and how to drive the truck?'

'What?'

'I don't want to take up all your time, and I can get the job done much faster if I drive myself. So, I need to learn how to drive the library truck. Will you teach me? Please?'

'I can, but …'

'Thank you.' Lou bounced off the stool before he could finish. She suddenly seemed very eager to be gone. 'That's great. Tomorrow? The day after? Text me when you're free. I have all the time in the world, but right now I have to go. I'm Zooming with my parents back in Sydney shortly. See you soon.'

'Okay. Bye.'

She was gone before he finished speaking.

Jake picked up the last potato. His promise to Luca was kept—or at least the first part of it was. As for the rest … well, he'd do the best he could.

He glanced up at the door. If Lou found out, she'd be furious. She might never speak to him again, and he was beginning to think that would hurt him more than he might have imagined all those months ago when he made his promise to Luca.

Next morning, Lou had the shed doors open long before Jake was due to arrive and start the lesson. She'd woken early and for the first time, in the bed. When she had talked to her parents, they'd been supportive of her decision and when the call was over, she'd unpacked her clothes into the empty wardrobe, wondering as she did where Luca's clothes had gone. She'd taken a long relaxing bath, made a light dinner and eaten it on her lap while watching a movie. It had all seemed so … normal. As did getting into bed. Luca's shadow didn't seem so strong or so strange now.

As she waited for Jake, she climbed into the driver's seat and settled herself comfortably. The pedals were hard to reach and she guessed it was set up for Jake rather than Luca. Although, come to think of it, she didn't know how tall Luca had been. Apart from that one photograph, which she hadn't looked at since she'd found it, she knew nothing about what Luca had looked like. She knew so little about the woman who had given birth to her and that was starting to play on her mind more than she liked. Despite her adoptive parents' support for her quest, it still felt disloyal to be here in Luca's home, learning about her. Of course, her feeling for her parents would never change. She was doing this for her own peace of mind.

When Jake finally appeared, exactly on time, she jumped down from the cabin.

'I'm ready,' she said. 'How do we do this?'

'Well, good morning to you too.' His smile took the bite out of the words.

'Sorry. I'm a bit excited. It's going to be really cool to be able to drive a truck.'

'Slow down a bit. It's not quite that simple.'

'I know. But I want to try.'

'Let's get started then. I've found a place you can have a go safely. Come on.'

The three of them fitted quite comfortably into the truck's cab, Ollie between Lou and Jake.

'He's never been in the truck before,' Jake said. 'I hope he behaves.'

'You didn't have him when you were driving with Luca?'

'No. I didn't get him until a couple of months ago.'

'He'll be fine, won't you, Ollie?' Lou scratched the excited Labrador's head as Jake started the engine and pulled the library truck out of the shed. They drove out of town in the opposite direction to the road to Sydney. Lou watched everything Jake did. She looked at the speed when he changed gears and listened to the engine noise.

'Do they do these things in automatic? That would be so much easier.'

'Luca would never have been happy with an automatic. She liked the driving part of the job almost as much as she liked the books.'

A few minutes later, he turned the truck through some gates. A wide gravelled area lay beyond, a large set of stockyards set to one side.

'I do some work here sometimes,' Jake said, 'and they're happy to let me use it today. Just don't drive into any of the fences. I'll have to rebuild them.'

Lou chuckled.

'Don't laugh, because you'll be helping.' He cast a sideways glance in her direction and she felt her heart give a little skip. This was going to be fun. Useful too, of course, but fun.

Jake parked the truck and turned the engine off. 'Let's switch seats, but don't turn the engine on. There's a lot you have to know first.'

She listened carefully to everything he said about gears and air brakes and turning circles. It was forever before he finally told her to start the engine.

'But first check you are in neutral.'

'I know. I've got this.'

And she did. Sort of. Starting the engine was really no different from starting a car. She put the truck in gear, keeping one foot on the clutch and one on the brake. The ground was flat, so she had no fear of the truck rolling as she moved her foot to the accelerator and revved the engine a little. So far, so good. Very conscious of Jake's presence next to her, she began to release the clutch. The truck jumped forward and stalled. She heard a hint of a chuckle.

'Don't you dare laugh at me!'

'Never.'

The second time, she pressed harder on the accelerator. The engine roared loud enough to almost scare her, then stalled as she released the clutch far too quickly. She gritted her teeth in determination.

'Third time lucky.'

This time the truck moved forward. Not smoothly, but it kept going.

'Turn left,' Jake instructed as the yards suddenly loomed.

She turned the wheel, but the truck was slow to respond. With visions of mowing down the fence ahead of her, she reefed on the wheel and slammed a foot on the brake. The library shuddered to a stop—and stalled.

'Sorry.'

'That's fine. Just remember, at this slow speed, it's going to take a little longer to turn. You're doing fine. Start her up again.'

The next forty minutes were surprisingly enjoyable. Lou was determined to get it right so she listened to every word Jake said and followed every instruction carefully. She pretended not to hear his sharp intake of breath as they passed dangerously close to a fence, or see him wince each time the gears screamed when she missed a change. This truck driving business wasn't easy, and by the time Jake called a halt, her lower lip was sore from being bitten. It was very clear, even to her, that she needed a lot of practice before she'd be safe to drive on a public road.

'Let's walk around for a few minutes before we head back. You've been so tense all this time; you need to relax those muscles.' Jake jumped lightly down from the passenger seat. She tried to do the same, but landed with a bone-crunching jar.

They fetched Ollie, who had been tied up next to the water trough in the yard to keep him out of the way during the lesson.

Lou rotated her shoulders and stretched her arms and legs to ease the stiffness. 'I didn't do very well, did I?'

'You did okay, but you've got a way to go yet. You've never driven a truck before. And this old girl has a few quirks. She also doesn't have a lot of the modern technology to make driving easy.'

'I know.'

'More importantly, have you thought about what it takes to get a licence to drive this? I assume you only have a car licence.'

Lou frowned. 'I hadn't thought about that.'

'It's not as easy as getting a car licence. It will take some time.'

Her heart sank. He was right of course. It could take weeks, even for a small truck. And if she failed her test, what then?

'Why don't I just drive you? I don't mind the time. It's no problem, really. And Ollie and I can be pretty good company on the road.'

His words were a life jacket tossed to a drowning swimmer. 'That would be so much easier. Thank you.' Lou sprang towards him and, standing on the tips of her toes, she enveloped him in a hug.

'You're very welcome.' His arms came around her and pulled her close.

She gradually loosened her hold and his arms slid down her back. But he kept hold of her waist and as her eyes met his, she found herself unable to move. Like actors in those old films that Jake liked, they simply looked at each other for what seemed like a few very long seconds. In those moments, Lou sensed her feelings for Jake shift from friendship to … possibly something more.

She stepped back quickly, slightly confused. 'We'd better get back now. I've taken up too much of your time. Thanks again.' The words tumbled all over themselves. She didn't dare look at Jake's face for fear he would see something there that would give her away.

Jake glanced at his watch, appearing not to notice her sudden turmoil. 'I do have to get to the pub soon. If you're not doing anything, pop by. It should be fairly quiet, and I know Val won't be there.'

'I've got some stuff I have to deal with, but I'll try. Come on, Ollie.'

She hoped the walk back to the truck and the fuss over getting the dog safely settled in the cab would give her the time she needed to bring her errant emotions back under control. She'd come to Wagtail Ridge to sort out an inheritance. Now she was trying to get to know her birth mother and starting to wonder about her biological father. That was enough emotional upheaval for anyone.

The last thing she needed was to fall in love.

CHAPTER 12

Lou wasn't going to the pub. She had a shower and put on some better clothes because she needed to freshen up. Her hair was due to be washed and if she put on some lip gloss and mascara, it was because, after a few days of sorting through the house and library, not to mention the truck driving lesson, she simply wanted to feel a bit girlie. It had nothing at all to do with Jake, and this most certainly was not a date.

She left the cottage because it was a nice evening and she was in the mood for a long walk. She still wasn't ready to listen to strangers telling her about Luca and that would happen if she went to the pub. She might be feeling better about being in the cottage, but she wasn't ready for that kind of conversation yet. She certainly wasn't going to the pub because Jake was there. That little moment after her driving lesson had been exactly that—a little moment. There was nothing in it. Jake was a nice guy who was helping her. Sure, he was good looking but that didn't mean anything. She was in no fit state right now to think about anything but the task at hand: satisfying her need to know about Luca. And maybe find her biological father. Then she was going back to Sydney to get on with her life. She didn't need any sort of romantic relationship distracting her. Particularly with someone she'd be leaving behind in a couple of weeks … or maybe even months. She needed more time than she'd planned to do what had to be done, but she would be leaving eventually and she didn't want to make this harder than it already was. And she really didn't feel comfortable having that kind of relationship with someone who, for now at least, knew more about some aspects of her past than she did. It would be better to keep things with Jake all about the library. So having dinner at the pub when she knew he'd be there was not a good idea. She was not going to do it.

She repeated all that to herself as she walked towards the main street and then past the supermarket. She kept telling herself that right up to the moment she pushed open the door and walked into the pub.

As Jake had predicted, the bar wasn't busy. A few people glanced up as she walked in, but to her relief, there was no sign of Val from the post office—that hair made her easy to spot. There was no sign of Jake either. Lou assumed he was in the kitchen, so she waited at the bar. When someone appeared, she'd order a drink. Just one. She really wasn't hungry. One drink and she'd walk home again.

The door to the kitchen swung open and Jake emerged, a plate in each hand. He smiled when he saw her and Lou firmly instructed her insides to stop churning.

'Hi, Lou. Glad you could make it. I'm on my own tonight. Let me deliver these and I'll be right back.'

He carried the plates to a table where a young couple sat staring into each other's eyes, hands tightly clasped. They almost jumped when Jake put the plates down in front of them. He exchanged a few words with them and, a moment later, was back behind the bar.

He turned his smile on in full force. 'What can I get you?'

'Small glass of white wine please.'

'Sure thing. And to eat?'

'Well, I'm not really sure …'

'I can recommend the Caesar salad. It comes with prawns, if you like. Or I could grill a chicken breast for you.'

'Um … prawns sound good.'

'Fine.' He placed the wine in front of her. 'Take a table, any table. Or, if you want to eat at the bar, I could keep you company. It's Deb and Shane's night off so I'll have to keep serving, but it's quiet. A bit too quiet really. The meals are almost all done. So unless anyone else comes in, it's just drinks.'

And with that he vanished back into the kitchen. A thumping at her feet attracted Lou's attention. Ollie was almost sitting at her feet, staring up at her with a grin. He was struggling so hard not to jump his hindquarters were quivering a couple of centimetres off the floor.

'Oh. Such good manners. You are learning.' She bent down to pat him. He squirmed a lot, but still didn't jump up. 'Good dog.'

Lou slid onto a bar stool and sipped her drink, trying hard not to pay any attention to the couple wrapped in a fuzzy haze of love, or lust perhaps, on the other side of the room. After a while, a middle-aged woman approached the bar, carrying two glasses. Lou tensed, waiting for the question. Then Jake appeared.

'Hi, Sarah. Be right with you. Let me deliver this.' He carried another plate of food to a man sitting alone at a table and was back in a minute. 'Same again, Sarah?'

'Yep.'

Jake retrieved two glasses from under the bar and began filling them. 'By the way, Sarah, this is Lou. Lou, this is Sarah. She and her husband Geoff teach at the school.'

'Nice to meet you.' Sarah nodded in a friendly fashion. 'Thanks, Jake.' She took the beers and headed back to her husband.

Jake looked at Lou and raised an eyebrow. It was clear what he was saying: she didn't have to be afraid that everyone would want to talk about Luca.

'One prawn Caesar coming up.' He vanished again.

The salad he placed on the bar in front of her when he returned looked good. 'I hope you like the dressing. I make it myself.'

She picked up her fork, skewered a prawn and ate it. It was fresh and tasty and the dressing was wonderful. She licked her lips with great exaggeration.

'Thanks,' Jake said.

She didn't say much while she ate. Jake amused her with stories of Ollie's puppy training sessions and occasionally served another customer. By the time she was finished, Lou had relaxed. She had put Jake firmly back into the correct corner of her mind—friend, nothing more—and she was no longer afraid that every time she looked at him, he'd see something in her face that would further complicate her already far too complex reasons for being in Wagtail Ridge.

When she was finished, Jake took her empty plate back to the kitchen and topped up her wine.

'Tell me about the library.' The question popped out as she took the glass from him. She realised she actually did want to know. 'When I went to the library in Scone, they said the mobile library wasn't theirs any more. That it was privately funded.'

'That's right. It was before my time, but I've been told people around here were pretty upset when the council decided to close the mobile library.'

'But the library in Scone isn't that far away.'

'It wasn't all about that.' Sarah had come back to the bar. 'Sorry, I don't mean to butt in, but that mobile library was about more than just books.'

'What do you mean?'

Sarah handed the glasses to Jake and nodded. Then she propped herself on a bar stool. 'When I was a kid, we didn't have the internet and only two TV channels. Gosh—that makes me sound old. The point is that getting to Scone was difficult because my father and mother were always working just to keep the farm afloat. But I could ride my pony into the Ridge to meet the mobile library. It was a lifesaver.'

Jake placed the beer on the bar and took her money.

'Thanks, Jake.' Sarah made no move to go back to her table. 'Back then it wasn't much, and it wasn't Luca driving it of course, but it was an escape for a lonely kid. There were people and places, whole worlds in the pages of those books for me to discover. Then when Luca took it over, when it was still part of the council, she really improved the range of books. And she'd go out of her way to get special orders in. By then I had kids of my own, and they loved the library as much as I had. They loved Luca too—despite the internet and streaming and everything else, she kept them interested in books. She kept them reading. They both have uni degrees now. They work in the city and I miss them, but I'm glad they are making good lives for themselves. In part, I have Luca to thank for that.'

'Were you one of the people who helped keep the library going?'

'Sure. Almost everyone was. We were all so angry when the council decided to close the mobile run. It was more than just a chance to pick up a book. People would make a point of coming into town that day. They'd meet friends and chat over a pub lunch.

Grab their groceries. Whatever they needed to do. It was something of a social event. We didn't want to lose that.'

'It must have been hard to raise the money.'

'Not as hard as you think. People cared. They donated a lot of books. The computer was second-hand—it came from Matt, the real estate agent. We held a B&S ball. That bought the truck at auction and raised petrol money for a year. The folk over in Spring Ridge looked after registration and insurance. Rocky Glen had a picnic race meeting and that pretty much all went to Luca. It wasn't charity. It was payment for her work in keeping the library running.'

Lou could hear the emotion in the woman's voice. She felt her own throat tightening too. It was the first time talk of Luca had drawn a positive emotion from her and she wasn't really sure how to react to that. All this time she'd been angry at Luca for giving her up just because being a single mother was too hard. But now she was beginning to think there must be another reason. The stories she was hearing painted a picture of a mother who loved her child. The woman people were describing—the woman who wrote those letters—would not have given up her child easily.

'Thank you for telling me. I … well, Luca was my biological mother. She gave me up for adoption when I was small so she is a stranger to me. I'm trying to learn more about her.'

Sarah nodded with a sad smile.

'You knew?'

'She talked about you a lot. And you look exactly like her, you know.'

'People keep telling me that.'

'If you spend much time around here, she won't be a stranger to you for long. Luca was one of those people who are the heart of the community, and not just here in the Ridge. The other nearby towns too.'

'I'm taking Lou on the library run,' Jake said.

Sarah smiled. 'Good for you. Both of you. Make sure you let everyone know where and when. They'll be so pleased to have it back, you'll be swamped with customers.' She picked up the drinks Jake had placed on the bar in front of her. 'I'll leave you now. This is date night, and I don't want to leave Geoff alone for too long. Some hot young thing might try to steal him away from me.' The affection in her voice was as palpable as the glow in her eyes as she looked across at the balding middle-aged man with the thickening waist who was waiting for her.

'Have a great evening.'

The woman patted her on the hand, and then wandered off.

'That was nice,' Lou said, partly to herself and partly to Jake.

'Sarah and Geoff are good people.'

'We have to be careful not to get people's hopes up too much,' she said firmly. 'About the library, I mean. I'm not really reopening it. One run, to try and find the letters. Then I have to sell the cottage and go. I've only just got my degree. If I want a career, I need to find a proper job.'

Being a mobile library is a proper job. He didn't say anything, but she was certain he thought it. There were other hopes she didn't want to raise. The silence that settled between them seemed to cut them off from the rest of the people in the bar and surround them with questions that she didn't want asked—or answered.

Jake's eyes flickered to the doors as Lou heard someone enter the bar behind her.

'Look out. It's Val,' he whispered in a conspiratorial tone. 'Do you want to sneak out before she spots you?'

'Yes, please.'

'There's a side door that way.' Jake tilted his head. 'We can talk tomorrow about the details of the library run.'

'Thanks.' Lou stood up and hurried out.

CHAPTER 13

Three days later, Jake and Ollie arrived at Lou's cottage early to find she was already up. The shed doors had been opened and as he walked down the driveway, he could see Lou moving around inside.

'Good morning.'

'Hi, Jake.'

Ollie stayed at Jake's side, looking up at him with begging brown eyes. 'Go on.' The dog gave a tiny woof and bounded towards Lou.

She bent down to give him a hug. 'He really is starting to learn some manners.'

'We've been working pretty hard.'

'The coffee is on, if you want one before we leave.'

'I'd love one.'

He followed her into the kitchen, which smelled strongly of fresh coffee. What looked like a packed lunch sat in boxes on the table, alongside a folded map of New South Wales. He cringed a little inside. He'd been about to ask how she'd spent the last couple of days, but now he didn't need to. The answer was clear.

'I did some research about our route yesterday. It was that or clean house. I had a go at mapping out our run.' Lou handed him coffee and opened the map.

He made a non-committal noise, hiding behind a sip of coffee.

'So, I marked Wagtail Ridge and you said today we were going to Blackville. Here.' She indicated with her finger.

'That's right.'

'And you said the other towns were Breeza and Spring Ridge and so on.'

Jake could see she had marked each town on the map. He knew what was coming next and mentally scrambled for the right answer.

'That doesn't seem like very many stops. There are a lot of other small communities in the same area. Did Luca visit any of them?'

'Yes, she did.' That at least was a truthful answer.

'Then we could add some more. The more places we visit the more chance of finding what we're looking for. And if we map the route carefully, we could do more than one in a day, and get it done faster.'

'Towards the end, Luca didn't do all the towns. She was really too ill to be out at all, so I tried to make it easy for her and we only did one town each day. Sometimes she was too sick to go and a stop was missed. The route was very irregular at the end.' That was also true.

'So you think if she left me letters, they will only be in these towns she still visited right up until … until she died?'

It was the first time he'd heard real sadness in Lou's voice when she talked about Luca. He wanted to hug her and tell her everything, but he'd made a promise.

'I think that's likely.' He didn't think. He knew. He knew exactly where Lou would find those letters.

'I guess that makes sense. And if the route was so irregular, I guess you don't know which towns the letters might be in.'

He didn't answer that. He didn't want to lie. Lou was so engrossed in her planning, she didn't seem to notice.

'But can we still do more than one stop on each trip? Maybe change the route here and here … that way we'll get to them all faster.'

'I hadn't really thought about that. Let's look at that when you see what happens on this first trip. You might not want to do too many at once. And besides, I do still have a job at the pub, and I'm booked to do some work on a couple of the studs. And install wheelchair ramps in some housing commission properties. I don't know how much time I'll have to drive you.' He hated being so discouraging, but it was the only way he could see to avoid direct lies.

'Yes. Sorry. I didn't mean to just assume. Of course you have other things to do.' Lou started folding the map and gathering her things to hide her obvious discomfort. 'Really sorry.'

'No, don't be. It's fine. But we had better get going.'

The three of them settled into the cab of the truck.

'Right. We're off. Ollie, settle down.' Jake started the engine and slipped the truck into gear. It slowly moved out of the shed and into the sunlight. They pulled out of the driveway and into the street. Once they reached the intersection with the main road, their route was west.

'Tell me about our first stop.'

'Blackville. It's about sixty kilometres from here, so it's not a long run. There's not much there. A post office and a tiny school. About fifteen or twenty houses. There are probably more people on the surrounding farms than in the town itself.'

'How will they know we're there?'

'I hope you don't mind, but I rang their post office and told them we were coming. Everyone would have found out within about ten minutes of that call; small-town grapevines are very efficient. And besides, we're pretty hard to miss.'

Lou fell quiet and settled back in the seat, one arm around Ollie, to watch the scenery. There'd been good rain recently and everything was fresh and green. The cattle and horses grazing in paddocks near the road looked fat and shiny and the crops were flourishing. With the window wound down, the air smelt fresh and clean, with a tinge of eucalyptus.

Jake had expected this journey to feel the same as driving Luca, but it didn't. Everything was very different. Driving Luca had been doing a favour for a friend and for the community he was part of. Of course he knew how vital the library was to the towns they visited and he'd like to see it revived. But this was more. This was about someone who was fast weaving her way into his life without meaning to. This was about helping her get past a difficult time, because he was beginning to hope that once that happened, there might be room in her life for something more. Something else. Maybe for him.

Lou was surprised at the contentment she felt being on the road with Jake and the dog. Jake had hooted the horn as they'd driven past the small school at the edge of town. All the kids had rushed to the fence to wave and Lou had felt like she was an explorer, being waved off on some great trip of discovery. Well, maybe she was.

She looked sideways at Jake. He looked totally at home. Eyes on the road. Hands firm and assured on the steering wheel.

'How often did you drive Luca?'

'During the last six months, all the time. She wasn't able to drive.'

At last Lou summoned the courage to ask the question that had been on her mind for some time. 'How did she die?'

Jake glanced her way. 'Cancer.'

The word cut through Lou like a knife. She closed her eyes for a few minutes and let a familiar pain and anger wash over her.

'Are you all right?'

She had to take a deep breath before she could answer. 'Yes. I'll be fine. It's just that I lost someone I cared about to cancer a few years ago. My grandfather.' She saw Jake frown, his head moving slightly to one side. 'My adoptive grandfather. Although as far as I was concerned … as far as I am still concerned, the Taylors are my real family.' The unintentional emphasis on the word 'real' didn't escape her. It would not have escaped Jake either.

'Cancer is a cruel disease.'

'Yes. It is. My grandfather fought it as long as he could, but in the end, it took him. After months of treatment that was almost as bad as the disease itself.'

'That sounds a lot like Luca's story. She just wasted away. The chemo took her hair and her strength … but it never took her courage.'

Lou found herself nodding. She understood exactly what Jake was saying. She felt a twinge of sympathy for Luca. At least her grandfather had been surrounded by his family as he fought and fought and finally lost. Luca hadn't had anyone. Or maybe she had.

'Thank you, Jake.'

'For what?'

'For being there with her. I mean, it's really got nothing to do with me, but I am beginning to understand that you did a lot for her. That was kind and generous of you.'

'It wasn't just me. Deb spent a lot of time with her too. And some of the others. She was our friend.'

The tone of his voice made it clear that was reason enough.

'I'm really glad she didn't have to face it alone. No-one should have to do that.' Even if the reason she was alone was because she had sent her daughter away.

She didn't say the words out loud, but Lou wouldn't be human if she didn't feel some resentment, or even anger, at that thought. But more than ever, she was beginning to wonder why. She was very conscious of Jake sitting beside her. If he'd done these same journeys with Luca, maybe she'd talked to him about her reasons. He might be able to help Lou understand, but they'd only known each other for such a short time that she wasn't ready to go there—yet. Maybe at some point in the future she would, but right now, she didn't want to make herself any more vulnerable than she already was.

She took a slow breath and turned her head to gaze out the window at the passing landscape. Jake took the hint and said no more, although a slightly anxious Ollie did push his head under Lou's arm. Whether he was trying to comfort her or demanding comfort for himself was a moot point; she felt better for his touch.

Some time later a tall wooden sign told her they were arriving in Blackville. She was glad of the sign, for without that she wouldn't have suspected she was entering a town. Compared to this, Wagtail Ridge was a bustling metropolis. There were just a handful of homes. If there was a pub, she must have missed it. A small school sat on a crossroads and Lou guessed that was the only reason for the town, if you could call it that, to exist. Jake hit the horn twice as they passed the school, and used a larger space a little further up the road to turn the library truck so he could park with the door opening onto the footpath.

'This is it.' He turned the engine off. 'Let me help you get everything set up.'

He swung down from the cab and began what she imagined was a familiar routine. He opened the library door and caught it back so it wouldn't swing. Then he opened two small hatches beneath the door and pulled out the metal steps. Once they were firmly in place, he darted up the steps and she saw a light go on.

'I haven't turned the air con on,' he said as she climbed the stairs to join him. 'But feel free to turn it on if it starts getting hot.'

'That's fine.'

'I think you're set. Anything else you need? Would you like me to hang around to help you get the feel for how it all works?'

'Thanks, but I think I'm better off doing this on my own.'

'I'll leave you to it. I'll take Ollie for a good long walk. Have fun.' He vanished into the bright sunlight.

Lou dropped into the chair behind the desk as a flood of panic threatened to overwhelm her. What was she thinking? She wasn't a librarian. Wanting to know more about Luca was no excuse to pretend she was. The people in these communities needed a real librarian. And they needed someone who would come back again and again, not appear once for their own purposes and then desert them.

She had almost talked herself into giving up this crazy scheme when a head poked through the doorway, followed by a body. A schoolboy. Then another. Then a girl with plaited brown hair.

'Have you got the last two Harry Potters? I still haven't read them.'

'Yes, we do. Over there, third shelf from the top,' she answered without thinking.

'Great.'

'The Brumby books?' A tentative question from the little girl.

'Of course I have those. They're over there.' Lou pointed the girl in the right direction and was rewarded with a smile.

She had spent the past couple of days tidying and dusting the books on the shelves and trying to memorise some of the titles. She'd also added a few books from Luca's living room until the library was practically overflowing.

A woman who Lou guessed was the schoolteacher followed her charges into the library. 'We've missed the library so much. Our school library is pretty small, so this helps us no end. We need to spend our money on school books, so the kids were missing out on really important reading. And fun reading too.'

Lou felt a surge of something very like guilt.

'I was so sorry to hear about Luca. The kids all loved her.'

Did this woman know about her relationship with Luca? Before she could frame the question, Lou found a small blonde girl standing in front of her.

'I've read all this now. What other books like it do you have?' She placed a book on the desk. Lou stared at the words 'Wimpy Kid' on the cover, and her mind went blank.

'Why don't you have a look on the shelves over there and see if there's anything that appeals to you.'

Luckily the child accepted that as an answer and went looking for herself.

The kids were starting to queue at her desk now, each one clutching a book or two. Lou opened the metal tin ready to check them out. She gathered up the small collection of empty book sleeves and put them to one side.

'What's your name, miss?' The Harry Potter fan handed over a library card and the two books that he'd been seeking.

'I'm Lou … Miss Taylor.' She glanced at the card the boy had offered. 'You're William Sparkes and you're a Harry Potter fan.'

'Yes, Miss Taylor. I promise I'll have these both read and ready to bring back next time.'

Lou opened her mouth to tell him there wasn't going to be a next time. At least not for her. But then she stopped. He was so pleased to have the library back; they all were. She wasn't going to spoil the event by telling them it was only this once. And he'd probably ask why. She had nothing to tell the boy. She certainly couldn't tell him that this last library run had nothing to do with helping him and his friends to learn more about the world outside their tiny town. It had nothing to do with bringing books to their community. It was for her own sake, as she struggled to cope with her past and the mother she had never known.

'That's good, William—'

'Billy.'

'That's good, Billy. Enjoy the books.' She collected the book sleeves and attached his library card before placing the bundle in the empty tin.

'Thanks.' He vanished, to be replaced by the little girl, clutching a pony book.

'Can I have this one, please?'

'Of course you can.'

The last of this group of readers was the teacher, who exited carrying a couple of historical romance novels with covers that suggested they were of the more raunchy variety.

When the trailer was empty, Lou let out a deep breath and tried to gather her thoughts. She had quite enjoyed recommending books and chatting to the kids, but when it came to her reason for being here, she'd learned nothing.

She counted the book sleeves in the tin. A lot of books had found new readers today. The idea of using cardboard book sleeves and membership cards was so old-fashioned. She was sure everything had been replaced by computers long before, even in a mobile library. She glanced over at the empty desk where a computer had obviously once sat. Why hadn't Luca used that? Maybe she had, but today's visitors had seemed totally familiar with the manual card system. Of course, that didn't explain the empty book sleeves she'd found. She gathered them up, put a band around them and put them back in the tin.

The room darkened for a few seconds as a new visitor climbed the stairs into the trailer.

'Hello. It's so lovely to see you here.' The older woman came to where Lou was sitting and placed an egg carton on the desk. 'I used to give Luca eggs every time she came. I have more than I can ever use. I thought you might like some. From my own chickens of course.'

'Ah … Yes. Thank you.' Lou liked the idea of fresh farm eggs. If she didn't stay in Wagtail Ridge long enough to eat them, she could always take them back to Sydney. Her mother would love them. 'How much?'

'Oh, no. Just take them. I would hate to see them go to waste.'

'Are you sure?'

'Of course.'

'That's very kind of you. Thank you.'

'It's nothing, really. I'm glad to get them out of my kitchen. You'll enjoy them. Luca always said my eggs were the best she had ever tasted. And they make great cakes too.' The woman turned away and headed for the crime section.

With the school kids all gone, the town's adults were arriving. At least twenty of them came and left, clutching books. She wouldn't have thought the town had that many residents, although of course some may have come from the surrounding properties. Most people greeted each other as friends and, from the level of chatter as they gathered outside the library waiting for their turn in the tiny space, Lou guessed they didn't see each other on a daily basis. Library day was obviously something of a social occasion for the people who didn't get many chances to just chat.

She was starting to tidy up for the day when a grey-haired woman entered.

'Well, you must be Lou. It is a pleasure to meet you. I'm Dot. I run the post office.'

Lou wasn't surprised the woman knew her name; small-town grapevines always run through the post office. 'Hi, Dot. What are you looking for today? A bit of crime. Romance?'

'Actually, I've come to return a book.' She placed it on the desk.

'Oh.' The words on the cover were so familiar to Lou. She placed the tips of her fingers on the lettering. *Seven Little Australians*. 'This was one of my favourite books when I was young. Did you like it?'

'I loved it when I read it as a child. And my daughter loved it when I read it to her. Now my granddaughter has joined the club.'

'It is that sort of book,' Lou said as she opened the cover. The book sleeve was missing, of course. She reached for her tin. Sure enough, there was the book sleeve among those without library cards.

'Oh, that's strange. I'm sorry. But your card isn't in here.'

'I know. Luca didn't take it on her last visit.'

'Oh.'

'She gave me something instead.' Dot glanced down at the book.

Lou followed the glance and realised there was something inside the book's front cover. An envelope. She opened the cover long enough to recognise the handwriting, then closed it again.

'Thank you.'

'You're welcome. Luca asked me to hold it for you. She wasn't sure you would ever come for it, but she hoped. I'm glad you have.

Now, I'd better get back to work. It was nice seeing you, Lou. I hope you'll come back. It would mean so much to us to have the library calling regularly again.'

She was gone before Lou could form an answer.

Lou sat there looking at the envelope. A small part of her panicked, and a tiny voice deep inside urged her to simply tear it up. She'd already become too involved in this woman's life. But she wasn't going to listen to that voice. She had set out to learn about her biological mother, and that was what she would do. But not here, when someone was likely to walk through the door.

She put the tin of library cards back in the desk drawer and put the letter in her bag. As she did, Jake put his head through the door.

'Are you ready to go home?'

'Yes, I am.'

CHAPTER 14

My Darling Daughter,

So, you've decided to take the library on the run. You must have, if you're reading this. Thank you. There really is so much I have to tell you. Is Jake helping you? I guess he must be. That old truck was never easy to drive.

Did Margaret bring you some eggs when you stopped at Blackville? I hope so. Her hens lay the most wonderful eggs. I don't know what makes them special. Maybe it's what she feeds them. Of maybe it's because she talks to them when she does.

There I go rambling on about eggs when I should be telling you my story.

How do I explain what happened that terrible day? The day my mother wasn't there waiting for me when I came home from my travels. How can I show you a grief that almost destroyed my life when I had barely begun to properly live it?

I was coming back to spend my twenty-first birthday with her. I'd been working as a camp cook. Well, an assistant to a station cook in the Northern Territory, and that meant a bit of camp cooking. It was a great job. I spent a lot of time sleeping under the stars. Have you ever been to the Territory? The sky at night is so wonderful ... you feel you can almost reach up and touch the stars. This was the 1990s of course, so women on properties weren't that unusual. But still I felt special. Privileged, I guess, to be able to live the type of lifestyle that defined us as a country—or at least did in my eyes.

But there I go again, wandering off. Some of my memories are so very clear, even with this cursed illness and the drugs. Those are the happiest memories, and a lot of them involve you. Others are hazy. I wonder sometimes if my mind is trying to avoid the things that hurt the most.

It was a long journey home from the Territory. I took buses mostly. I couldn't afford to fly, but even if I could, I sort of like long bus rides. Watching the scenery roll past. Looking out into the darkness at night. I don't really have any religion. To me, the bush at night is a kind of spiritual experience.

I was so excited as we pulled into Scone. I hadn't seen my mother for nearly six months. When I jumped off the bus, I expected she'd be there waiting for me. Smiling that wonderful smile of hers. Waiting to hug me. There was so much I wanted to say. So many adventures to tell her about. But most of all, I just wanted to tell her that I loved her, and hear her say the same thing to me.

She wasn't there. There was a policeman instead.

My mother had been hurt in a road accident the day before. While I was on that bus heading south, someone had driven their ute into the side of her car at high speed. I learned that day how very fragile life is.

The policeman took me to the hospital. I barely recognised my mother. Most of her head and face were covered with bandages and the rest was swollen and bruised. She had drips and tubes running into her, and machines to keep her alive. I sat there with her for three days but she never woke up. The doctors told me she wasn't in any pain because of the drugs, but that was hard to believe. Sometimes she moaned a little and once I thought I heard her say my name … but that could have just been me wishing to hear it. Then she died. I never got the chance to tell her I loved her or to say goodbye. It was only weeks later that I realised she had died on my twenty-first birthday.

I cannot begin to tell you what it was like to lose her. It wasn't just the grief, although that was so strong at times I could barely breathe … there was guilt too. If only I'd come home a day earlier, she might still be alive. That's foolish, of course. Her death wasn't my fault. But there was no-one to say those words to me. My last memory of my mother was a vision of suffering that would haunt me for years.

I was alone. Unutterably alone. There was not one person in the world who loved me. Sure, I had friends I'd met on my travels, but those friends came and went as we all moved on to different places, in search of different things.

My mother had friends in Wagtail Ridge and I'd been to school with their kids. They knew me, but they didn't really know *me. Not the way she and I knew each other. We'd always been each other's best friend. There were things we had shared with no-one else. And now I had no-one to share those things with.*

Not only that, there was no-one in this whole wide world who loved me. Not real, unconditional love. I hope you never have to experience such emptiness. There were times I hated her for leaving me like that. And there were times I cried so hard I thought I would never stop.

I stayed in our cottage in the Ridge and for a long time, I was just hiding. But you can't hide forever in country towns, and after a while, I found myself being dragged out of my solitude by people who brought me small gifts of food, or who dropped by to check I was all right. I won't say I got over it. You never get over a shock like that. But slowly, I got better. And that's when I vowed that no child of mine would ever suffer as I had. No child of mine would ever have to sit in a hospital as I had and watch their whole world be ripped from under them. No-one should ever feel that alone and lost.

I need you to understand that.

Your loving mother,

Luca.

Tears pricked Lou's eyes as she put the letter down. Tears for whom? Until now, she hadn't shed a tear for Luca, because Luca was a stranger to her, but that stranger had lost her mother in such a terrible way. Luca's mother Christina was a stranger too, but the thought of her death squeezed Lou's heart until it ached. Why? Perhaps it was the thought of her mother, Fiona, and her grandmother suffering in a similar way. The thought of losing her real family was heartbreaking.

Her real family? Who were her real family?

When she was small, Lou had been the victim of schoolyard bullies. Mean girls who'd told her she was somehow not as good as the rest of them because she was adopted. Because she didn't have a 'real' mother and father. With Fiona's guidance, she'd come to understand that 'real' was a surprisingly flexible word. What was a 'real' mother after all? Someone who loved you and helped you grow into the person you were supposed to be. Fiona had done that for her.

But maybe Luca was, in her own way, doing the same thing now?

If she was, she wasn't making it easy. If she wanted Lou to know her, why hadn't she come forward and told her all this in person? Lou could understand, even appreciate, that she hadn't wanted to disrupt a child's life, but Lou hadn't been a child for some years now. Luca should have found her and given her a chance to hear all this firsthand. She focussed on that thought, like a child scratching an annoying itch until it starts to bleed, until the tears went away and the pain was replaced by something else that could almost have been anger.

She got to her feet and started making a cup of tea, her third for the morning. She didn't really want it, but doing nothing was driving her crazy. She and Jake hadn't set a time for the next library trip, so she was stuck here in the Ridge with no friends and nothing to do. She paced the kitchen while the kettle boiled, and then went back to the living room without bothering to make the tea.

'It's time I started doing some research,' she said to herself and powered up her laptop. She had friends who were into genealogy, tracing their ancestors back to the days of the first European settlers, or even before that. She'd never really cared. She was interested in the future, not the past. Or rather, she had been. Now the past was haunting her. Luca's letters weren't enough. She wasn't sure when, or even if, she'd find another one. She opened a browser and a search engine.

The name Luca Bonnet produced links to a project manager, two young men with bad facial hair and many pictures of knitted caps for babies. A search for Christina was equally without result. Of course, Christina hadn't been part of the internet generation, so that wasn't entirely unexpected. It wasn't the most cheerful route to take, but maybe a local newspaper had an archival story about the accident in which she'd died. There were a couple of regional news organisations that had been around for twenty-five years or more, but a lot of traffic accidents had occurred in that time. It would help to know when Luca's birthday was, because just randomly looking wasn't going to get her anywhere.

She slammed the laptop shut in frustration and grabbed her keys.

The afternoon was warm, but not hot enough to be discouraging, so she decided to walk into town. It would do her good to stretch her legs. She passed a few cottages that were not all that different from the one she had inherited from Luca. A couple of kids playing on a swing waved at her and she waved back. When she reached the main road, she turned in the direction of the shops and pub. Some of the locals nodded a greeting or passed a comment about the weather as they went about their business. At first it felt strange greeting people she didn't know, but she began to realise that this was how people were in Wagtail Ridge.

Lou stopped walking when she reached the real estate agent's window. She peered through the glass at the notices. Sections of land near the town had been subdivided for residential use. They weren't expensive. There were two cottages similar to hers for sale in the town itself. They weren't that expensive either. Well, not compared to Sydney. But if she sold the house she had inherited, it would still leave her with a tidy sum of money, enough to fulfil those travelling dreams. She leaned closer to the window. The 'For Sale' notices looked as if they'd been faded by the sun. They were a bit saggy at the corners. Those houses had been on the market for a while.

The office door opened and a man appeared. 'Hello. Can I help you?'

'No, thanks. I was just looking.'

'Of course. You're very welcome. If you're thinking of buying or selling, I guess I can help. I'm the only agent in town. Matt Ambrose.' He held out his hand and Lou shook it.

'I'm Lou Taylor.'

'Oh, of course. Luca's daughter. Pleased to meet you.'

'I was wondering how long these cottages have been on the market?'

He nodded. 'You're very astute. It's a small town and these sorts of sales move slowly. If I had to rely on those, I'd be out of business. But the farm sales keep me going.' Ambrose had a pleasant, open face, not handsome, but he did exude an aura that suggested honesty. It was a good face for a real estate agent.

'How hard would it be to sell Luca's—my cottage?'

His brow furrowed. 'It's hard to say. It could use a refresh. Some paint, a bit of work to present it nicely to the market. You're not staying then? I thought … we all hoped that now you had the library up and running again …'

She didn't bother asking him how he knew about the library. She was beginning to understand how the Wagtail Ridge grapevine worked. 'I'm not sure yet. I'm checking my options.'

'Of course. Well, any time you'd like me to come over and do a valuation for you or give you some thoughts on how to prepare it for the market, I'm happy to do so.'

'I'll remember that, thank you.' She started to move on but stopped when the door to the office swung open.

'Daddy?' The high-pitched voice trembled on the edge of a scream.

'It's all right, Vicki. I'm here.' Matt swept the girl into his arms. She clung to him as if her life depended upon it.

'I was scared, Daddy. I thought you'd gone away too. Just like Mummy.'

'No. I'm here, Vicki. You must have had a little dream. Did you fall asleep?'

The girl nodded, wiping her face.

'Well, it was just a dream. I'm here with you, sweetheart.'

The girl's big blue eyes were still filled with tears. She looked at Lou. 'I thought I heard Mummy talking.'

The anguish on Matt's face was raw, and Lou wasn't at all sure he would be able to answer his daughter.

'Hello, Vicki,' she said, hoping to give the man a chance to recover his composure. 'My name is Lou.'

'Hello.'

'Miss—Lou is the new library lady.' Vicki didn't notice the forced lightness in Matt's voice.

Before Lou could jump in and say she wasn't, Vicki's face lit up.

'Oh. I like the library.' Just as quickly the joy faded. 'But the other library lady went away. Just like Mummy did.'

Lou was beginning to understand the tragic cause of the little girl's fear. There was no way now that she could say the library wasn't reopening. Perhaps Vicki would forget about it. Kids forgot things, didn't they?

'Will you read the books to me, Daddy? Just like Mummy used to?'

'Yes. But first, you go in and finish your drawing. I'll be there in a minute.'

Vicki frowned. 'Promise?'

'I promise.' Matt kissed his daughter's cheek and lowered her gently to the ground. She vanished back through the door into the office. He waited until it closed before speaking. 'I'm sorry about that.'

'No, please don't apologise. I understand.'

'We lost her mother over a year ago. Poor Vicki was so afraid, she never wanted to leave the house. But then she started going to the library—but only if I would take her. She would sit and chat to your mother. When Luca died, she just retreated again. She gets scared if she can't see me.'

Lou couldn't find any words to answer that—perhaps because there was no answer to the grief in every line of the man's face.

'I'm sorry.'

Matt took a deep breath and Lou could see the strength it took for him to gather his thoughts and emotions again.

'I'll think about what you said about the cottage,' she said.

'Would you also think about the library? It means a lot to Vicki. To all of us.'

Lou nodded and made her escape from the pleading look in his eyes. She let her feet take her where they willed while she tried not to think about the encounter. Strangely enough, that was to the pub. She pushed the door open. The only person present was Deb.

'Hi, Lou.'

'Hi.'

'Can I get you something?'

'Um … lemonade, lime and bitters?' She didn't want a drink, but what other excuse could she give for coming here?

'If you're looking for Jake, he's not here. But he will be a bit later. He's doing dinners.'

'No. I wasn't—' Lou saw the look on Deb's face. 'Well, yes I was looking for him. But only to ask about when we could do the next library run.'

Deb nodded in a knowing fashion. 'Of course. How did the Blackville trip go?'

'Okay, I guess.'

Deb didn't say anything.

'When I say okay, I mean good. It was kinda nice to see all those kids so eager to read. The adults too.'

'I think that's a thing in small towns. There are not a lot of places to go or things to do. People read.'

'Do you?'

'Oh, yes. All the time.'

'Did you get books from the library?'

'Of course. We all did.'

'But it's not far to the library in Scone. And surely they have ebooks you can borrow online?'

'That's true. And they do. But nothing is better than meeting friends with a shared love. Spending time chatting about the books. And Luca was so very good at finding new books for everyone to try. She used to get boxes of books from all sorts of places. She'd go through them carefully and read a lot of them too. She had this … I guess you'd call it a gift. When she recommended a book, you could be confident you'd enjoy it.'

Lou was excused from answering when a couple of men came into the pub. She decided she'd come back later and look for Jake. In the meantime, it couldn't hurt to take a look through the library shelves and get to know the books a bit better. She didn't know how many more towns she'd have to visit before she found all of Luca's letters. There could be a lot of people walking up those stairs and asking her for recommendations. She really should be more familiar with the books on her shelves. Perhaps that 'gift' of recommending books could be inherited.

CHAPTER 15

'Lou was here looking for you,' Deb told Jake as soon as he arrived for work. 'She might come back a bit later.'

'All right. Thanks.' He made sure Ollie was settled behind the bar before turning towards the kitchen. If he'd expected to escape Deb that way, he was wrong.

'Not so fast!' She followed him. 'How did the run to Blackville go?'

'Fine.' He began pulling vegetables out of the pantry.

'Fine? Come on, Jake, you know what I mean.'

Jake sighed. 'Yes, she got a letter.'

'Did she say anything?'

'No. I saw her put it in her bag before we left. And she was very quiet all the way back.' Much as he'd wanted to talk to Lou, it seemed better to follow her lead. The trip back had not been as enjoyable as the trip out. He'd missed their easy chatter, the sound of her laughter and her voice.

'She didn't tell you she had the letter?'

'No. Why should she? It's not really any of my business. Or at least, it shouldn't be.' He stopped his preparations and looked at Deb. 'I'm starting to feel uncomfortable about this whole thing.'

'What do you mean?'

'When I agreed to this, I was doing Luca a favour. I had no problem with that, especially knowing what was ahead for her. It seemed the right thing to do. But now that I've met Lou it seems … wrong. Like I'm helping manipulate her. I don't like it.'

'It's what you promised Luca you'd do. We both made promises to her.'

'I know. And of course I'll keep my word. I'm just not happy about it.' He picked up a potato and began vigorously peeling it. 'You know what she asked me?'

'What?'

'She asked me how Luca died.' He still felt the sadness of watching his friend slowly fade away in those last weeks and months and he knew his feelings were shared by Deb.

'That must have been hard. But surely that's a good thing? If she's asking questions about her mother, that must mean she's starting to feel something.'

'And what's the point of making her feel something for someone who's gone? All it can do is bring her sadness.' Jake sliced through a potato with unnecessary force.

Deb shook her head slowly. 'I see what you mean. But it's already started. I don't know that we can stop now. We'd be breaking our word to Luca, and I don't think that would help Lou either. When's the next run?'

'I guess that's what she wanted to talk to me about. I actually do have some work booked over the next couple of days. And I have to take Ollie to puppy class, so it's going to be two or three days. Maybe Monday of next week. That might not be a bad thing. It'll give Lou time to absorb whatever that letter said. Maybe she won't want to do any more trips.'

Jake didn't believe his own words. Lou was on a path now and he didn't think she would turn from it. He knew her well enough to understand this hadn't been an easy decision, and she wasn't likely to back down. But he would wait until she was ready to take the next step. It was the least he could do.

Lou's face showed her disappointment when he told her she'd have to wait a few days for the next library run. It was late and he'd finished work for the night. They were sitting in the beer garden behind the pub while Ollie snuffled around hunting small imaginary creatures.

'I'm sorry, Lou.' Jake didn't have to pretend the sincerity. 'There's nothing I can do. I have to take Ollie to puppy class, and I've got two days' work on one of the studs. They're planning to build a spelling facility. This is just a start, but if it goes well, I could get a lot of work out of them. And working at the studs is important to me. I can't afford to let them down.'

'Of course not.' Lou looked contrite. 'I'm sorry. You're doing me a favour. I'm grateful for whatever time you can give me. I had hoped to wrap this up fairly soon, but it looks like I'm going to be around longer than I thought.'

'Is that such a bad thing?'

'No. Of course not.'

Her smile set a little spark of hope alight in him. They sat in silence for a short while. Jake found himself enjoying the night sounds, and the stillness and the feeling of Lou next to him.

'How many towns are there to visit?'

He paused for a moment to count. 'The full run was twelve—no, wait, thirteen. Fourteen if you include the Ridge. But we didn't do all of them in those last few trips.'

'Luca opened the library here?'

'Of course. It was her home. The Ridge was always the last stop on the run.'

'So when can we do the next one?'

'How does Monday sound?'

He almost felt her shoulders slump. 'That's fine.'

He was pretty sure it wasn't. Some of the gloss seemed to have gone out of the evening. He didn't know how to get it back. 'The next stop will be Walhallow. I'll let them know we're coming.'

'Thanks.' Lou sighed. 'It's late. I should head back to the cottage.'

He wondered if she would ever call that cottage or Wagtail Ridge 'home'. 'Do you need a lift?'

'No. I'll enjoy the walk.'

He wanted to offer to go with her, but he sensed she would say no. The Ridge was perfectly safe for a late-night walk, and he wasn't going to tell her he was offering because he enjoyed being with her. She was a long way from being ready for that.

'All right. Goodnight.'

'Goodnight.' She stood up and walked away.

Ollie trotted over to Jake and whined softly as he watched her leave. Jake knew exactly how the pup felt.

CHAPTER 16

Lou managed to keep herself busy. She read a lot. She went into the shed and looked through the boxes stored there. They seemed full of all kinds of assorted … not quite junk. A couple of boxes were filled with what seemed like costumes, perhaps for a play. There were some musical instruments that had seen better days. The same could be said for the sports gear. It seemed a strange collection for a librarian's shed, but perhaps Luca had just offered the place as storage for her friends. Lou probably should try to find out who owned all this stuff and get it back to them. That was a problem for another day. She might be trying to fill the long hours until the next library trip, but her mind was already too full … of thoughts of Luca and the letters, a sad little girl, and a kind man with a cute puppy. She was just not up to tackling another task.

When she had filled as much time as she could in the house and the shed, she still had the weekend to kill. Lou stood in the middle of the living room and wondered what to do with it. If she had to spend two whole days in this house, looking at the letters lying on the sideboard, she'd go stir crazy. Back home in Sydney she could meet up with friends, or cycle or go to the movies. She really didn't want to drive back to Sydney to simply turn around and drive back the next day. Beside, her mother would look at her with those loving but far too discerning eyes and she'd find herself telling Fiona everything, despite the fact that she wasn't entirely sure what 'everything' was yet.

There had to be something happening somewhere nearby to distract her. A quick internet search provided the solution and within half an hour, she was in her car, heading out of town in the opposite direction from the city.

She soon discovered that country markets were very different from those she'd frequented in Sydney. For a start, there was a vast area in an empty school field just for parking. There were plenty of stalls, set up in a rough circle rather than neat rows, and in the centre a couple of musicians were playing country music. It wasn't quite Keith Urban, but Lou was soon nodding away to it. There was none of the tourist tat she saw in every Sydney market. Instead, a good number of the stalls were laden with homegrown, often organic, vegetables, and homemade jams and cakes. This really was a local market in every sense of the word. The stallholders weren't in a rush to make a sale although they clearly took a great deal of pride in their wares and were more than happy to chat for a while.

'Those are what they call heritage tomatoes in the posh shops,' an elderly woman with short grey hair and a smiling, weather-beaten face told her. 'My mum used to grow these, and her mum before her. All from the same plants. We save some seeds every year for the next crop. You won't taste anything better. Here, try one of these.' The woman held out a small plate with a few cherry tomatoes rolling around on it.

Lou tried one. 'That's really tasty.' It wasn't, not more than the heritage tomatoes sold in the 'posh' shops in Sydney, but the smile on the woman's face grew broader.

'There you go. You can't beat home grown.' She turned away to serve someone else, leaving Lou pleasantly surprised by the lack of sales pressure. She would come back in a bit and buy some tomatoes to make a pasta sauce for dinner. Maybe she'd even invite Jake and Ollie around.

A few steps away, she did start reaching for her money when she found herself standing in front of a stall featuring the most delicious-looking cupcakes. The woman running the stall was helping a young boy decide between a pig and a cow. The little girl standing next to him, presumably his sister, was carefully cradling a pink iced cake with tiny white horse ears and a gold unicorn horn. Lou was happy to wait until a cow was decided upon. The children handed over their money and took their purchases across the grass to another stall.

'These look lovely,' Lou said.

'Thank you.'

'I'd like one of those with the roses please, and do you happen to know if there's somewhere here I can get a cup of coffee to go with it?'

'Sure. There's a coffee stall over that way.' The woman pointed as she took Lou's money.

'Wonderful. Thank you.'

'You're welcome. Come back again.'

Lou acquired the coffee and as she perched on one of the plastic chairs clustered in the centre of the circle, she wondered if she would ever come back. Probably not, although the cupcake was worth it. So was the atmosphere. It was very different from her favourite markets in The Rocks. Sure, there was none of the bustle and excitement, no expensive eateries and fancy shops. But this market had something else—it felt like a community. Like a home.

Licking the last of the icing off her fingers, Lou disposed of her paper coffee cup and wandered through the rest of the market. It wasn't long before she pulled out the bags she always carried and began filling them with locally produced honey and homemade jams. She bought some tomatoes from the grey-haired woman and, after some hesitation, a primrose plant growing in an old blue and white china gravy boat. She would take that home to Sydney and give it to her mother, who had once owned a similar gravy dish before it was broken by her young daughter Lou.

She had almost decided it was time to go when she saw the stall selling quilts. The colours were the first thing to catch her eye; the stall was ablaze with pinks and blues, greens and yellows, browns and creams and reds. Completed quilts hung over the sides of the stall, while others lay folded on the table. On a second table, piles of neatly cut squares of fabric were gathered into beautifully colour-matched bunches. A woman sat behind the tables, hand stitching some fabric.

'They're beautiful.'

'Thank you so much.' The woman put down her work. 'There's a group of us who love to quilt. There's work here from everyone.'

Lou stroked one of the completed quilts, feeling the soft fibres inside. She could imagine how warm and snuggly it would be on a chilly night.

'What colours do you have in your home?' The woman began spreading the quilts out so Lou could have a better look.

'It's mostly cream. The colour tends to come from the bookshelves. They are everywhere, loaded with books.' Lou spoke without thinking. It wasn't until she stopped that she realised she had described the cottage in Wagtail Ridge. Her real home, in

Sydney, was painted in darker shades. As the woman rearranged the quilts, she shook out one in lovely tones of cream and brown. Small squares dotted with cream and dark red flowers formed an intricate pattern and Lou could only imagine the hours of painstaking work that had gone into its creation.

'How much is this one?' She knew it would be expensive, but she really didn't care and when the price was mentioned, she reached for her wallet without blinking.

'Thank you,' the stallholder said as she tucked the money away.

'Is this the only place you sell the quilts? These would be such a hit in the Sydney markets.'

'We can't afford the stall prices in Sydney, but we do go to the bigger markets in Tamworth and we try to find a stall in Newcastle leading up to Christmas. I never sell more than one, sometimes not even that here. There's not a lot of money about, unless a tourist bus stops. But I always come to the market. If we stayed away, and then someone else did … well, the market would just cease to exist. It's as much about keeping the market alive as it is about making money … although we like to do that too when we can.' The woman smiled.

The quilt wouldn't fit in her tote bag, but the stallholder handed her another larger bag sewn from scrap fabrics. 'Here you go. I hope you can get it safely home before the rain hits.'

Rain? Lou looked up and saw the clouds gathering. She'd been having such a good time, she hadn't noticed the change in weather. She thanked the woman and set off back to her car. The first drops of rain fell as she pulled away from the car park. By the time she was back in Wagtail Ridge, her wipers were working at full speed. She parked the car as close as she could to the cottage and gathered all her purchases together for a mad dash for the veranda. Once safely under shelter, she paused for a moment and took a deep breath. She loved the smell of rain. There was a freshness and a sense of joy and renewal about it. It smelled so much better here, away from the city. There was so much about the bush that she loved. Why, then, did she not love this town as much as she had some of the others she'd only passed through? She knew it was all linked to her biological mother. And her unknown biological father. Right now, she didn't want to think about that.

She carried her purchases inside, wishing that she'd made a second stop at the cupcake stall and bought another treat. Instead, she placed the primrose in its whimsical pot on the coffee table, made herself a cup of tea and pulled the quilt over herself as she lay down on the sofa. The room was dark because of the rain, so she flicked on the light and picked up *Seven Little Australians.* In a short time, she was so lost in the story, she decided not to invite Jake for dinner after all. This evening, she was happy to be alone.

CHAPTER 17

It was still raining on Monday, so Jake drove to Lou's cottage rather than walk. He parked his ute next to the shed, but Ollie wasn't in the mood for good behaviour. By the time Jake had the shed doors open and was calling the pup into the shelter, he had already jumped in a couple of puddles and rolled on the wet grass.

'Come here.' Jake reached into the back of the library cab for a towel he kept there for just this purpose. 'Sit.' He wiped the mud off the dog's paws. 'If Lou sees you like this, she won't like you any more. She'd probably say you have to stay home because she doesn't want your muddy paws all over the library truck. And who could blame her? If you want her to like you, you'd better start behaving.'

'I assume that's Ollie you're talking to.' Lou appeared in the shed doorway. 'Because I'd probably still like you, Jake, even with muddy paws.' Her laugh was like a ripple of the high notes on a harp. It made Ollie wriggle in his grasp, and it made Jake smile.

'I think there's going to be a lot of wet dog smell on the run today.'

'That's fine. I can live with a slightly damp Ollie … and a slightly muddy you.'

Jake let go of the dog, stood up and looked down at himself. There were a couple of clear muddy paw prints on the legs of his best jeans and a muddy smear across his shirt. So much for making an effort to impress Lou. But as he watched her hug the dog, gaining her own mud stains, he guessed that she wouldn't have even noticed that he'd made the effort. She really wasn't like any other woman he'd ever met.

Jake pulled the truck out of the shed and Ollie and Lou joined him in the cab once the shed doors were safely closed. A few minutes later they were on the road out of town.

'How was your weekend?' Jake asked.

'Very relaxing. I went to some markets. I even bought a few things. Some amazing homemade jam. I had it on toast for breakfast. It was wonderful. And I bought this marvellous handmade quilt. I spent most of the weekend wrapped up in it reading.'

'Anything in particular?' If Lou was exploring on her own, maybe she was starting to feel more at home.

'*Seven Little Australians*.'

'A classic, that one. It was one Luca recommended a lot, and not just to kids.'

'Yeah. It was the copy that was returned at Blackville. There was a letter inside …' Lou's voice trailed off.

'If you want a sympathetic ear, I'm here for you, Lou.' He glanced at her. 'But you don't have to tell me anything you don't want to.'

'Thanks. I'm struggling a bit with all this.'

The feeling of guilt that lived at the back of his mind surfaced again. He ignored it and kept driving. The regular swish of the wipers across the windscreen seemed to lull both of them into silence. Even Ollie settled and closed his eyes.

Their journey was almost done before Lou spoke again. 'Tell me about Walhallow.'

'In a bit, we'll turn onto Caroona Mission Road. That's named after the old mission that was here. This was all Gamilaraay land, and the school at Walhallow is all First Nations kids. There's probably less than twenty of them, and they all come to visit the library. It's a very close-knit community. This was always one of Luca's favourite stops.'

They crossed a river and turned right, and a couple of minutes later had parked outside a small wooden building that was the school. Lou barely had time to break out the steps and open the door before she was surrounded by eager young readers, a group of adults not far behind them. There was no doubt this was a town event. And no-one seemed to pay any attention to the rain that was still falling, or to the muddy puddles that were forming. Lou saw a long evening ahead cleaning the library floor.

She needn't have worried. With teacher supervision, the kids all did their best not to track mud through the truck. Their eager hands almost stripped the shelves of reading matter and Lou knew she'd have to restock before the next run, whenever that might be.

As the last of the kids left, Jake appeared at the bottom of the stairs, a large cardboard box in his arms. Lou recognised it as one of those from the shelves at the back of her shed. It was full of costumes and props for a play.

'I got your message,' Jake said to the teacher. 'Here you go. All you're going to need for Mary Poppins. There's a CD in there with the music as well.'

'Thank you.' The teacher made to take the box from him.

'It's fine. Just show me where you want it.'

They disappeared in the direction of the school.

Lou put two and two together. Now she understood those boxes stashed in Luca's shed.

She helped several adult readers check out some books then began packing up, fighting off her disappointment. There had been no letter.

She had locked up and was about to slide the metal steps back into their hatch when the schoolteacher came back.

'Do you need another book?'

'No. Sorry. I almost forgot this. I'm new. I only started working here last month. The previous teacher left this with me, and told me to give it to the librarian when the mobile library came back again. It's been sitting in my desk all this time. I almost forgot. Anyway, thanks for today. The kids are all very excited to have the library back. We'll see you again soon, I hope.' She handed Lou a book and was gone.

Lou turned the book over and read the front cover. *Picnic at Hanging Rock*. She remembered this one too, remembered reading it with her friends at school. They'd seen the film too and spent hours arguing over what had actually happened and what they would have done in the same circumstances.

There was an envelope inside the book. As she stared at it, a drop of rain fell onto the white paper. Then another. She closed the book over the envelope and thrust both into her bag. As she did, Jake appeared, looking a little damp around the edges after his walk with Ollie.

'We should get underway.'

She nodded. The sooner they left, the sooner she would be alone with the book and the letter. She jumped into the cab and settled her bag on her knees. She could feel the hard cover of the book through the bag's soft sides. Her eagerness to be alone was not a reflection of her eagerness to read the letter. Luca's last letter had stirred emotions in her that she was still struggling with. Did she really want to know more? Could she bear not to?

The rhythmic beat of the windscreen wipers almost pounded the questions into her brain. *Read the letter? Don't read the letter? Walk away? Stay?* Any moment now, she would scream.

'Shit!' The library swerved violently as Jake struggled with the wheel.

Lou caught a flash of movement and a kangaroo vanished into the trees on the side of the road. The seatbelt bit into her ribs as Ollie fell against her. She grabbed the dog and held him tightly as the truck slid slowly to a stop, the rear wheels well off to one side of the road.

'Are you all right?' Jake's hand gently touched her arm.

'Yes. We're fine.'

'Roos.'

'I saw. Did you hit one?'

'I'm not sure. I'm going to check. Stay here.'

Jake disappeared into the rain and was back in a few seconds. 'No sign of any of them. They're gone.'

He started the engine. Lou was amazed to see his hands weren't shaking as he put the vehicle into gear. Hers were, and she wasn't the one behind the wheel. Jake revved the engine. The library lurched but went nowhere as the revs climbed and the engine noise turned into almost a scream.

'What's wrong?'

'We're stuck. That rear wheel is in a bit of a ditch.'

'Oh.'

Jake revved the engine one more time and dropped the clutch. The library shook as the wheels spun in the mud, but it didn't move.

'Nope. We're not driving out of this one.'

'So now what? We can't exactly push this out.' Lou dug around in her bag, moving the book and the letter it contained aside as she looked for her phone. 'If there's a signal I can call for a tow truck.'

There was no signal.

Jake was unconcerned. 'We just have to wait. It won't be too long.'

Lou admired his optimism, but suspected he was wrong. On a quiet country road like this, it could be hours before another car appeared.

He wasn't, of course. Not more than ten minutes had passed when she saw a tractor approaching through the bright sunlight that had so quickly replaced the rain. The driver skilfully turned the big machine and backed it to the front of the truck.

He jumped from his seat. 'I saw you were stuck,' he shouted. 'Let's get you on the road again.'

'Stay here where it's dry. You too, Ollie.' Jake jumped out.

It didn't take long to get the tow line attached and he climbed back into the cab and started the engine. Seconds later, the tractor engine roared and the truck was pulled free.

Jake disappeared again to help the tractor driver uncouple the line then, with a wave, the man was gone.

'Let's try again, shall we?'

As they laughed over Jake's stories of getting bogged in other places and the kind-hearted souls who had rescued him, Lou felt her mood lifting, and before long, they were back on the familiar approaches to Wagtail Ridge.

CHAPTER 18

My Darling Daughter,

Let me tell you about the library.

After I came home and found I was alone, I decided to stay in Wagtail Ridge. At least for a while. I really had nowhere else to go. I figured I could always start travelling again later, although I never did. I guess I had found my place at last.

I needed a job, so I started helping out at the pub, but that wasn't what I was looking for. I thought maybe a job in Scone and bought a clunky old car so I could get there. I didn't have much success job hunting and one day, tired and disappointed, I just walked into the library for somewhere to rest. The moment I entered that building, I fell in love. So, so many books. Moving about as I did, I had to travel light. I read books, but then I had to give them away or swap them for something new because I couldn't take them with me. I hated saying goodbye to some of them. Favourites that I knew I would want to read again. It was like saying goodbye to friends.

I'd visited some libraries in my travels of course, and some of them were much bigger. But this was different. This was MY library. Does that make sense? And they had a job for me. Knowing I could spend my life in that room surrounded by literally thousands of books was a gift.

I must sound so naive to you. The libraries at your university must make our little country library seem a poor thing, but I hope you can understand that I loved it. And not just for the books. I made friends with the staff and with the readers. I learned to help people choose books. I was pretty good at that even though I wasn't a trained librarian.

Then I was given the mobile library to run. What a perfect combination: books and the open road. I got to know the people on my run. I would pick out books I thought they'd like. Some became friends and would give me things. Like Margaret at Blackville with her eggs. Sometimes it would be a cake. Or some homemade jam. Their kindness was heartwarming. When you came along, some of the women gave you clothes and toys their own kids had outgrown. It wasn't charity—it was kindness.

When the council finally decided to close the mobile library, all those people decided that they didn't want to lose it. I guess Deb or Jake has probably explained that to you by now—the fundraising and community effort that went into saving the library.

You probably think my system of cards and book sleeves is old and inefficient. Perhaps it was, but it was all I needed. When you know your books and your customers that well, a lot of it is based on trust. That's why I turned to the library users for help when I realised I wanted to try to explain everything. I knew they would honour my request and get the letters to you, if you decided to come looking for … well, looking for me, I suppose.

I know I could have just written to you. Or left the letters at the cottage. But I wanted you to see how I lived my life. I will never know the woman you have become, but I wanted you to know me. Just a little. I thought spending time in the library and with my friends would help you do that, so that when you have read them all and you decide to leave—to go back to Sydney and get on with your life—you might take some of me with you. Just as I have always held some of you with me.

I love you. I always have.

Your mother,

Luca.

'How did you know I went to uni? Were you spying on me?'

Lou's words echoed around the empty kitchen. Her only answer was silence.

She tossed the letter on the table next to the cup of tea she hadn't touched. She'd waited to read the letter until after she got back to the cottage. Jake had parked the library in the shed, backing into the restricted space with the ease of much practice, and then left to run some errands. She had wanted the privacy, but after reading that letter, she could have used someone to talk to.

'I don't understand,' she said to the empty house. 'You gave me up. The lawyers told Mum and Dad you wanted to stay out of my life. We never heard a word from you. So how did you know I was at uni?'

Someone was lying to her, and she was certain it wasn't her parents. She reached for her phone.

'Hi, Mum.'

'Lou. How are you?'

'I'm okay.'

'You don't sound it. What's happened?'

'Mum—I have to ask … You said Luca never wanted to be a part of my life. That she withdrew and never got in touch again.'

'That's right.'

'Then how did she know I went to uni?'

Her mother was silent for a few seconds. 'I don't know, honey. What have you discovered?'

'We took the mobile library on another run today.'

'By we, I guess you mean Jake is driving for you.'

'Yes. There was another letter. Mostly she talks about the library. It was pretty much the only thing she loved.' Lou didn't care if the bitterness showed in her voice. 'But it mentioned me being at uni. How did she know that?'

'I don't know. Perhaps she found you on social media?'

'But she said she didn't want anything to do with me. Why would she look for me on social media? I feel as if she was stalking me.' Lou suppressed a shudder.

'Stalking is a harsh word, Lou …'

'If she was looking me up without letting me know or trying to make contact, what else should I call it?'

'Maybe she did try to make contact and you missed seeing it.' Her mother's voice stayed calm even as Lou's stress level was rising.

'Mum. You were always at me for the amount of time I spent with my nose buried in my phone. I wouldn't have missed it. And now I feel as if she is manipulating me. Forcing me to find all those letters.'

'Do you want to stop? You can just come home if you want to.'

Lou took a deep breath. 'I can't do that. Not now that I've started.'

'Why don't you ask Jake? Or someone else in the town? They knew her. They were her friends. They can probably answer a lot of your questions.'

'Because I don't want them to tell me about their friend. I want to find out about my biological mother. They are not the same person. Does that make sense?'

'Yes, it does. I wish I could make this easier for you. Would it help if I came up there for a couple of days?'

Lou blinked rapidly as her eyes began to fill. 'Thanks, Mum, but I have to do this alone. I want to keep this separate from our family.

After all these years of not caring that I was adopted, it now seems really important … no, that's not right …' She struggled to find the words. 'Your adopting me has always been important. Knowing you wanted me enough to bring an unknown child into your home has always, *always* made me feel valued and loved. That will never change. But I do need to know now why she gave me up. And if I can, who my father was. The thought that he could still be alive somewhere, maybe even here in Wagtail Ridge, is preying on my mind. I have to see this through.'

'I understand. We're here for you. Whatever you need.'

After she ended the call, Lou made a cup of tea. She had another call to make, and needed a few minutes to gather her thoughts. When she opened the pantry to get her newly purchased teabags, she saw the boxes of fruit teas left behind by Luca. She took them out of the cupboard and stared at them.

'Why are you doing this to me, Luca? Why? You gave me away. Wasn't that enough? You say you loved me, so why did you decide to torture me like this after you died?' She took the tea and tossed it in the bin.

The call to the law offices of Curtis and Moore didn't take long, but was almost as much an emotional strain as her conversation with her mother. She told them what she wanted, and they agreed. Afterwards, Lou decided to go for a walk. She could avoid the main street and hopefully not see anyone. She pulled on a baseball cap to help give her the anonymity she sought and set out.

The streets were lined with trees, either growing on the footpath or in front gardens. For the most part, the people of Wagtail Ridge lived in plain wooden houses of the type found in any country town, with the occasional newer brick house. Most showed signs of care, not affluence to be sure, but love of a home isn't dictated by money. Once or twice she saw people gardening in the yards or sitting on their verandas, reading. She returned their casual waves. As she walked, she felt the tension draining from her body and her steps became lighter. She turned a corner and froze. She recognised the building ahead of her on the corner with the main road. It was the church and beside it was the small graveyard where, in all probability, Luca and her mother Christina were buried.

She was about to turn around and go home when she noticed that between her and the church was a big hall, and Jake's car was pulling up in front of it. She hesitated and in that time Jake released Ollie from the car. The Lab must have scented her, because, with a joyful bark, he began running her way.

'Ollie. No. Come here.'

Lou froze. Ollie skidded to a halt and looked over his shoulder at Jake.

'Ollie. Come here.'

The look the dog cast her as he turned to walk back to his master would have been heartbreaking if it wasn't also so funny. She had to fight to stop herself laughing.

When Ollie was sitting obediently at his master's feet, Jake looked up at Lou and smiled. 'Sorry about that, but he shouldn't run off like that, even if it is you.'

'That's fine.' She walked over to join them. 'A dog has to learn manners. Especially a budding guide dog.'

'Exactly. Are you listening, Ollie?' Jake rubbed the dog's head affectionately. 'Are you doing anything special, or just out for a walk?'

'Who? Me or Ollie?' Lou asked.

Jake smiled in the way that lit his eyes and left her unable to do anything other than smile too.

'Seriously,' she added, 'I was only out for a walk.'

'I don't suppose you've got a few minutes to give me a hand with something?'

'Sure. What do you need?' After all he had done for her, what else could she say? And besides, a bit of Jake's company right now would take her mind off Luca.

'I've got some bits and pieces to drop off at the hall. Nothing too big, but I have to get to the pub to get ready for the dinner rush.'

'We'd better get to it then.'

The back of Jake's ute didn't seem overly full, but Lou picked up a couple of boxes. They weren't heavy. She followed Jake up the front stairs of the hall where he somehow managed to unlock the door despite the load he was carrying. The hall was larger than it looked. Lou guessed the whole town population would easily fit inside. It was built for practicality rather than looks, with plain wooden walls and a floor that was showing signs of much use. A line of trestle tables stretched against one wall. Jake set his boxes there and she did the same. Three trips was all it took to bring all the boxes inside, leaving Lou very much with the impression that Jake had asked for her help just to spend some time with her. Hiding the pleased smile that thought evoked, Lou took more time to look around. Folding metal chairs had been laid out in almost straight lines in front of the low stage, which held a table and six slightly better chairs. From the assortment of slightly dusty and faded decorations that hung from the ceiling and floors, she guessed the hall was used for a lot more than town meetings.

'The hall gets a lot of use.'

'Yep. Meetings, weddings, christenings, birthday parties and whatever else we can think of to celebrate.'

'The town really is very close-knit, isn't it?'

'Yes. It's one of the reasons I like it here.'

'Doesn't your family miss you?'

'I do get to see my parents fairly often. As for my siblings … well, the stories I could tell. Why don't you come over to the pub with me? We can trade embarrassing stories about our families while I set up dinner. You could even stay—it's fish and chips night.'

When he looked at her like that, she wanted to say yes. It wouldn't be a date, not as such. Just an evening with a friend who happened to be tall and nice looking with a smile that made her go a little weak at the knees. She'd happily peel a few potatoes at the same time. 'That sounds good, but …'

'I know. I can steer you clear of people who are likely to talk too much about the wrong subject. And you can always hide in the kitchen with me.'

She started to chuckle and he joined her.

'Sorry, I guess that's not the most impressive invitation you've ever had.'

'I don't know. It sounds pretty good to me.' Lou realised she actually wanted to spend an evening with people. She'd been too much alone recently. And besides, there was Jake. It wasn't that she had the hots for him or was falling for him or anything silly like that. But he was good company. He was kind, and right now, she needed a bit of both those things.

She accepted Jake's lift to the pub, even though it was a short walk. She liked sitting in the ute's broad cab with a smiling Ollie between them. He parked the car and they walked through the front doors together.

Shane Fraser was rearranging the chairs and tables in the lounge, while his wife was behind the bar getting ready for the evening.

Shane looked up. 'Hi, Jake. You're early.'

Lou cast a sideways glance at her companion, who had insisted that he needed her help because he was going to be *late* for work. She decided he looked even cuter than ever when he blushed.

CHAPTER 19

'Do you think Val's noticed that I'm avoiding her?' Lou giggled then caught herself. Giggled? No, she wasn't a giggler. And she wasn't drunk. She was sure she hadn't had more than two glasses of wine while perched on a stool talking to Jake and helping him cook. Well, 'helping' was perhaps a bit of an exaggeration. Mostly she'd washed and peeled and sliced vegetables while marvelling at his efficiency. She was feeling a little high spirited, but that wasn't enough to cause her to giggle. The pub was closed now, and Jake was walking her home. He didn't seem to have noticed the giggle, just as he didn't seem to have noticed that he was the one responsible for it.

'I'm pretty sure she hasn't. Val doesn't pick up much in the way of subtleties.'

'Subtleties? I vanished into the kitchen the minute she walked through the door and didn't come out again. Not very subtle.'

'Well, maybe she thought you wanted the pleasure of my company.'

'I did.'

Their steps faltered for a second, long enough for Ollie, who was running ahead of them, to notice, look back and give a short bark.

'We're coming, Ollie. Don't rush us.'

Were Jake's words a hint? Had she rushed in? A car drove past, illuminating them, and Lou glanced across at Jake again. His face looked … happy. Not at all rushed. She relaxed again. Her school and university years had been filled with what she imagined was a normal number of crushes and dates and boyfriends. Nothing had become very serious, because she was too young for that. But as she felt her heart thumping a little louder than normal, she began to wonder if maybe things were different this time.

They turned the corner away from the main road and walked in silence for the block and a half to the cottage.

Ollie raced up the steps ahead of them and stood by the front door, his tail wagging wildly.

'No, Ollie. It's rude to invite yourself in like that.' Jake's voice echoed with barely contained amusement.

'Would you like to come in?' Lou tried not to hold her breath. She wasn't entirely sure what she wanted him to say. She'd be disappointed with a no, but a yes would take her already complicated life up a notch.

'I wish I could, but Ollie and I have to be up early tomorrow. I have to drive up to Tamworth to collect some stuff from the plane. I won't be back until after lunch.'

'Oh. Of course. I understand.'

'I'll be doing a bit more work at the hall in the afternoon. If you have nothing better to do, I can always use an extra hand.'

Her heart lifted. 'All right. I'll see you there.'

'And then the day after tomorrow I could do another run with the library, if you wanted to.'

'That would be great. Thanks.'

'No worries. Goodnight, Lou.'

She was still trying to hide her disappointment when he leaned forward and kissed her gently on the cheek. Then he turned and, calling Ollie to follow, he walked away. She stood by the door watching, hoping he might turn around and wave goodnight. When he did, she waved back then went inside, feeling ridiculously pleased by such a small gesture.

Her mood was light as she prepared for bed, and this time, it definitely wasn't because of the wine. She ignored the letters and the books they had come in, and searched the shelves for a good romance to read in bed. Tonight was all about her. Luca and her puzzle could wait.

Two steps inside the bedroom, she stopped and gazed at the bed. It had been staring her in the face all this time: where do people hide things? Under the bed, of course. In all her searching for clues about Luca, she hadn't looked in the most obvious spot. She turned on the light and dropped to her knees beside the bed. When she lifted the bedspread and looked under it, she saw a single suitcase and a smaller cardboard box. With a bit of effort, she pulled both out.

Kneeling on the carpet, she opened the suitcase first. As she dropped the lid back, she saw the shawl. It was woven of fine mohair, in shades of pale blue and cream. It had been folded carefully on top of the piles of clothing beneath. As she reached out to pick it up, Lou could have sworn she smelled jasmine, but it was so faint it vanished a second later. Her hand stilled. Was that Luca's perfume? It seemed familiar, as did the shawl that lay millimetres from her fingertips. It was almost as if she could feel the softness of the fabric before she touched it. Perhaps because her fingers could remember the feel of it from many years ago.

She slammed the lid of the suitcase shut and pushed it back under the bed. She would deal with that another time.

The cardboard box was very light as Lou lifted it onto the bed and sat down beside it. Cautiously, she opened the lid. The first thing that caught her eye was a photograph. It was quite old, taken long before digital photos and phone cameras came into being. It showed a girl of about twelve with an older woman. Lou held the photo up to the light. It could almost be her in that photo, except when she was twelve, she was living in Sydney with the Taylors. The clothes the girl in the photo was wearing looked old-fashioned and the older woman was a stranger to Lou. The truth folded itself around her mind with absolute certainty. This was Luca she was looking at. Luca and her mother, Christina. That explained the likeness that all three shared. She gently touched her grandmother's face. Whatever animosity she held for Luca, it wasn't Christina's fault. Her grandmother was not the one who'd rejected her. She set the photograph to one side and turned her attention back to the box.

There were other photos, all quite old. Some showed an older Luca with people that Lou assumed were her friends. She tried to guess the dates on the photos. Could one of the young men be her father? Without knowing when they were taken, it was impossible to tell, so she wouldn't waste her energy on that. At least not now. She also set to one side photographs and postcards of places Luca must have visited. There was a postcard from Queensland's Big Pineapple and another from the Northern Territory that dated from a time when Uluru was still mostly known as Ayers Rock. Lou found a tiny carved wooden whale, a seashell gone white with age, a card which testified that Luca Bonnet had won the grade 6 three-legged race. Lou was sifting through the cherished mementos of her biological mother's life. These were the clues she had been looking for.

Right at the bottom of the box was something not faded and made brittle by age: a small velvet bag, deep blue in colour and tied with a silver ribbon. As Lou lifted it out, it was surprisingly heavy. She opened it and tipped the contents into her palm.

The necklace was an intricate silver chain, only slightly dulled by lying untouched for a long time. The pendant that hung from the chain was a piece of rock crystal, smooth and polished at one end, but retaining the distinctive geometric shapes at the other. At the top, where it was held by a graciously curved silver band, the crystal was a purple so dark it was almost black, the colour fading to a sparkling white where the crystal remained rough and unpolished. Lou had taken some geology classes at uni and recognised the stone as amethyst. She held it up to study it more closely. It spun slowly, glinting as it caught the light. The necklace was unusual, probably expensive and very beautiful. It didn't fit with the cheap and cheerful travel souvenirs in the house. Nor did it seem to fit with anything she was learning about Luca.

Lou packed everything else back in the box and slid it under the bed. She would look at it all in more detail another time. The necklace she kept with her. She leaned back against the bed head and held it up, watching the light as it spun, wondering how Luca had come by such a thing. She was still wondering as her eyes closed and she fell asleep on top of the bedspread.

When Lou awoke next morning, she was under the bedclothes. At some point during the night, dazed with sleep, she had sought their warmth. She looked around quickly and saw the necklace lying on the bedside table. For a while there she thought it might have been a dream. When she dressed, she hung the pendant around her neck.

It wasn't visible beneath her T-shirt, but she could feel it against her skin. Every now and then she would reach up and touch it. She didn't know why, but knowing it was there gave her a sense of contentment.

She spent the morning doing housework. She watered the primrose plant, which had some pretty new cream and yellow flowers about to open. The quilt looked lovely lying across the back of the couch, so she left it there. When it started getting chilly, it would be nice to have while she was watching TV. Maybe with Jake? She probably wouldn't still be here when it got really cold, but she did like the way the quilt looked. It seemed to match the plain walls and the overflowing bookshelves, giving a homely feel to the room.

She went to the kitchen to look through the cupboards and make a shopping list. There were still a lot of library stops to make. Obviously she'd be here a little longer. It wouldn't hurt to pick up a few more things. She couldn't eat at the pub every night.

Armed with a list and her tote bags, she set out for the shop, but on the way she diverted to walk past the hall. Sure enough, Jake's car was there. The hall was a hive of activity. Jake was assembling more tables and folding chairs while Kelly from the store was covering the tables with paper tablecloths. Sarah, who Lou had liked when they met at the bar, was carrying boxes through a door at the back of the hall. Lou guessed it probably led to a kitchen. Both women called a greeting as they saw her. She nodded back and crossed to Jake.

'What's all this activity about, anyway?'

'This weekend is the town dance.'

Lou raised her eyebrows. 'A town dance? Any particular reason?'

'It's a fundraiser.' He held up a hand before she could speak. 'And so you don't get mad at me for not telling you—yes, it is a fundraiser for the library. We've done it every year for the past six years.

It's our biggest social event. It's important for the town as well as for the library. No-one actually decided we should keep doing it when the library stopped. It just happened.'

'Oh.' Lou didn't know what to say. It was hardly her place to say anything really, except that she owned the library now. Any money raised might come to her and that wasn't right. She looked around at the other workers in the hall. 'Is everyone expecting me to take over the library now? Because I'm not going to. This is a one-off run while I find those letters Luca left for me.'

'What other people expect isn't the issue. You'll do what's right for you. As for the funds, in a town like this, there's always someone or something that needs helping. Whatever else happens, the town will be here on Saturday night for a party. Would you … would you come? With me?'

'Oh … um …' Lou struggled with the thoughts that whirled around in her head. She was tempted. So, so tempted. Jake was her friend, but unlike what was supposed to happen with a friend, every minute she spent with him she wanted another … and another. And another day. But not a lifetime. No. She was only twenty-three. She was only in town for a short time. As attractive as the idea was, she couldn't afford to have a fling with Jake. Because she was beginning to realise that if she did, it wouldn't be just a fling. And she wasn't in an emotional place to deal with that right now.

'No strings.' Jake was starting to look uncomfortable. 'I thought maybe you'd feel more relaxed with someone you know. And if you're with me, it will stop some of the pushier town matrons trying to matchmake me with any single woman in the room. You would be doing me a favour.'

Despite herself, Lou began to chuckle as her mind filled with images of Jake fleeing elderly women towing daughters behind them in some kind of modern Jane Austen scene.

'All right. Just to save you from that fate.'

Jake feigned overwhelming relief. 'Thank you.'

'It's the least I can do after all you're doing to help me. In the meantime, can I help here?'

'Well, you could check with Sarah in the kitchen to see if she needs a hand.'

In the kitchen at the back of the hall, Lou found Sarah and another woman unpacking and washing an assortment of plates and cups and teapots. Almost immediately a tea towel was thrust into her hands.

'Lou, meet Alison. Thanks for pitching in. We can always use an extra hand.'

'Sarah will badger anyone into anything.' The second woman winked at Lou. 'She even had the local MP out here drying dishes once.'

'If he wanted my vote, he had to earn it.' Sarah and Alison laughed.

'Did he break anything?' Lou asked as she reached for a dripping plate.

'A cup,' Sarah said. 'I don't think he'd ever held a tea towel before. To cover his embarrassment, he offered to donate some replacements. I think he was afraid we might tell the press or something.'

This time Lou joined their laughter. Rather than feel excluded by what was obviously a long-term friendship, she felt herself folded into their closeness. She felt welcome.

The three of them chatted happily and the work vanished at a rapid rate. Not once was the library or Luca mentioned. By mid-afternoon, when everything was finished, Lou was singing softly to herself as she walked to the shop to buy her groceries.

CHAPTER 20

Jake slowed down as he approached the cottage. Beside him, Ollie whined and wiggled. 'I know.'

If the dog was looking forward to seeing Lou, it wasn't half as much as Jake was. He and Lou were heading for Breeza. Jake had always liked the town, and there was a special treat there for Lou. He couldn't wait to see her face when they pulled up in the park.

Lou was waiting for them in the shed and looked as pleased as he was at the prospect of their day. 'I guess you've let them know we're coming?'

He nodded as he settled himself into the driver's seat.

'Thank you again for doing this for me. You must tell me if I'm taking up too much of your time.'

'That's fine. I always enjoyed driving the library routes.' He might have his own reasons for the route they were taking, but he also wanted Lou to do this at her own pace. If it became too much for her, she might leave and his promise to Luca would be broken. That promise was not the only reason he wanted Lou to stay.

They set out, both singing along to the local country music radio station.

Half an hour into their journey, he began to slow down and turned in to a truck stop. 'We need petrol.' He pulled up to the bowser and got out.

When the bowser clicked off, Lou turned in the direction of the shop. 'Do you want anything while I'm there?'

'I'm fine, thanks, but you're not paying for the petrol.'

'Of course I am. You're doing this for me. I'm not letting you pay.'

'I'm not paying. There's still some money in the library fund. The petrol money is coming out of there.'

She tilted her head as she always did when she was trying to make a decision. He liked the way she did that. 'All right. I just want to be sure that it's not coming out of your pocket.'

'You keep Ollie company. I'll be right back.'

He walked swiftly into the shop, hoping she didn't follow. If she saw him pay with his own credit card, she'd start asking more questions and he was already uncomfortable with the lie he'd just told her. But he didn't have much choice: he didn't have the library account payment card and didn't want to ask her if she did. Whatever her answer, that would start a conversation he didn't think she was ready for.

Most people would say the town of Breeza didn't have much going for it. It had no school, post office or pub. But it did have two things of which Jake was rather fond. The first was Sheila Baxter, who was already waiting for them when he parked the library truck by the town's small park a little ahead of schedule. Jake had met seventy-something-year-old Sheila on his very first library run with Luca and the two had quickly established a mutual liking and respect. While Jake pulled out the metal stairs and prepared the truck for visitors, Sheila almost marched Lou over to the second thing of which Jake was fond. He watched them examine the faded hand-painted billboard that stood so proudly in the centre of the small park. Lou's head was tilted as she listened to Sheila holding forth on the subject of the bushranger Ben Hall.

When they returned, Sheila vanished in the direction of some nearby picnic tables, while Jake and Lou went inside the library.

'So now I know more about bushrangers than I think I ever wanted to.' Lou laughed.

Jake couldn't resist joining her. 'Sheila does love that monument. It's officially called Ben Hall's Wall, but I tend to think of it as Sheila's Wall.'

'I can see why. She clearly loves telling that story. I guess she tells everyone who's new to the town.'

'Yep. Even if they are simply passing through.'

'The paint's fading. It could use some TLC.'

'I'd be careful about saying that in Sheila's hearing. Before you know where you are, she'll rope you into helping.'

'Maybe I could help. I did an elective course working in the museums while I was at uni. I learned a bit about preservation of wooden artefacts ...' Her voice faltered. 'But I guess I won't be here long enough to help.'

'It would be a shame to see it rot away.' Jake deliberately ignored her last comment. 'I think it's pretty great. Well, maybe the art is not technically great, but I love that a town as small as this one finds something to be proud of. That says a lot about country towns, I think.'

Any further conversation was interrupted by the appearance of Lou's first customer in the doorway.

'I'll leave you to it,' Jake said. 'When you're done, you'll find me hovering next to Sheila's lunch basket. She won't let me eat anything until you get there, so don't take too long.' He grinned to show her he was joking, but she had already turned her attention to the newly arrived readers.

Sheila opened her esky and handed Jake a cold can of lemonade as he joined her. Ollie was already sitting patiently in the shade under the table. 'How's she handling everything?'

Sheila had never been one to mince her words.

'She's doing better than I think I would if our situations were reversed.'

'Her mother was a strong woman. I hope she has inherited some of her strength.' Sheila placed a couple of Tupperware containers on the bench and Jake peered at them, trying to determine what was inside. Among her many good qualities, Sheila was an excellent cook.

The library was starting to get busy now. A few people raised an arm in greeting as they made their way up the stairs.

'Is she going to stay?'

It was a reasonable question, but Jake had no answer. 'I don't know. She told me she has just graduated uni. Something environmental. She must want some sort of career. And she's too young to tie herself to a place like Wagtail Ridge.' Too young and too smart and too pretty, he could have added, but didn't. His companion was a shrewd woman more than capable of reading between the lines, even if there was nothing written there.

As it was, she cast him an inquisitive look. 'We've missed the library. If she goes back, would you take it on?'

Jake shook his head. 'It needs someone who loves books. I like to read, but this is not for me. Besides, I have my other jobs. I can't fit another one in.'

'Well, then, I guess I have to hope she stays. Or at least passes the library to someone else. There's little enough keeping us afloat.

Some of us are barely holding on and losing the library might be the final straw. These months of waiting have been tough, but if we lost it altogether …'

'Try to not let Lou hear you say that. There's enough pressure on her already.'

'I know. But it might be good for her to know just what that old truck and all those books mean to us.'

'I think she's starting to figure that out for herself.'

The number of people going up and down the metal stairs clutching piles of books told Jake he was right. He lifted the top of a cake tin, helped himself to a biscuit—and got his hand slapped.

'You wait for Little Lou.'

'Ah. You might not want to call her that. She doesn't like it.'

'I'm not an idiot, Jake Barnes.' Sheila placed a thermos on the table with a little more force than might have been absolutely necessary.

A few minutes later, the last of the customers left the library and Lou appeared in the doorway. She came over to the table where Jake and Sheila were waiting.

'You really didn't have to go to all this trouble for me,' Lou said, indicating the picnic.

'It was no trouble. We used to have the whole town here for a picnic when the library came. But I thought this time you might prefer it quieter.'

'That's thoughtful of you. Now, please tell me more about Ben Hall.'

Sheila would have noticed the abrupt change in subject, but she didn't bat an eyelid as she switched to the story of how Breeza mistakenly became known as Ben Hall's birthplace.

Jake relaxed and ate the sandwiches Sheila had brought. Then he helped himself to a slice of cake. Ollie nudged him, so they went for a stroll. As he made his way back to his seat, he saw Sheila hand Lou a book.

'Ah. *The Silver Brumby.* I loved all these books so much. Give me a minute and I'll check this back in and get your card.' Lou started to get up.

'There's no need. I still have my card.'

Realisation spread across Lou's face. Jake saw her open the book and find the envelope inside. The way she quickly closed the book again said so much about how distressing these letters were for her. Jake guessed that, much as Lou wanted to find them, she dreaded reading each one. He just wanted to put his arms around her and comfort her. Or even tell her not to read it. To forget about her mother. He wanted to tell her all about the promise he'd made to Luca. And then he wanted to break that promise.

'Thank you.' Lou's voice was soft, but she didn't sound fragile. Silence reigned for a few moments and when Lou spoke again, she sounded far more confident. 'Sheila, you knew Luca fairly well, didn't you?'

'I did. We spent many hours sitting in this exact spot talking, swapping stories and maybe even the occasional bit of gossip.'

'Tell me something about her. Just one thing. And please be honest with me.'

Jake could see that Sheila was thinking carefully about her reply and he wanted to hug her for her kindness.

'Luca liked to laugh. She had a great sense of humour, but she wasn't one of those people who laugh at others. She would never poke fun at anyone, or laugh at someone's misfortune. Her laughter came from her heart, and she had the kindest heart of anyone I have ever met.'

'I don't remember her. Not at all. But I find it hard to reconcile that kindness with the woman who gave me away.'

'Was your childhood with your adoptive parents happy?'

'Yes. Very happy. We had our ups and downs, of course. What family doesn't? But they are wonderful people and I love them.'

'Then perhaps Luca was being kind when she sent you to them.'

Jake broke the awkward silence that had fallen. 'Maybe we should be getting back.'

'Yes. Thank you, Sheila.' Lou turned and walked away, clutching the book and the letter it contained to her chest.

'Take care of her, Jake,' Sheila said softly as he turned to follow Lou.

'I will.'

When they were back in the cab Jake hesitated, the ignition key in his hand.

'Can I tell you something about your mother too?'

There was no answer.

'Even when she was ill, Luca's laugh was one of the most joyful sounds I have heard. And when you laugh, you sound a lot like her.'

He turned the key to cover the fact that Lou didn't answer.

CHAPTER 21

My Darling Daughter,

The day I found out I was pregnant with you was the second happiest day of my life. Second only to the day you were born. I hope that, despite everything, you will believe that. And I hope you'll give me a chance to explain.

I was content living in Wagtail Ridge and running the mobile library. I didn't have a lot of money, but it was enough. There were times when I was lonely and I grieved for my mother, but the community became my family. Here in the Ridge and at all my stops along the library run, people opened their homes and their hearts and let me in. I felt loved. I had a family. There was always someone there when I needed them. Have you met Deb at the pub? I guess by now you must have. I can't imagine you have spent more than a day or two at the Ridge without meeting Deb and Shane. They are the best people. Deb is my best friend. You know you can rely on them for anything you need. Just as you can rely on Jake.

Deb and Shane are so good together, and she wanted that same happiness for me. She used to make sure I met men—nice, eligible bachelors. But from the day I met your father, it was too late. I was only twenty-two, but he was the one and only love of my life.

Then I discovered I was pregnant.

I guess some women would have found the prospect of being a single mother terrifying. I didn't. I knew I couldn't give you the sort of home other children had. But I'd mostly grown up with just Mum, and I knew we would be happy, you and I. I had so much love in my heart and I was ready to give it all to you.

I had such an easy pregnancy. Very little morning sickness. I was healthy. People say pregnant women glow—well, that's how I felt. It seemed even then that we would be happy together. I kept driving the library run, but in the last few weeks of my pregnancy, Shane drove for me.

Finally my time came. Deb and Shane took me to Tamworth and you were born there. The moment they handed you to me, I fell in love—totally and utterly. I thought I knew how good it would feel, but I didn't. I had no idea what a joy and a privilege being a mother could be.

You had the most beautiful grey eyes when you were born. They got darker of course, but they remained beautiful. Your little hands and feet were so perfect. I cried the first time your tiny hand curled around my finger. And the first time your eyes really focussed on my face, and I knew you recognised me. These are the memories that I hold the tightest, because I was denied so many other memories that a mother and daughter should share.

You were denied so many memories too. Or rather, you and I didn't share them. I hope you had them with your adoptive mother. I hope she was kind. I hope she loved you even a fraction as much as I loved you. Because if she did, you were a very lucky little girl.

After everything that has happened, do you believe me when I say I love you? I hope so. Because those are the truest words I have ever said.

Your mother,

Luca.

Lou tried to imagine how Luca must have felt. She had been younger than Lou was now when she became a single mother. A single mother with no family to support her emotionally or financially. Lou leaned back in the sofa in Luca's living room and tried to imagine how she would fare as a single mother. Even with Fiona and Richard helping her, it would be hard. How much harder would it have been for Luca? If nothing else, Lou had to admire the courage it had taken her birth mother to face that. Not just to face it, but to want it and seem happy at the prospect. What had changed? What had caused her to give up this child she professed to love?

Lou took off the necklace she was still wearing under her T-shirt and held it high, watching the purple crystal catch the light as it spun on the end of the chain. The necklace was beautiful and not cheap. In her letters, Luca had given the impression that she didn't have a lot of money to spare. Why, then, did she own this silver pendant? Luca must have had a reasonable wage when the library was run by the council, but even so, for a woman who lived alone in a small country town, the necklace seemed a huge extravagance. And what about later? When she was no longer working for the council and facing medical bills? A necklace like this could have brought her a useful sum of money, so she didn't have to rely on others. She didn't know Luca at all, but everything she'd read in the letters or heard from Luca's friends made her believe Luca would not want to be a burden. She must have had some strong emotional attachment to the piece. Lou wondered how long she'd had it. Had she ever worn it or had she kept it locked away under the bed with her other secrets?

Lou got down onto her knees and reached under the bed for the cardboard box. She didn't touch the suitcase. Luca's clothes wouldn't tell her the things she needed to know. The box of memories, though, might hold clues she could decipher. She carried the box and the necklace through to the kitchen table and started to spread out the contents for closer study.

She piled the photos to one side. They would be her biggest clues. She sorted through the souvenirs of Luca's travels, but they didn't tell her much, except that, like her, Luca had enjoyed wild places, travelling and the outback. There were no dates on any of the souvenirs to suggest when Luca had been to these places, except for the fact that they were all old and more than a little faded. It would appear Luca's wider travels had come to an end when she settled in Wagtail Ridge and took over the library. Perhaps her itchy feet had been satisfied by her visits to communities like Blackville and Breeza.

Lou wasn't sure what to do with the souvenirs. They had no real value and she had no emotional attachment to them. For now they could go back under the bed. That accomplished, she spread the photographs out over the table, checking each one for a date or any names written on them. There were a couple of photos with printed dates on the back, no doubt added when the films were processed. That was quite a few years ago, and they were no help because there were no names to add to the faces in the photos.

She sorted out the photographs with men in them and checked the backs of those for dates. Not one was dated. She turned them face up again and scanned the images.

'Is one of you my father?'

She looked at the men's eyes and the shapes of their faces, searching for a resemblance, but she couldn't see any. Luca was the one she looked like, not her father, whoever he might be.

She got up from the table and walked through into the living room. She stood in the middle of the room and slowly turned in a circle.

'Luca … you started this. I was settled and happy and you brought me here with your letters and your inheritance. I didn't want any of it. But now that I'm here, for God's sake, stop mucking around.

Tell me what you wanted me to know and let's be done with this so I can get on with my life.'

She waited for a moment as if expecting an answer that she knew would never come, and started when someone knocked on the front door.

Trying not to laugh at herself, Lou opened the door to find a delivery man outside, clutching a parcel. As she signed for it, she noted the time. It was getting late. Back inside the house, she tossed the package on the table alongside the photos. It was the paperwork she'd requested from the lawyers, but, eager as she was to find the answers she was seeking, now wasn't the time. The afternoon had drifted past. Jake was coming by shortly. They would walk to the hall together for tonight's dance, or party, or whatever it was. She'd spent all her time these last few weeks worrying about the past and all the things that she didn't know. She'd thought of little else since that first letter from Curtis and Moore had arrived at her parents' home. Tonight she wanted to escape all that.

Jake checked his watch and slowed his pace, just a little. He was going to be early and he really didn't want to be early. That might make him seem too eager. Lou might laugh at him. What was he doing? He was acting like a nervous schoolboy going on a first date, not a grown man meeting a friend who happened to be a woman. A very pretty woman, with smiling eyes and a joyful laugh. And a way of tilting her head when she was thinking that was captivating. But it didn't matter how captivating she was, he was not going to even try to step beyond the role of friend. He wasn't going to read anything into that one kiss on the cheek. He could see how much she was struggling. She was in no place to even think about anything other than unravelling the mystery Luca had left her. Much as he had admired and respected Luca, he wished now that he had never promised that he would try to convince Lou to stay and take over the library. At that time it had seemed he was simply granting a dying friend's wish. But now he had become part of Luca's plan and he was the one guilty of manipulating Lou.

The small cottage was visible ahead of him. He checked his watch again and nodded. He reached the door at exactly the right time and knocked.

The door opened and someone punched Jake in the guts. Or at least that's how it felt.

Lou was wearing some sort of pinkish or purple-ish dress. The fabric was floaty and soft and moulded to her body in such an innocently beguiling way he had to fight back the urge to reach out and touch it … touch her. The late afternoon sun was streaming onto the veranda, making her blonde hair shine like polished gold. Her head was tilted on one side, and as he looked into her brown eyes, he wondered how any man could say blue eyes were best. Nothing on this planet could be prettier than those eyes that smiled back at him, flecked with the same gold as her hair.

'Jake?'

'Oh. Sorry. Hi.'

'Hi.'

She was trying not to grin, but failing. She knew exactly what had left him semi-stunned in the doorway. And he could tell she liked that she could do that to him. He could kiss her hello, a simple peck on the cheek to highlight that tonight wasn't about work, it was about enjoying themselves. A quick kiss would be no different to the way they had said goodnight after he'd walked her home from the pub a few nights ago. But he didn't do it, because a friendly kiss on the cheek was not what he really wanted.

'You look very nice.'

'So do you.'

He shrugged to hide the fact that he was absurdly pleased by her words, and so she would never guess that he'd spent the afternoon ironing his best shirt and jeans and polishing his boots.

'Do you want to come in for a second?'

He did. 'No. I'll just enjoy the sunset until you're ready.' He needed the space to get his emotions under control.

'I'm almost set. Give me a minute.'

When she returned, the first thing he saw was the pendant she'd fastened around her neck. He'd seen it many times before and it reminded him again of the promises he'd made and the secrets he was keeping from Lou. He wished she hadn't chosen to wear it.

Lou didn't seem to notice the slight change in his demeanour. 'It might seem silly,' she said as she almost bounced down the stairs, 'but I'm really looking forward to this. It's been ages since I forgot about everything and had some fun.'

Since seeing the pendant, he felt exactly the same. 'I hope you can. But there will be people there wanting to talk about Luca. You know that, don't you?'

She nodded. 'I think maybe I'm more able to deal with it now. And who knows, I might learn something useful.' She touched the stone that hung at her neck. 'This was hers. Did she wear it often?'

'Yes.'

'It's beautiful. I wonder if wearing it will make me feel a bit more connected …' Her voice trailed off, then she smiled again. 'No, I'm not going there. Tonight isn't about Luca, it's about me and you and having some fun.'

He admired her optimism, but he knew that Luca's name would come up, more than once as Lou met her mother's friends. Everybody at the dance would remember that necklace. He wondered if he should warn Lou, but the moment had passed. She looked so happy, he didn't want to do anything to dampen that smile.

The sun had decided to dress the sky in its very best for them as they set out to walk to the hall. The underside of the few clouds turned gold, then pink and finally purple. Birds raucously greeted the end of the day.

'I like this time of evening,' Lou said. 'It's not just a pretty sunset. There's a feeling of both an end and a beginning. There's anticipation of the stars coming out. You really don't see the stars very well in Sydney. But out here, they're wonderful.'

Jake looked up but saw no evidence of any twinkle. Maybe later.

They heard the activity at the hall long before they turned the corner to see its welcoming lights. A few others were making their way into the hall and two figures were leaving. As they approached, Lou spoke gently.

'Hello, Vicki. What a pretty dress. Is that your party dress?'

The girl nodded shyly, never letting go of her father's hand.

'Hi, Matt.' Jake greeted the real estate agent, a little surprised that Lou seemed on such friendly terms with his daughter. As Matt nodded his acknowledgement, Lou knelt down and brushed the little girl's hair out of her face.

'Did you go to the dance with your daddy?'

Again her only reply was a silent nod. Lou didn't seem to notice.

'Well, I'm about to go to the dance too.'

'We had to leave because it's her bedtime,' Matt offered. 'But I hope the two of you have a good time.'

'Goodnight, Vicki.' Lou tried one more time, and this time was rewarded with a small smile.

'I didn't know you knew Matt and his daughter,' Jake said as they walked away.

'I spoke to Matt about the cottage. And Vicki was there. She seems a very sad little girl.'

'It has been a tough time for both of them,' Jake agreed, but his heart sank. There was only one reason Lou would be talking to Matt about her cottage, and that was if she was thinking of selling it and going back to Sydney. That wasn't an idea Jake even wanted to consider. And he wouldn't. Not tonight. Tonight was a chance to convince Lou that maybe she didn't want to move back to the city.

Pushing all such thoughts aside, he climbed the steps and walked into the brightly lit hall with Lou by his side. The hall was crowded with people, a few of whom raised their hands in welcome when they saw Jake. He nodded back. Against one wall, the trestle tables were groaning under the weight of the food displayed. Beside him, Lou waved a hand at Deb, who was helping a couple of other women with the food. On the wall opposite, three men were running a cash bar from a couple of ice-filled bathtubs where bottles of beer and wine and soft drink were cooling.

'Is all that food donated?'

'Most of the women bring a plate.'

'Why didn't you tell me? I should have brought something.'

'It's fine. This is a library fundraiser, remember? No-one would have expected you to bring anything.'

'But still …'

She was frowning, and Jake could have kicked himself. This might not turn out to be the evening he'd hoped for.

There was a sudden explosion of sound as the band on stage started up. Jake knew them well. They were a local group with a wide repertoire of all the country favourites, and while they might not be big names, they were pretty good.

Lou's head was already nodding in time to the beat. She leaned towards him. 'I didn't expect a band. You realise I am going to expect you to dance with me. So I don't feel like a wallflower.' She grinned and batted her eyelashes wildly.

'Wallflower? You? I don't think so. But if I am going to make a fool of myself on the dance floor, I might need a drink. What do you want?'

'Beer, please.'

'Sure thing.' He made his way to the bar.

'Hi, Jake. Is that Lou's daughter?' the barman asked as he pulled two bottles out of the ice.

That hadn't taken long. 'It is, but she's hoping to forget all that tonight.'

'Of course.' If the man thought he was talking about grief for her mother's death, that was fine. Jake took the beer and went looking for Lou. She'd found her way to the food tables and was chatting to Deb and a few other local women. As he approached, he heard Luca's name mentioned and cringed slightly. But the smile on Lou's face didn't fade. She seemed happy talking to her mother's old friends.

'Now you get out of here and leave us women to talk.' Deb waved him away after he'd given Lou her beer. Lou was smiling, so he shrugged and wandered off to find his friends and talk about the weather and politics and football.

As he moved around the room, he kept one eye on Lou. He told himself it was in case she needed him to run interference with Val from the post office again. He'd already caught a glimpse of Val's impossibly orange hair across the room. But it might really have been that he was keeping an eye on Lou because he liked looking at her. She already appeared to belong in Wagtail Ridge. She was chatting to people as she handed out plates of food. Every now and then, when the band fell silent, he heard her laugh. It seemed as if that laughter rose above the rest of the clamour and found its way directly to him.

One of the advantages of a small town like the Ridge was that his car was safely parked at home and another beer was not out of the question after he'd finished his first. He was headed to the bar when the band returned from a break and the music started up again. A few people moved forward and started to dance, forcing the audience to draw back a little and opening up a dance floor.

'Come on.' Lou appeared at his side and grabbed his hand. 'Let's dance.'

He wasn't much of a dancer, but he let her drag him onto the floor as an impromptu line dance started to form. He and Lou joined them, and he kicked up his heels as best he could. Lou's face was glowing as she danced next to him, her skirt floating around her knees, giving tantalising glimpses of her legs as she did a high kick or two to accompany a loud 'Hee Haw!' from the band. Like most of the dancers, Lou's face was flushed as the country set trailed off, replaced by something slow and rhythmic. Without even thinking, Jake did what he had been longing to do. He pulled Lou into his arms, holding her tight as they swayed together and caught their breath.

She smelled wonderful. And felt even better in his arms.

His resolve crumbled when she looked up at him and smiled. He'd tried to give her space. He'd tried to give her time, but he didn't know how much longer he was going to be able to do that before he did something foolish like kiss her again.

The music stopped far too soon and with an effort, he let her go.

They were heading for the bar in search of another drink when Val appeared in front of them, an eye-watering vision in a red dress that clashed terribly with her orange hair.

'Well, hello, Little Lou. Jake.' The way she said it spoke volumes.

Lou blushed. The red glow on her cheeks only made him wish even more that Val's insinuation was true.

'Hello, Val.'

'I see you're wearing your mother's pendant, Lou. It is so lovely. Do you know how she came by it?'

Beside him, Lou stiffened. 'No. Do you?' He wasn't sure if that was hope in her voice or fear of what Val might say.

'No, dear. She wore it so often, but never told anyone where she got it.'

'We all have our secrets, don't we?' Lou said with a smile. 'Oh, there's Kelly. I need to speak to her. I may see you later, Val.'

'Good for you,' Jake whispered as they moved away.

Time passed too quickly for Jake. Quite a lot of people came to introduce themselves during the rest of the evening. A few made comments about Luca, but Lou handled it all with a grace and a strength that seemed new to him. It sat well on her. He didn't dance with Lou again. There were others queueing for that honour and he didn't mind, because even when she was dancing with someone else, her eyes would flash back to him, and her mouth would curve into the smile that was quickly becoming the thing in the world he wanted most to see.

It was close to midnight as they made their farewells and left. The party was still going, but Lou had decided it was time for her to leave, and he was more than happy to walk her home.

'Thank you,' she said as they strolled along, so close they were almost touching.

'I didn't do anything.'

'You made me come tonight. It was so good to forget everything and just have some fun. Everyone was lovely.'

'I hope they didn't bother you too much, talking about Luca.'

She shrugged. 'A few people talked about her. Everyone seemed to like her.'

'She was easy to like.'

Lou didn't reply. They walked in silence for a while, and then she stopped and looked up. Above them the inky sky was filled with stars.

'See what I mean?' she said. 'You never see anything like that in Sydney.'

'Will you miss it when you go back?'

'Yes.'

He allowed himself a small hope that she wasn't talking about the stars. They kept walking until they were standing at the front door of Lou's cottage.

'Thanks again,' she said as she slipped the key in the door. 'Do you want to come in for a coffee or something?'

He did. 'Thanks, but no. I've got an early start tomorrow. A job in Merriwa. And Ollie will be looking for a walk about now as well.'

Did he sense a hint of disappointment in her smile?

'Well, say hi to Ollie for me.' She kissed him gently on the lips. His arms moved around her and he pulled her close as the kiss deepened into something that was way more than simple friendship. It took all of his will to finally let her go.

'Goodnight,' she whispered, and she was gone.

Jake listened to the door softly click shut before turning to make his way down the steps and towards his home.

CHAPTER 22

Lou sat at the kitchen table, a glass of orange juice next to her hand and her bowl of cornflakes untouched on the table. She was thinking about last night. About Jake. She'd had such a good time at the dance. The townsfolk had been so welcoming. She'd danced, drunk beer, talked and laughed. There hadn't been any awkward moments. Even the few conversations about Luca had passed easily. She'd learned quite a bit about her birth mother—mostly that she had been held in very high esteem by everyone who knew her.

And then there was Jake. He'd made the evening even more special. She was sure he felt the same. They'd talked so easily on the walk home. She'd been feeling so happy. The happiest she'd been since all this started. And then … she'd kissed him. That had taken a bit of courage on her part, but in the end, she simply couldn't not kiss him. The very best part was that he had kissed her back. She could sit there all day thinking about his handsome face in the moonlight, and the way the corners of his lips curved when he smiled. And the feeling of his arm around her on the dance floor.

The line dance had been fun, but when the band had played that romantic ballad, Lou had felt like she was dancing on air.

She knew she was acting like a teenager, but right now, she would be hard put to even remember the names of any of her previous boyfriends, far less their faces. Not that she cared, because they all paled into nothingness compared to Jake. He was helping her through the most difficult time of her life. And he was doing it because he liked her. Not only that, he seemed to understand how unsettled she was by suddenly finding her birth mother and wondering for the first time about her birth father. That understanding was like a rock to support her in the moments when she struggled. There had been a few, and she suspected there were more to come. She would need Jake.

And now it was time to stop daydreaming. Lou didn't want to open the envelope that sat on the table in front of her, the solicitor's name printed boldly on the top, but she had to face the documents she had requested. She pulled the envelope towards her and tore it open quickly, before she could lose the courage.

Now the pile of papers sat in front of her without the comforting anonymity of the envelope. If she looked down, she'd have to read it.

She looked down. A letter lay on the top of the small pile. She could read it without touching it. The solicitor was pleased to enclose all the final documents, including their own schedule of fees, which they had taken the liberty of paying out of the estate account. In delivering the documents, they had discharged the last of their duties to Luca Bonnet's estate, but they would be more than happy to represent Miss Taylor in any further legal matters, including the sale of the cottage if that was still her wish. They remained hers faithfully, etc., etc.

That, it seemed, was that. She looked around at the cottage and its contents. What was she doing here? She shouldn't be wasting her time trying to find all those letters. Luca was gone and she didn't matter at all. Not one bit. Lou needed to get this house sorted and sold and get on with her life. She had a degree that she had worked hard to achieve. She might not know exactly what she wanted to do with it, but she did know she wanted to contribute to preserving the wonder that was the bush. She had a career to plan and she needed a job to start that plan. It was time to get this thing finished while she still knew who Lou Taylor was and what she wanted.

She put the letter to one side and flicked through the next few papers. There was a bit to do with the house. Apparently Luca had owned the place outright, which was good; it meant there was no mortgage for Lou to worry about. It also explained how Luca could live off the money raised by the local community. There were also two bank accounts with funds that she could access. The first was in Luca's name. There wasn't a lot of money, but Lou could survive on that if she committed to this journey that Luca had started. The second account had slightly more money in it and was in the name of WRML. There was a debit card attached to that account in the pile. Before she could think about what those four letters meant, her eyes fell on the next document. It was a death certificate. Putting the bank paperwork to one side, she read it. There was the diagnosis. Cancer. There was a date of death. There was no marriage certificate and no clue as to why Luca had given up the child she professed to love so much.

The last item in the pile was a birth certificate. Lou's birth certificate. She'd never seen that before, but had imagined her mum and dad had a copy. She'd never thought to ask before all this happened, and then she'd been too distracted. With hands that trembled slightly, she smoothed the certificate out on the table and looked at it. There was her name—Susan Luca Bonnet. It looked so very strange to see Bonnet, not Taylor, written there. She hadn't really expected to see her biological father's name, but still felt a twinge of disappointment that it wasn't there.

Lou pushed all the papers back into the envelope and laid it on the table alongside all her other clues. Those legal documents, a few old photos and five letters from a dead woman. The truth of who she had been born and why she had grown up as someone different lay in those meagre piles of paper. The only way to know that truth was to finish what she had started the day she first drove into Wagtail Ridge.

She turned her attention back to the collection of photographs she'd found under the bed and selected all the images with other people in them, the most recent on the top. Twenty years had passed since most were taken. She might not recognise someone in these photos even if she met them. But maybe someone would recognise a younger version of themselves. Or someone they knew. She would start showing them to people. She found a spare envelope and placed the photos inside.

Happy at the thought of taking some positive action, she reached for the phone to ring Jake. Then she remembered that he wouldn't be home—he had more work at one of the studs. It would be at least four days before they could go out with the library again.

Four days! Waiting to put this new plan into action would drive her crazy. There was one thing she could do though. She walked through to the bedroom and started throwing clothes and cosmetics into her overnight bag.

Twenty-four hours later, she was having lunch with three friends at a favourite restaurant overlooking Sydney Harbour. The sunlight glinted off the water and the chilled glasses of prosecco on the table in front of them. Food had been ordered and it was time to catch up.

'I've got a new job,' her friend Annie said eagerly. 'I just found out yesterday. It's with … drumroll please … The Belden Agency!'

Lou had never heard of them, but she understood from her friends' chatter that this was a big name advertising agency. She congratulated Annie on a job that would suit her.

'But what about you, Lou? We've hardly heard anything from you since uni broke up. What have you been doing? Are you planning to become a full-time academic, or have you found a job?'

'No. Well, not a long-term job. I've been doing some work with a library.' Apart from a few texts, this was Lou's first catch-up with her old friends since before her graduation.

'A library? That doesn't surprise us at all. In fact, it's perfect for you. It's not going to be a full-time job?'

'No. I'm still looking for something else. You'd think with all the concern over climate change, there'd be plenty of work for an environmental scientist, wouldn't you? But apparently not.'

'You'll find something that suits you soon, I'm sure of it.'

The conversation continued and Lou found herself strangely quiet. She didn't want to tell her friends about Wagtail Ridge and Jake and she didn't want to talk about Luca either. After her arrival back home yesterday afternoon, she and her parents had talked about all that well into the night. Now she just wanted to forget and have some fun doing something she couldn't do at the Ridge.

Their food arrived. Lou had ordered a salad with prawns and mango. It was good, far better than the salad Jake had made for her. Yet she'd enjoyed that one more.

'Let's go shopping when we've eaten,' she suggested. That would take her mind off Wagtail Ridge and everyone she had met there, including Jake.

'Good idea.'

The four of them spent the afternoon window shopping in the Pitt Street Mall. It was something they'd done a dozen times, but Lou wasn't having as much fun this time. The city seemed busier than ever before, and the crowds harder to manage. The clothes in the shop windows were not particularly enticing and the jewellery not as interesting as the purple amethyst pendant she had left sitting in a dresser drawer in the cottage. The air in the city tasted of smog and the noise never ended. When the friends stopped at a trendy new bar for a cocktail at the end of their day, Lou found herself wishing she was drinking a lemonade, lime and bitters in the pub kitchen with Deb. Or with Jake.

She returned to Wagtail Ridge the following day and the two more days she had to wait before Jake was free passed quickly and restfully, as she curled up on the couch, reading the books Luca had left with her letters. When he arrived on the morning of the next library run, Lou was a little afraid that things between them might have changed because of that kiss. She was right. Things between them had changed, but in a good way. He kissed her again. Just a quick kiss, and then stood back, studying her face. She saw a hint of her uncertainty in his eyes.

'Hi.'

'Hi,' she replied and when he smiled, they both knew everything was all right.

They set about the library run much as they always had, for which she was glad. If something was growing between them, she had no desire to hurry it.

On the road to Spring Ridge, she told him her plan for showing the photos to the library customers.

'That's a good idea,' Jake said. 'I can't help with that, I've only been here a few years. But some of the longer term residents might recognise the photos.'

'That's the plan. Or at least the hope.' She gave Ollie a scratch under the chin and was rewarded with a very sloppy dog kiss.

'So you're trying to focus now on finding your father?'

'My biological father, yes.'

'Can I ask why?'

'I think I'm coming to know Luca a little because of her letters. But how will I ever know if I've found them all? Maybe I'll never truly understand why she gave me up. And while it never really mattered to me before, I now find it hard to forgive her for what she did. I thought maybe if I found my biological father, that might help me understand. Or maybe, if I got to know him, I'd feel this has all been worthwhile. In her letter, Luca said she fell in love and never even looked at anyone else. It's nice to know they were in love, and now I want to meet that man. I just have to give it a try. I don't want this hanging over me for the rest of my life.'

'How do your adoptive parents feel about all this?'

'They understand. They know I love them. Whatever happens, they'll always be my mum and dad.'

'That's good.'

A few minutes after eleven o'clock, Jake guided the library into its parking place next to the Spring Ridge Community Hall. They alighted from the cab and set about preparing for library visitors. They had already fallen into a routine. Jake made sure the steps were in place and safe. Lou took care of the library itself and as visitors came and went, Jake and Ollie went for a walk or chatted to the locals. Spring Ridge was a slightly larger town than some they'd visited and soon there were people gathered outside waiting their chance to enter the library. Lou had the tin of book slips on the desk next to her. The four slips that didn't have names inside had been kept separate from the rest.

A man appeared at her desk with two large tote bags. 'Do you have a use for these?'

'Are they books for the library?'

'Well, they're for the library, but they're not books.' He placed both bags on the floor and pulled from one a box of coloured pencils. The other bag contained sketch pads and other art materials. 'These were my daughter's. She just won a scholarship to art school.'

'Congratulations. You must be very pleased.'

'We are. It's what she has always wanted. These are her old art things. The scholarship included all new materials, and she wanted to give these to the library for other kids to use.'

'That's very kind of her.'

'She's just returning the favour. Without the donated art supplies Luca brought her, she might never have won that scholarship.'

'I'll make sure they're put to good use.'

'Thank you. And thank you for bringing the library back. We have all missed it a great deal. You'll always find a big welcome when you come to Spring Ridge.'

The man was gone before Lou could tell him this was a one-off trip. She lifted the bags of art supplies onto the desk and wondered why she'd told him she'd get them to someone who needed them. Unless that someone was at one of the few remaining library stops, the only way she could keep her word would be to take them with her when she went home to Sydney and give them to a charity there. Come to think of it, there were all those boxes of things in the shed. They'd been donated by this community for this community. She really couldn't take them to Sydney and give them all away. She'd talk to Jake soon about what to do.

She heard more footsteps on the metal stairs. Another customer was arriving, so she tucked the bags behind her desk. She would worry about giving them away when the time came.

Lou was starting to feel like lunch when the crowd finally dispersed. She closed the tin in disappointment. No more books with letters inside. Then she heard someone running up the stairs.

'Sorry, sorry. I'm late.' A teenage girl breathing heavily from running stepped into the library.

'That's fine. Come on in. What are you looking for? Perhaps I can suggest something. I have some new books.' Well, she hoped they might be new. She'd restocked again from the shelves in Luca's house, taking pleasure from the nice display they made.

'No. Thanks. I only came to return this.' She held out a copy of *The Thorn Birds*, and Lou knew instantly it was one of the unclaimed tags in her tin. She opened the book and, sure enough, there was one of the familiar envelopes.

'Thanks.'

'Oh, what a pretty necklace.'

Luca's hand went to her chest, where the purple pendant hung. It was a bit fancy for jeans and a Western shirt, but she liked the feel of it. And it was, as the girl said, very pretty.

'My mum has a necklace like that. Dad bought it for her in a craft show in Scone.'

'Do you know who he bought it from?'

'No. But I could ask if you like.'

'Please. I—I'd really like to know.'

'Sure.'

Lou wrote her number on an old card and handed it to the girl. 'Text me if he remembers. It's important.' She had the envelope of old photos in the desk, but there was no point asking this girl about them. She was far too young to have known any of the people in those faded images. 'Did you know Luca very well?'

'No. I only met her once, I think. She and my mum were friends. Mum's away today. She had to take Grandma to the doctor. But she made me promise to bring this book back. A lot of worry over a late library book, I guess. Anyway, I'm off. Bye.'

In a flash the girl was gone, leaving Lou with a book and a letter.

CHAPTER 23

My Darling Daughter,

I cannot begin to describe to you how happy I was during our time together. I hope one day you'll find out yourself when you have a child of your own. I was besotted by you. I could not believe that somehow I'd created this beautiful, perfect human being. How I wished your father could be there to see you. I know he would have loved you. I missed him so much, but the joy you brought me was enough.

At least, that's how it was most of the time and those are the times I like to remember, because it wasn't always like that.

I try not to think about those first few months. It wasn't just that we didn't have much money; there were times when I felt overwhelmed by everything. The responsibility of caring for you terrified me. What if I did something wrong or made a mistake? What if I accidentally hurt you?

I'd never spent any time around a baby before. I'd had no chance to learn what being a mother is all about. People say instinct takes over. For some women, perhaps, it does, but for me, it didn't work that way. I thought there was something wrong with me. I'd always been strong and capable, but here I was reduced to shivering panic.

When it all became too much, Deb Fraser or one of the others would come around and care for you while I sat in the dark and cried, driven almost to incapacity by my fear.

I'm not the first mother to suffer like that, and I won't be the last. I didn't have a husband to help and I was spiralling quickly downwards. At the time there wasn't much support out here for someone with postnatal depression. No doctors or health workers calling every day. I don't know what would have happened if it hadn't been for my friends. They were my lifeline. They told me how common my feelings were. Some had gone through the same thing. They shared their experiences with me, looked after you when I couldn't. They helped me heal.

It took months, but I began feeling stronger again. I began to believe I could be a mother to you. And when I looked at you then, my heart was so full of love. I promised you that I would never again let you down.

I went back to work and you came with me in the library, your baby seat safely strapped in. Everywhere we went, people commented on how beautiful you were and how good. They were right on both counts. You laughed and smiled far more than you cried, and I was the happiest mother in the world each time your little hand curled around my finger.

Have you ever heard that old song—'You and Me Against the World'? It may seem corny but that's how I felt. We were so happy together, you and I. I've been told most people don't remember anything from when they were that young. I wish you could. I wish you shared those memories, because they have kept me going all these long lonely years.

I don't know why people talk about the terrible twos. You weren't terrible. Well, you were a bit, but I would've been worried if you weren't. You were a happy, healthy, smart toddler, always getting into trouble, but I loved you for that as well. I had such big plans for your third birthday. But that's when everything went wrong.

One day, I collapsed. We were home alone, just you and me. You were asleep, safely tucked away in your cot. I was doing things in the kitchen. I was never sure how long I was unconscious, but when I woke you were screaming. My first thought was for you, left without anyone watching you while I was lying on the kitchen floor. It was only later, when it happened again, that I began to worry about me.

It's pointless now to go into details, but I was diagnosed with a degenerative illness. A few years, the doctors told me, and I would die. And during those years, I would become less and less able to function … or to look after you. My nightmares were not about dying, they were about you. Two things haunted me. The harm that could come to you if I collapsed again and left you alone. And the almost unbearable grief I felt when I watched my mother die. I did not want you to go through that.

I knew I had to let you go.

Almost four years later, I found out it was a misdiagnosis. The doctors were wrong and, with changed medication, I was perfectly able to live a normal life. But by then it was too late. You were gone. You were my whole reason for living and I had sent you away on the basis of a doctor's mistake. All I had left ahead was time to regret that decision.

I did think about trying to find you. I wanted to. But by that time, you had lived longer with your adoptive family than with me. I didn't even know if you would remember me. Could I drag you away from the people who were your family? From the place that was your home? I didn't even know if the law allowed it.

And the irony of it all was that about twelve months ago, I discovered I had cancer. So I guess the doctors weren't all wrong … but how I hate them for robbing me of all those years to watch you grow into a young woman.

I would happily have given my life to have those back.

Your loving mother,

Luca.

Lou dropped the letter on the kitchen table and wiped the tears from her cheek. Six letters lay in front of her, along with the collection of photographs. Her hand was shaking slightly as she picked up the photograph of herself as a baby with the woman whose tragic story was unfolding in front of her. The smile on Luca's face in that photo seemed so real and so filled with love that another sob caught in Lou's throat. It had been so easy to hate her. To blame her for giving away her daughter. But she was beginning to understand that there really are two sides to every story.

'Oh, Luca. I am so, so sorry for everything you went through.'

She flicked through the pages of *The Thorn Birds*. She'd never read it but she knew it had a lot to say about families and love. Perhaps it was one of the books that Luca would have recommended to her as she got older, had they stayed together. Maybe they would have sat around this very kitchen table discussing the book. She closed it gently. She would add it to the pile of books Luca had sent her. Something in those books had been special to Luca and perhaps when Lou read them, knowing what she now knew, she'd find that something special too. Some comfort in the words.

And she did need comforting, of that she was certain. She glanced back at the letter. Her mother had turned to Deb Fraser for help. Maybe Deb could help Lou as well. She carefully put the letter back in its envelope and hesitated before dropping the envelope on the table. Deb may have been Luca's closest friend and she seemed a kind person, but Lou wasn't ready to share the contents of the letters yet. Not with anyone.

She picked up her phone and checked again. There was no text about the necklace. Perhaps the girl in Spring Ridge had forgotten.

When she got to the pub, it was almost empty. Shane Fraser was behind the bar and there was no sign of Jake.

'Hi, Lou. Can I get you a drink?'

'No, thanks. I actually came to see Deb. Is she about?'

'Yep. In the kitchen. Thursdays are usually pretty quiet, so she does the cooking.'

'Not so much cooking as reheating the things Jake has left.' Deb's head appeared in the doorway. 'Come on through, Lou.'

Once she was perched on a stool by the big centre table, a glass of cold water in her hand, Lou wasn't quite sure where to start. Deb was chopping vegetables and didn't try to hurry her.

'You and Luca were friends for a long time.' It wasn't a question.

'Yes. We were friends before you were even born.'

'Did she tell you about the letters she was leaving for me to find?'

'She said there were letters, but didn't tell me where or how many.'

'It seems she didn't tell anyone. The only way I can find them is to keep taking the library out.'

'Is that what you plan to do?'

'I have to. But I kind of feel as if she is manipulating me, trying to force me into moving into her house and taking over the library, even though it's not what I want from my life.'

'Don't think that. That wasn't Luca. I'm sure she had her reasons for doing it this way, but she would never have wanted you to do anything you didn't want to. She loved you too much for that.'

'Do you have a letter for me?' The question seemed almost rude, but Lou had to ask.

Deb didn't look away. 'I think she hoped the search for the letters would help you understand her … as well as the past.'

'She says you helped her a lot.'

Deb's hands stilled. 'She didn't have an easy time. Losing her mother in such a terrible way and then being alone and pregnant. But she found her way back. You know why, don't you?'

'No.'

'Because of you. She loved you so much. Giving you up was the hardest thing I have ever seen anyone do.'

'In a letter she said she thought she was dying, but the doctors got it wrong.'

'They did.' Lou could almost feel the anger in Deb. 'They told her she would become more and more frail and unable to control her body. She would certainly never be able to look after you. And then, they said, she would die. You know that's why she gave you up, don't you?'

'Because she couldn't look after me?'

'Yes that, but more importantly, she didn't want you to have to watch her go downhill. Remember, she watched her own mother die. She wouldn't do that to you. People here in town would have helped her look after you, but in the end she believed you would be alone. And heartbroken, just as she was. She gave you up rather than do that to you.'

'I was angry at her at first. But now I think I feel sorry for her.'

'You're entitled to feel angry. And to feel sorry for her. You are entitled to whatever feelings you have. What you're going through isn't easy. Just as what Luca did wasn't easy. When it comes to families and love and pain, it's never simple.'

'No, it's not.'

Silence fell in the kitchen. Deb went back to chopping vegetables. Without thinking too much about it, Lou picked up the spare knife on the table to help. There was comfort in the familiar movements, and in doing something vaguely useful.

Deb broke the silence. 'How many letters have you found?'

'Six so far. But I don't know how many there are.'

'And she's telling you the whole story.'

'So it seems …' Lou paused and frowned. 'Come to think of it, I seem to be getting all the letters in the right order. I wonder …' Her voice trailed off as she thought it through. The letters were coming to her in exactly the order Luca must have wanted. The story was unfolding in such a way as to best help her understand. But how could that happen? If the run had become erratic in the last weeks, as Jake had said, how did Luca know what order Lou would visit the towns? Unless …

She dropped the knife back on the table, causing Deb to jump.

'What's wrong?'

'Is Jake coming in tonight?'

'Probably not. I know he had a job in Scone today. He's usually pretty late back after a day there.'

'Thanks.' Lou got to her feet and started to leave, before realising she was being rude. She turned back. 'Deb, thank you. Thank you for helping my mother. And for helping me as well.'

'You're very welcome.'

'I have to go now. If you see Jake, can you tell him I'm looking for him?'

'Sure.' Deb paused. 'Do you realise that's the first time you've called Luca your mother? She would be very happy to hear that. I'm here to talk about her, any time you want to. I still grieve for my dear friend, and talking to you helps me too.'

Lou had driven to the pub, so when she left she drove past Jake's place just in case he'd arrived home, but there was no sign of his ute. When she got back to her cottage, she texted him: *I need to see you.*

Then she sat and stared at her phone, waiting for a reply. The longer she stared, the angrier she became, and not only because he wasn't replying.

At last the phone beeped.

Job isn't going to plan. I won't be back until very late. Sorry. Tomorrow then?

I have to be back here at daybreak. All week. But I can do another library run early next week if you want.

Did she? Probably. But right now, the last thing she wanted was to spend a couple of hours in a truck cab with Jake.

Call me when you can.

She wondered if he would get the hint that she was upset with him. If he didn't notice now, he certainly would when they spoke. She'd thought he understood her struggle and wanted to help. He might not have lied to her, but he was supposed to be her friend at a time when she really needed one. And he certainly hadn't treated her like a friend should.

CHAPTER 24

Lou's car was parked next to the cottage when Jake and Ollie walked up to the cottage, but there was no answer when Jake knocked on the door.

'She must be in the shed,' he said to Ollie. He was tired after three long days working on stockyards just outside Scone. He was back early today, and every time he moved his right arm, he was reminded of the reason why. The arm was bruised and swollen and it hurt, but in one way he was lucky: he could have broken the arm and that would have put paid to helping Lou. There were only two more places he had to take Lou. Well, three, if you counted the Ridge. Then he could tell her everything. What a relief that would be. She'd seemed upset in her texts, and she hadn't answered when he finally found time to call her yesterday while waiting at the hospital for an X-ray on his arm.

He was looking forward to spending the day with her. Right now all he wanted to do was kiss her again, to see if it was as wonderful as the last time. Just one kiss. That would keep him going for a little longer. Until he'd fulfilled his promise, and there was no barrier left between them.

The shed door was open. So too was the door to the library. Ollie bounded up the stairs ahead of him, obviously as eager as he was to see Lou.

'Hi. Sorry about being away …' The rest of the words died in his throat when he saw her. She was seated at the desk, the open tin of library cards in front of her, and a pile of letters next to it. She hadn't even welcomed Ollie, who was looking up at her with a hurt expression on his face.

'Lou? What is it?'

'You lied to me.'

'No. I have never lied to you.'

'She told you to do this. Luca. She told you to take me around and collect these letters.' She indicated the pile on the table. 'Don't bother to deny it. She must have. You told me the route became a bit muddled and irregular towards the end, and yet I'm getting these letters in exactly the order she would have wanted. You arranged this with her, didn't you?'

His first reaction was relief that it was out in the open at last. But then he read the anger in her voice and the disappointment and hurt on her face. 'Yes. She did ask me to do this for her. I never lied about that. The only thing you ever asked me was if I know who your father is. And I honestly don't.'

'But why didn't you just tell me you knew where all the letters were? So we could collect them more easily?'

'I knew the stops, not who had the letters, although I could probably have guessed at least some. But Luca asked me not to tell you.'

'And that was more important to you than telling me the truth.' It was a statement, not a question, and he heard her voice break a little as she spoke. 'I trusted you, Jake.'

'Let me tell you everything now.'

When she didn't respond, he pulled out the library's second chair and sat down. 'I told you I drove the library for her when she was sick. Especially towards the end.'

Lou nodded. As she did, she absently slipped a hand off the desk to pat Ollie. Jake took that as a good sign.

'She knew you'd struggle with all this,' he said quietly. 'She thought it would be easier if you found out everything a little bit at a time.'

'She was wrong.'

'Maybe, but she meant well. She made me promise to help you if you came to the Ridge. To take you out with the library and, yes, she did tell me what order to do the stops. I knew she'd left you one letter in the library. She asked me to make sure you found it. I honestly didn't know about the others. It wasn't until you started to collect them that I realised what she had done.'

'You should have told me.'

'I wanted to. But Luca was my friend and she was dying when she made me promise not to say anything to you. I couldn't break my word.'

He hoped her silence was a sign that she understood and maybe even would forgive him.

'Luca didn't say this outright, but I suspect she had other reasons for this secrecy.'

Lou tilted her head. 'What?'

'I think she hoped to keep you in the Ridge for a while, until you started to get to know her. I think she hoped you would come to love this place and the library as much as she did. I know she wanted the library to continue. Maybe she hoped you would do that.'

'That's ridiculous. I've got a whole career in front of me. And a whole world to explore. I'm not ready to settle in a backwater town like this. I mean—it's nice, but still …'

Jake tried not to wince. He was only a couple of years older than Lou and he had most happily settled in this 'backwater town', working in the pub, doing odd jobs and raising guide dog puppies. He was happy here. He suddenly realised that, deep down, he had hoped maybe Lou was too. That she might stay so he'd have someone to share it with. So much for that.

'Luca wouldn't have wanted you to do anything you didn't want to. She wasn't like that. But she knew how important the library was—not just to the Ridge but to all the other towns as well. She wanted you to know that. And I think she wanted you to understand how important it was to her, too.'

'It's just a library, for goodness' sake. It's not life or death.'

'Not as such no … but for some of these towns, losing the library would be part of a slow death. First it's the library, so people start driving to Scone for their books, and then they shop there as well. You must have noticed that Kelly's store is struggling.'

She nodded.

'The pub too. The library brings people in and they might go to the pub to chat over lunch. The margins on a country pub are pretty small. Losing a social occasion like that can cause it to fail.'

'Deb hasn't said anything.'

'Of course she wouldn't. These places are communities, and as each little bit is chipped away, the towns become less and less viable. Until one day there are more houses boarded up and empty than there are people living here and a whole way of life will be lost.'

'No!' Lou shook her head. 'You can't lay all of that on me! It's not my job to save the town. And it's not my fault if it dies. It's just life and sometimes life deals you a shitty hand. You just have to do the best you can with it.'

Her shoulders were heaving as she fell silent and Jake knew she wasn't talking about the towns. He kept silent until she seemed more composed.

'So what do you want to do?'

'How many stops are left?'

'Just two more. And the Ridge. It was always the last stop.'

Lou stared at the pile of letters on her desk. She folded them and stuffed them into a cardboard box on the desk. Jake saw some old photos already in the box. He wanted to ask her about them, but this was not the time.

'What are the towns?'

'Mullalee and Gwabegar.'

'Are there more letters waiting for me?'

'I don't know. Probably.'

'Show me.' She pulled a map from the desk drawer and unfolded it. He pointed out the two towns. 'Can we do them in one trip?' she asked.

He thought carefully. 'I guess so. But we couldn't fit both in one day. Not if you're going to open the library properly at each site. You're still going to do that, aren't you?'

She hesitated and his heart fell.

'Yes. I will,' she said. 'But then I'm done.'

'All right. I can't do it for a couple of days until my arm is better. I'm okay with a car, but wouldn't be safe driving the truck.'

She blinked in confusion then looked at his arms. Her eyes widened. 'Oh. Jake, I didn't see … Are you okay?'

'Yep. They X-rayed it and there's nothing broken. It didn't even break the skin, but it hurts like … well, it hurts.'

'What happened?'

'A metal rail slipped and fell. I failed to catch it.' He made a self-deprecating face.

'You're not Superman. Leave those rails to fall. They don't break. Bones do.'

'Yes, ma'am.'

She grinned, and just like that, everything was better. His arm still hurt and there were still more letters from Luca to be found. They hadn't solved the question of Lou's father. She would still be mad at him when this moment passed, but that was fine. He deserved it. But when she smiled at him like that, he believed that everything would be all right, because he saw a light in her eyes that was a tiny reflection of the hope that lived in one corner of his heart, growing stronger each day.

'Do you want to stay for dinner? You can't cook with your arm like that.'

'I would love to say yes, but I'm tired and this hurts. I'm planning to walk home, take a fist full of painkillers and sleep it off.'

'All right. Call me if you need a hand … or a spare arm. I hope it feels better in the morning.'

It wouldn't. Jake knew that it would be worse as the bruising really started to show. He had a couple of very uncomfortable days ahead, but he'd be fine. He'd be back on the road with Lou soon enough. It was time to get this thing done.

It took more than a couple of days—Jake didn't feel it was safe for him to tackle the long drive until the middle of the following week. He wasn't sure who was most restless by the time they were in the library and heading out of town—him, Ollie or Lou. Two overnight bags were stored on the shelf behind the seats and he'd booked a couple of rooms at the nearest pub to Gwabegar. They'd visit Mullalee first and then drive on to the pub. The residents of Gwabegar were expecting them the next morning, which left plenty of time to get back to Wagtail Ridge before dark.

The drive seemed longer than it should. They were both feeling the pressure of their task. Lou sat staring out the window, only occasionally speaking to him or Ollie. The pup whined, sensing the atmosphere. Jake gave him a quick pat each time, but mostly kept his eyes fixed on the road, giving Lou the space she so clearly wanted. When they'd set up the library near the school on the corner of the aptly named Black Stump Road, Jake called Ollie and set off for a walk. If there was another letter here for Lou, he didn't think she would want him around when she received it.

The tension she'd felt all through the drive was still sitting heavily on Lou's shoulders when her first reader arrived, asking about rural romance novels. The woman was delighted to discover the range on the library shelves and would have taken them all, had not Lou pointed to the sign on the wall saying maximum of four books per reader.

'I'm sorry. I didn't know. Four books are fine. There's such a fabulous choice there. I'm new in town and this is my first visit to the library. I didn't realise we had one until I saw the notice in the shop window yesterday. When are you coming back?'

Lou tensed a fraction more at that. 'I'm not sure.' The woman was so pleased to have discovered the library, Lou didn't want to say 'never again'.

'I'll keep an eye open for another notice in the shop. Now, how do I join, or sign up or whatever?'

The question floored Lou. She had no idea. It had never occurred to her that she might find new customers on this journey to find Luca's letters.

The woman reached into her bag. 'I guess you want ID.'

'Yes. Please.'

The woman's face was bright as she held out her driver's licence. 'I'm just so excited about this. I can't afford to buy a lot of books, and downloading books from the main library … well, I prefer proper books. And out here there's not much to do. My husband's a truckie, you see, and away a lot. So books are my company.'

Lou opened the desk drawers until she found a package of unused file cards. She sat down and took the offered driver's licence then copied the woman's details. Then she put the card in her tin, attached to the book sleeves.

'That's wonderful, thank you so much. You have really made my day. I'll see you soon.' The woman was almost bouncing as she left the library.

Lou barely had time to sit down again before the next customer appeared. Mullalee was a small town, but if the number of people wanting books was any indication, they liked to read. A lot. One woman asked after Luca, and her eyes glinted with tears when she heard that Luca was gone.

'Oh. I knew she was ill, but I didn't … Such a brave woman. A real fighter. And so kind. She brought a lot of joy into our lives. God bless her.'

At last the rush slowed to a trickle and then, ten minutes of nothing and no-one. Perhaps it was time to find Jake and set off. At least her mood had lifted. She wasn't really mad at him any more. Maybe they could have dinner at this pub he'd booked. Take Ollie for a walk to work out the kinks after a long drive. If there was a pool table, Jake could teach her to play.

She was about to go in search of them when a man stepped into the library. Silhouetted against the bright light outside, she couldn't really see his face, but his stooped posture told her he wasn't a young man.

'Hello.' She got to her feet. 'Are you looking for a book?'

'Not today. I came to return one.'

He gently placed a copy of *The Harp in the South* on the desk. Lou didn't have to open it to see what was inside. The corner of an envelope protruded from inside the cover.

The man turned to go.

'Please. Would you sit down for a minute and talk to me?'

'All right.' He sat and placed the hands holding his hat in his lap.

Lou could see him more clearly now. His face was lined. He was thin and wiry, no doubt from a life of hard outdoor work. Lou guessed he would be in his early seventies. The faint hope that this might be her father faded. It wasn't just his age, his demeanour was not that of a man who would have had a brief affair with a much younger woman twenty years ago.

'You must have known Luca well for her to give you this for me.' She laid a hand on the book, but they both knew she was talking about the letter inside.

'We were friends. I miss her still.'

'How long did you know her?'

'Almost twenty years. We met not long after she gave you away.'

Lou's hopes were fading even more, but she wasn't ready to give up. 'I have some old photographs here. I found them in the house. I was wondering if maybe you could tell me who some of the people are.' She reached into her bag for the envelope and spread the photos on the desk.

One by one, the man picked them up and studied them. On the fourth, his lips spread into a slow smile. 'Well, well. That's me.'

'Really?'

He handed her the photo of Luca and a group of people standing in front of the library. The photo was one of the more recent.

'That's me. And that's my wife, Joan.' The man pointed at a figure to the left of the photo. 'My late wife. I remember that day. It was the first library day of the new year and Joan brought a bottle of bubbly for a toast.'

Looking at the photo, Lou could see that Luca held what looked like a glass in her hand. The mood of the photo was certainly bright, almost celebratory.

'I'm rather pleased to see it again. That man in the hat, that's my friend Blue. And that woman there, she ran the shop but she retired to the coast a long time ago. That was a good day. I'm so glad Luca kept this photo to remind her of it.'

'Would you like it?'

'Oh, no. I couldn't take it off you.'

'Please do. It obviously means something to you. I'm sure Luca would have wanted you to have it.' She didn't add that if the photo had been taken after she was born, it was unlikely to be of any help in finding her father. And besides, the joy in this man's face as he looked at it had been wonderful to see.

'Thank you.' He picked the photo up carefully. 'Oh, by the way, my name's Ray. Ray Anderson.'

'Glad to meet you, Ray. I'm Lou.'

'Little Lou. I know. Your mother talked about you a lot to my late wife.'

It didn't upset her to be called that name this time.

Lou stayed sitting behind the desk as Ray left. She spread the photos out, examining the faces in a little more detail. Wondering about the people in them and the stories they had to tell until the sound of boots on the library's metal steps alerted her to Jake's return.

'How'd it go?' He sounded a little hesitant.

'It went well. I met a nice man called Ray. He knew Luca.'

Jake dropped into the chair Ray had so recently vacated. 'I know Ray. He's a good man. Did he …?'

'Yes. He had a letter.'

'I could leave you alone if you want to read it.'

'No. It can wait until we get to the hotel.'

'All right. Let's get underway.'

CHAPTER 25

My Darling Daughter,

I try not to think about that day. The day I said goodbye to you. It broke my heart.

For a long time afterwards, I would hear you crying in my dreams, and when I woke up, my pillow would be damp with my tears. I would lie there in the dark and wonder if you were awake and crying too. If maybe some connection between us still existed and you were feeling my pain. I could only hope that your adoptive mother was at that very moment picking you up, holding you. Comforting you. If there was any comfort for me, it was in knowing that you were cared for. That you would not have to face what I was facing.

The process itself was easy. I hired a lawyer because I didn't think I would ever do it if I had to do it myself. He made it all seem so simple and unemotional. Almost businesslike. He did say I could remain a part of your life. Your adoptive parents would be happy to have me. But I said no. I knew that I couldn't go on seeing you and being your mother. If I did, when

I died, you would still feel the loss I was trying to protect you from. Nor could I watch you become someone else's daughter.

That day … my heart still aches as I remember it. That day I parcelled up the things I wanted you to have. I put in your favourite books, the teddy bear you loved so much. At the last minute, I kept back one book. I needed something to connect me to you. Instead, I took a copy of The Magic Pudding *from the library, wrote my message in it and packed that into your bag. I hope you read that message when you were old enough. I hope you knew it came from the very core of my heart. I hope you understood what I was trying to say.*

I couldn't bear the thought of driving all the way to Sydney, where the law firm was based. Even more than that, I couldn't face the thought of driving all the way back with an empty seat next to me. So I arranged to meet the adoption agency team in Newcastle.

Once we were in the car, I realised that I never wanted that journey to end. You were there, in your baby seat, listening to the book recording I had done for you the night before. You smiled and you laughed. You had no idea what was ahead. Nor, to be honest, did I.

I carried you into the health care centre, along with all those things I wanted you to have. They were waiting for me in an office. The lawyer was very distant. The family services woman looked kindly at you, but I could see the disapproval in her eyes when she looked at me. Strangely enough, that helped. The woman had no right to judge me and what I was doing and why. That anger got me through the meeting, right up to the point where I had to turn my back on you and walk away.

I didn't think I could do it. But then I remembered that day when I came home and my mother wasn't waiting for me. I thought then about your father, and the sacrifice I made when I let him go. And I kissed you one last time and walked out the door.

In the months that followed, I couldn't sleep and I didn't eat. I became almost a shadow, which reinforced my belief that I had done the right thing.

If this was what my illness would do, you were better off away from me. In reality, I suspect it was grief that did it to me. Grief over losing you.

When the doctors decided they were wrong, it was a long time before they realised what my condition really was and that with medication, it was neither debilitating nor fatal, I wanted to scream. I had given you up for no reason. All I wanted to do was drive down to Sydney and bring you back. To have you back here where you belonged.

But of course I didn't know where you were. I had insisted on that. I knew I wouldn't be strong enough to stay away if I knew. I didn't want to risk disrupting your new life. I could have asked the lawyers, but that seemed like breaking a promise, so I didn't. It would have been wrong. Your adoptive parents were your real parents now. I couldn't break up your family. For all I knew you had brothers and sisters as well. What sort of monster would tear a child of six away from the home and family they loved? So I didn't.

When I set out to write these letters, I didn't understand how hard it would be for me. I hope you have had an easier time … because you are the innocent one in all of this. You did nothing to cause this crippling regret.

I wish I could say the same of myself.

Your loving mother,

Luca.

The teddy bear Luca had given her had been old even when Lou was young. Battered and bruised from a bit too much over-enthusiastic hugging, it still sat on a top shelf in her room in Sydney. It was vaguely yellow and went by the name of Ted. She'd never given much thought to when and where she'd acquired it. Ted had simply always been there and had always been loved. She closed her eyes and tried to remember. Surely she would have some recollection of the day her life changed forever? Or the days that followed. As a child, she wouldn't have understood what was going on. She must have missed Luca. Had she cried at night and needed Fiona to comfort her? She was pretty sure she had. All babies do. But had her crying meant something more?

She dropped the letter on the bed next to her and looked around the hotel room. The pub Jake had found for their overnight stay was clean and simple, not unlike the Wagtail Ridge Hotel. And the husband and wife team running the place were probably a lot like Deb and Shane. This town was even smaller than Wagtail Ridge. Tonight she missed the city. There was nothing she wanted more than to go somewhere busy. A crowded café, perhaps. Or a cinema. Maybe even simply go for a walk along the edge of the harbour to look at the lights. She missed the lights and people's voices. She even missed the sound of passing cars. Or maybe she just needed a distraction.

She slid across the bed and as she did, the copy of *The Harp in the South* slipped to the floor. She bent to pick it up and saw a second envelope sticking out from between the pages. Puzzled, she reached for it. There was no writing on this envelope. Nothing to suggest who it was for. Nor was it sealed. She shrugged and lifted the flap, pulling out a single rectangle of printed paper. She frowned as she looked at the letters written in the payee field. WRML. She had seen that before.

Lou roughly shoved it back into the envelope. She barely remembered to lock her room door behind her. Jake's room was across the hall, but when she banged on the door, there was no answer. She headed down to the bar, but he wasn't there either. When she asked the barman, he told her Jake had taken Ollie for a walk. She ordered a Coke, then went onto the pub's veranda. She pulled a chair up to one of the tables and sat down to wait.

As he and Ollie walked back to the pub, Jake saw someone sitting on the veranda. It was getting dark, but he recognised her immediately and raised a hand to acknowledge he'd noticed her. It was good to see her there waiting for him. Maybe they could have dinner together.

But as he got closer, he saw her face. 'Lou? Is there something wrong?'

She stood up as he approached. 'What is this?' She thrust an envelope at him.

He took it and opened it. Inside was a cheque for more than three hundred dollars, made out to the WRML Trust.

'Someone gave you this today?'

'Yes. It was in the same book as my letter. Given to me by Ray Anderson.'

'I know Ray.'

'Apart from the fact that no-one uses cheques any more, why did he give that to me? Is the WRML what I think it is?'

'It is. Ray and Joan—well, mostly Joan—ran the fundraising events for the library. I guess that's money he had waiting to give Luca.' Jake sat down at the table. Ollie, sensing the atmosphere, whined softly.

Lou didn't seem to notice.

'I saw a bank statement in the paperwork from the solicitors. I should have looked at it more carefully. There's a debit card to go with it. I have that card. So, Jake, when you bought that petrol for the library, you didn't use the library fund. You paid for it with your own money, didn't you?'

'Yes.'

'You lied to me.'

'It was only fifty dollars' worth of—' The look in her eyes stopped him. 'Yes. I didn't think it would matter. You have so much on your plate right now, I didn't want you to have to worry about something as simple as a bit of petrol.'

'It's not about the petrol. It's the lie. Lying matters, Jake. All my life I've known I was adopted. My parents never lied to me about that. But they couldn't tell me about my birth mother, about Luca, because she cut herself off from me. That's a form of lying too.' She paused and took a deep breath. When she spoke again, her voice was more sad than angry. 'I thought I could trust you.'

'You can, Lou.'

'I'm not so sure any more. Please don't lie to me, Jake. Not even a little white lie. Not even to make things easier for me. I need someone I can trust … and you're the only one I have out here.'

With that she got up and walked inside the pub. He wanted to call out to her, but the stiffness of her back and the way she held her head told him it would be no use. He could almost see a dark cloud of anger and confusion around her as she crossed the bar heading for the stairs.

Jake's childhood had been happy. He had a brother and sister, parents and grandparents. Like all families, they'd had their moments: arguments and mistakes and days of sadness. Sure, he had a few regrets about things he'd done or said when he was younger, but when it came right down to it, Jake knew his parents and grandparents and appreciated and loved his family. And was loved by them. But Lou had a whole side of her family, of herself, she didn't know. Jake wanted to help her find it, but he wasn't sure he was making anything easier for her.

He sat outside the pub for a while. A few people nodded as they went inside and he realised that the bar was starting to fill. That seemed unusual for a Thursday night. He went inside and saw some young guys carrying musical instruments in through a side door.

'You've got a band?' Jake asked the barman.

'Not normally. That's my son's band. They have a gig tomorrow night in Wee Waa. It's their first paying gig and they wanted to play here tonight as a final practice. I hope you weren't looking for an early night.'

'What sort of music do they play?'

'The only sort. Country music.'

'Great.'

'But if you and the lady want some dinner, it would probably be a good idea to order sooner rather than later. It's gonna get busy, I think.'

'Sure. I'll go and ask her.' It was an excellent excuse to break the silence between them.

He headed upstairs and stopped short of the closed door to her room. 'Ollie. Go on.' The Lab sat and looked at him, his head on one side in a way that strangely enough reminded Jake of the way Lou sometimes looked at him. 'Go on.' He pointed at the closed door. Ollie padded over to the door and sniffed it. He must have caught Lou's scent, because he sat down and sniffed at the bottom of the door again. Then he barked once.

Lou opened the door. 'Ollie?' Then she spotted Jake. 'Hi.' She didn't seem mad at him any more, but neither did she seem very welcoming.

'Hi. There's going to be a band downstairs later. It might get busy. If you want to eat, now might be good.'

'Okay.'

'It would be nice to eat together, if you want.'

'I do.' She smiled. It was like the sunshine breaking through clouds after a storm. 'And I'm sorry. I guess I overreacted.'

'That's fine. You had every right to be angry with me. I'll never lie to you again. I promise. So how about dinner?'

They found a table and ordered burgers. By the time Lou and Jake had finished eating, the band was ready and had struck up a rousing version of 'Way Out West'. Lou and Jake sang along.

Before the night was half over, the bar was full. It wasn't a dancing type of evening, but there was a lot of clapping and stomping. When the band disappeared for a break, Jake and Lou rescued Ollie, who had been left in Jake's room. They took him outside to do what had to be done, but they didn't go back inside. They sat in the beer garden, although garden wasn't really the right word to describe the grassy patch behind the pub where a few picnic tables had been installed.

'There are those stars again,' Lou said as she turned her face to the sky.

They didn't talk much, enjoying the peace and quiet. When the band started up again, they too seemed to be going for a quiet interlude. They played an old Johnny Ashcroft classic. The lead singer had a lovely voice and Jake watched the emotions play on Lou's face as she softly hummed the familiar words. 'Where's my daddy …'

'Luca loved that song,' Jake said when the music fell silent.

'I have always loved it too. I wonder if it's because she played it to me when I was little.'

'Maybe.'

'I always imagined how that little boy would feel. I loved that it had a happy ending.'

'You'll get your happy ending too, Lou. At least, I hope so.' He had never meant any words more than he meant those.

'Thanks.' She turned to look at him. As their eyes met, he knew he had to take her in his arms. He had to pull her close and kiss her. He had to do that as much as he had to draw his next breath. Because if he didn't, his life was over.

He took her in his arms and he kissed her.

They kissed for a very long time, revelling in the stars above, the night air around them and the touch and taste of each other.

CHAPTER 26

Lou felt good when she woke up. For the first time in weeks, her thoughts did not fly immediately to her quest. Luca and her legacy did not intrude. Instead, she hummed a country love song and thought about Jake: the sound of his voice, the feel of his arms around her and the taste of his lips. When they had finally come inside, the band was long gone and the pub was quiet. By unspoken agreement, they'd said goodnight outside Lou's room. This wasn't the night to be together. Not yet. But soon.

It might be a little too teenage to squee, but she did anyway, quietly, so no-one else could hear her, especially not Jake, whose room was opposite hers.

She glanced at the clock and leaped out of bed. Jake would probably already be out walking Ollie. She might be able to join them. She showered and dressed in record time, and went outside, where she met them returning. Without even thinking about it, Lou walked into Jake's arms and kissed him. He returned the greeting full measure. Ollie showed his approval by running in circles around them until they moved apart.

Lou patted him. 'Ollie, we don't need a chaperone.'

Jake looked at her and raised an eyebrow, which made her laugh and blush at the same time.

When they finally went inside, the publican was waiting to give them breakfast. Lou was feeling so good that she switched her usual toast for bacon and eggs. After all, today was special. Jake seemed to share her mood. When time came to pay for their rooms, Jake put his wallet away as Lou insisted the money come from her inherited library fund. She paid with her own credit card, assuring him she would reimburse herself later.

As they drove to Gwabegar, they sang along to a country radio station. Their voices matched so well. Although, Lou wasn't really surprised. They seemed to suit each other in so many ways, why not singing?

The singing continued as they set up the library in the park opposite the school.

'You sound like you're enjoying this,' Jake said as he slid the steps into place.

'I am enjoying it.'

'Does that mean you might consider staying around a bit longer?'

'Maybe.' Staying longer wasn't quite the same proposition as it had been a few weeks ago when she first stood outside the cottage she had inherited.

The look on his face was enough to turn a maybe into a yes.

'The library is here! Yay!'

A group of children appeared at the fence surrounding the school, indicating it was time for Lou to get to work. Jake gave her a wave and he and Ollie set out on their walk.

There was nothing to see or do in Gwabegar, so whenever he'd come here with Luca, Jake had usually gone for a walk in the nature reserve bordering the town. As he and Ollie walked along the paths through the timber, he wondered if he'd have enough time to walk down to Friday Creek. There'd been a bit of rain lately, so there might be water in it and Ollie always enjoyed a swim.

'Come on, Ollie.'

It didn't feel like such a long walk after all. Maybe it was because Jake was feeling so good this morning. He knew why—everything good about today had to do with Lou. He did not for one moment regret last night. He'd planned to keep his distance until Lou had done what she'd come here to do, but he was so glad he didn't have to fight his feelings any more. There was only one more stop after this one, and then his promise to Luca would be fulfilled and he could follow his heart.

He started singing softly to himself as he walked, while Ollie ranged all around him, enjoying the smells of the bush. There were a couple of reserves—or were they national parks?—around Gwabegar and all through the region. Maybe he could suggest to Lou that she look for a job up here. He wasn't entirely sure what an environmental science degree was all about, but surely a national park needed people with that kind of knowledge? It would be great if she could find work that she loved enough to keep her here. Maybe they could even figure out a way between them of keeping the library going. Doing these trips with Lou had reminded him how much he'd loved working with Luca.

When they got to the creek, there was enough water for Ollie to have a paddle. Jake decided to stand back and let the pup have fun. He found a log to sit on and pulled his phone from the back pocket of his jeans to transfer it to a safer pocket. He noticed a waiting message. There were no bars on the phone, so the text must be an old one. He read it once, then whistled for Ollie to come over.

'Looks like this is our last run, my friend. It's time for you to go to work.'

Ollie didn't know that his destiny was to be a guide dog, but the message had come from the training centre. They were ready for Ollie to come back and begin his training. Jake absently scratched the dog's head. He'd grown more fond of Ollie than any of his previous puppies. He wondered if Lou had anything to do with that. But in the end, his affection for the dog made no difference.

'You have a job to do, mate. Someone who needs you. Are you ready for that?'

Ollie barked.

'Good. Take another swim while you can. You have to start being a grown-up guide dog soon.'

The dog didn't need any more encouragement.

On the walk back to the library, most of the mud on Ollie's legs dried and Jake paused to brush it away. They'd been away longer than he'd anticipated. He guessed Lou would have another letter from Luca by now. She usually didn't read them until they got home because she preferred to be alone. She hadn't shown him any of the letters so far, and that was fine. If she wanted him to read them, he would, but he wasn't going to ask.

This afternoon might not be the best time to tell her about Ollie, but he would tell her. He never wanted any secrets or hint of lying to come between them again.

CHAPTER 27

My Darling Daughter,

I knew I had to make a life without you, so I buried myself in my library. I couldn't raise you, my daughter, and show you all the things I wanted you to know, but I could help other kids discover the magic of books. And I could help other lonely women in small towns find friendship and support. The library was more than just a place to find a book. It became a lifeline.

There's never a lot of money in these towns, but they all helped with the fundraising for the library when they could. I used what I needed for me. It wasn't much. The rest I put back into the library, because that's where it would do the most good for everyone. I even got an old computer donated and Jake set up some mobile wi-fi for me. I have no idea how it worked. And sometimes it didn't. But the kids loved it.

The library users became my family. I gave to them some of the love I couldn't give to you and lived with a hole in my heart that I knew I would never fill.

Everything changed when I discovered I had cancer. There was no mistake this time. I was going to die. And I didn't want to die without seeing you one last time. All those years, I think I had cherished a tiny flame of hope that one day we would meet and we would get to know each other. I knew now that wasn't going to happen. I didn't have enough time. Instead, I hoped I would maybe at least get to hold you one more time.

So, as I began to put my life in order, I convinced the lawyers to tell me the names of your adoptive parents.

You were so easy to find. All those years in one home. I was glad to hear that. It meant you'd probably had the stable childhood that I had wanted for you. Then I found you on social media. That told me what university you were at, and that's where I went. I didn't want to intrude by going to your home.

I was still able to drive my car, but it was a big deal for me to go to Sydney, so I made sure I knew where I was going. I went to the uni hoping to see you and maybe talk to you again. It was a desperate thing to do. I knew from your posts what you were studying. I sat on a bench near the department building and waited. Hoping.

I did see you. I recognised you instantly. You looked so much like my mother. You were with a group of friends and you looked so happy. I could hear the laughter from where I was sitting. Seeing you and hearing your voice ... You were everything I had hoped you would be. Happy and beautiful, confident. You were wonderful.

I couldn't take that away from you by suddenly appearing out of nowhere. And I was a coward. I couldn't bear the thought that you might just reject me and send me away. That instead of a reconciliation, I would find out that you hated me. I wouldn't blame you. So, instead of speaking to you, I took a photograph so I would have something of you to take home with me. You didn't see me do it. You walked away and I walked back to my car and cried for a long time. Then I came home.

Your loving mother,

Luca.

Lou's hands were shaking as she put the letter gently back on the desk, next to the copy of *My Brilliant Career* that had been delivered with it.

Something else was sticking out of the envelope. She slid out the piece of paper, unfolded it and looked into her own face. It was a computer printout of a photograph taken in a place that she knew well. She'd earned her degree and taught there. In the photograph she was walking out through the gate with two friends. Her face was in the centre of the image, turned slightly away from camera. She was smiling and looked happy.

Lou cast her mind back, trying to remember if she had ever seen a woman who looked a lot like her sitting on a bench outside her lecture halls. This photo had been taken about eighteen months ago; perhaps closer to two years. She was wearing summer clothes and her hair, which was longer back then, was caught up in a ponytail. The rucksack slung over her shoulder would have had her books and phone in it. The sky was endless blue. This was a picture of a perfect day for a young woman who was beginning to find her way in the world.

Her childhood hadn't been perfect, of course. She had been bullied sometimes and worried about her exams. As a teenager she had struggled with hormones and zits and crushing on boys who didn't return her feelings. But she'd survived all that because of the support and love of her parents.

And now this. She would survive this too. In fact, she'd do better than survive. Hard as this had been, she was stronger because of it. All she felt towards Luca was the sympathy she would feel for a stranger. How could she love a mother she had never known? But she was beginning to understand some of Luca's struggle and the anger was gone.

She looked at the image again. What if she had known? If someone had told her that her biological mother was there, a few metres away, what would she have done? She suspected she would not have handled it well. Now though, she was different. She could empathise with Luca and her loneliness and her fear. The silent library around her did not seem so empty or strange as it once had.

'You wanted me to know you,' she told the ghost in the empty library. 'Maybe even love you. I'm not sure if that will ever happen. But I understand more now. And I'm sorry that your life was not what you had hoped it would be.'

She wasn't sure what to do next. Jake had indicated this was the last of the stops he'd promised Luca they would make. But this letter gave no indication it was the last letter. Nor did it give any hint at the question that was now in the forefront of her mind: Who was her biological father?

She had hoped that Luca's letters would lead her to him. Until that solicitors' letter about Luca, she'd never really cared about finding her birth parents. She hadn't wanted to find Luca, but now that she had, she found herself longing to know about the man Luca had loved. Why hadn't he been there for her?

She heard a noise outside, and Jake and Ollie climbed the stairs.

'Sorry. Our walk was a bit longer than I thought it would be.'

'That's fine.'

Jake looked at the papers on the desk. 'Another letter? And you read it?' The surprise was clear in his voice.

'Yes. Did you know that Luca came looking for me when she was told she was dying?'

'No.'

'She found me.' Lou showed him the image of her and her friends. 'It's really sad to think of her sitting there, not able to come and talk to me. I wish she had. Although at the time, I might not have felt like that.'

'Maybe that's why she didn't.'

Lou nodded. 'I still have so many unanswered questions. But you said this was the last stop on her list.'

'Yes. Although the Ridge was always *the* last stop on each run. Perhaps she meant you to open the library there as well.'

'I would imagine if anyone there had a letter for me, they'd have already given it to me.'

'Maybe.'

Lou took the image back and carefully folded it and the letter and put them into the envelope. She set that to one side and opened the desk drawer to collect the bundle of old photos. 'I showed these to some of the older customers again but no-one recognised anyone.'

Jake moved a few of the photos around to look at them. 'That's a shame—' He froze.

'What is it?'

'This photo.'

He handed it to her. She knew it at once. It was a little older than the photo she'd given to Ray Armstrong the day before, and showed a young Luca with two men of about the same age. Both men had an arm around Luca and she was laughing as she looked into the face of one of them. This was the photo that Lou thought was most likely to include her father. He could easily be one of the two men.

'What about it?'

'That man with his arm around Luca. The one she's looking at. That's my father.'

CHAPTER 28

That's my father.

The words had ricocheted around Lou's brain all through the silent drive back to Wagtail Ridge. She didn't see the now-familiar landscape flashing past her window. All she could see was Luca's face in that faded photo and the way she was smiling up at the man with his arm around her. The man who was Jake's father.

Jake had been unusually quiet too and had left quickly after parking the library in its shed. She hoped it was because he wanted to give her time alone to read Luca's letter again. She didn't want him to know her true reason for wanting him to leave. That reason was still haunting her this morning, as she sat at the kitchen table after a restless night, the letters and photos strewn in front of her. If that man with Luca was Jake's father—did that mean he was also her father? That would make Jake her brother. Half-brother. And that made her want to scream.

She liked Jake. If she had a brother, he was exactly the sort of brother she would want. Except for one thing. She didn't *want* him to be her brother. She had strong feelings towards him and they were not sisterly feelings. And as for those kisses … she felt almost sick at the thought.

This had to stop.

She didn't just want to find out who her father was, she *needed* to. Because if what she feared was true …

She sorted the letters on the table into their correct order so she could read them again. Maybe she'd find a clue that she'd missed earlier.

She unfolded the first letter, and the words leaped off the page at her.

I hope you meet Jake. He's a good man. Like your father was.

How could she have forgotten those words? Luca had virtually told her who her biological father was in that first letter.

A wave of nausea swept over her. She raced to the sink and splashed cold water on her face. Then she found a glass and drank more water until at last she felt a little better. Then a surge of anger against Luca rose through her. This was so unfair! She'd more or less come to terms with her heritage and now this.

But if Jake's father was Lou's father, why hadn't Luca been clearer in the first letter?

A small glimmer of doubt—or was it hope?—formed in Lou's mind.

She needed to find out the truth and she needed to do it before she saw Jake again. He hadn't seemed concerned by the photo. At least, he hadn't said anything. Of course he hadn't—that would mean he was accusing his father of … No. Jake would never think that of his own father. He wouldn't be tormented by the same fears she had. But he'd know something was wrong the moment he saw Lou's face. And he'd ask her, in that kind way of his that made her want to open up and tell him everything. But what could she say?

I think your father is my father.

I think you are my brother.

I think your father cheated on your mother.

How could she do that? When they'd talked about his family, his voice had been full of love and respect for his parents. Pride too. How could she even think about throwing this at him? It might destroy his family. She loved and respected her parents, and could only imagine what an accusation like that might do to her family. How could she do that to Jake, just in the hope of finding a father she'd never seen? A father she didn't know and, at this exact moment, didn't think she would like very much?

No. She couldn't do it. She'd have to uncover the truth on her own.

She was pretty sure there was one way to find out. She couldn't go to the pub and ask Deb, because Jake might be there. And besides, Deb must have known that she and Jake were … Lou's thoughts shied away from that, and she instead accepted that if Deb knew who Lou's father was, she would have said something by now. But there must have been a lot of gossip when Luca was pregnant, and there was one person in town who would have known all of it.

Lou drove rather than walked to the centre of town and pulled up in front of the post office. The door was open, inviting her in. The woman inside that building had been in Wagtail Ridge for many years, and had known Luca. If anyone knew who Lou's father was, it would be Val. And if she didn't, Lou would learn as much about her birth mother as she could, then give up and go home to Sydney. She would sell that house and that stupid mobile library and get on with the life she had planned. She would forget about Jake and a relationship that could never be while this uncertainty hung over them.

Val's hair was visible inside the post office even before Lou walked through the door. 'Well, hello, Little Lou. I was wondering when you would come and see me.'

Lou cringed at the name, but kept a smile on her face. 'I know you were friends with Luca. I was wondering if you had some time to talk to me. About her.'

'Of course. Of course. I'm glad you've come. There's so much that I can tell you about your mother. Shall we go out back and have a cuppa and some of my homemade biscuits?'

That was going a bit further than Lou had wanted. She was wondering how to politely decline when movement in the street distracted her. It was Jake's car, heading in the direction of the pub. Now she wished she'd walked after all. When he saw her car, he'd probably come to the post office looking for her.

'Thanks, I'd love to.'

'Lovely.' Val lifted the wooden counter to let her through, then opened the door that led from the post office to the residence. 'Peter, look after the office,' she shouted to the house in general.

'Okay.'

Lou didn't see where the reply came from, but Val nodded happily. 'Now we can have a nice long chat without being disturbed.'

Val's kitchen was not that much different from the one in Lou's cottage. She took the indicated seat at the round table while Val made tea and retrieved her cake tin.

'There you go. Now isn't this nice.'

'Thank you.' The tea looked hot and strong, but was served in dainty cups on floral saucers. Obviously Lou's visit rated the good china.

'You poor thing. You must have missed out on so much home life. Being adopted away and all that.' Val patted her hand.

Lou gently extracted her hand, disguising the movement as reaching for the biscuit tin. 'My adoptive parents are the best people I know. They love me very much and I had a wonderful childhood.' She took a bite of the biscuit and almost coughed as the dry crumbs filled her mouth. She took a quick sip of tea to wash them down and balanced the remains of the biscuit on her saucer.

'Well, that's a good thing. I'm sure Luca would have been very pleased to hear that. Especially in her last months. Such a terrible time as the disease took hold. Thank goodness for young Jake. He was so kind to her, helping with the house and driving the library truck when she was too weak.'

The last thing Lou wanted to do was talk about Jake. 'You knew Luca for a long time, didn't you?'

'Well.' Val almost preened. 'There's some who might tell you they knew her longer, but no-one was ever a better friend to her than I was.'

Lou was beginning to doubt that, but now she had started down this path, she had to keep following it. 'Did you know her before I was born?'

'My goodness, yes. We were at school together. I was her friend despite … well, you know, her father.'

'Her father?'

'Well, he ran off, didn't he? Marriage was taken a lot more seriously back then, you know. There were some who bullied young Luca because of her father. But not me. I mean, she couldn't be blamed if her father was a faithless drifter. He was one of those assisted migrants, and you can't trust that lot. Her poor mother, left alone like that. With a child to care for. But I never held it against them. Not ever.'

Lou suspected that, despite the woman's protestations, the reverse was probably true. But she had learned something. Her grandfather was a migrant who had probably come to Australia seeking a new start. That was nice to know. She could admire someone who left everything they knew behind for a better life. That took courage; the same sort of courage she had seen in Luca's letters.

'Where did he come from?'

'I really don't know. Not from England though.'

'Did Luca ever talk about my father?' Lou hadn't really planned how she would broach the subject, but she certainly hadn't expected to do so quite that bluntly. The need to get away from this awful woman was growing stronger by the second. She knew now that anything Val said was unlikely to be true. Or at least, it would be Val's version of true and that was no doubt different from the real truth.

'Well, let me think now. Of course your mother was a very pretty girl. All the boys used to hover around her. None of the rest of us got a look in.' The woman barely paused for breath. 'Not that I minded, of course. I knew the right man for me would come along. Then she went away, all that travelling on her own. She became a bit of a hippie, really. There's no telling how many—' Val stopped speaking.

At least the woman had enough empathy to realise she was heading in the wrong direction.

'But of course, after she came back here, she didn't have anyone special that I knew about. She worked in Scone at the library for a while, as you probably know.'

Lou nodded, wondering how she was going to politely escape—and if she really had to be polite about it.

'There were rumours when you were born. Lots of rumours. But Lou wouldn't tell anyone. Not even me, her best friend. There were some people who suggested it might be a married man. But I didn't—'

'I'm sorry.' Lou could stand no more. 'I've realised I'm supposed to be calling my parents in a few minutes. I'd better get back.'

'Well, that's so nice that you stay in touch with them …'

'Yes. I have to run. Thank you.'

Lou was on her feet and out of that kitchen as fast as she could manage. She jumped into her car and was pulling away from the kerb before Val even made it to the door to wave goodbye.

She went straight home but she didn't call her mother for a quick chat. For once, she didn't think talking to Fiona would help. She simply sat at the kitchen table and stared at the collection of letters and photographs that held the secret she needed so badly to uncover.

There was a knock on the door, and she knew at once who it was. She considered pretending she wasn't home, but her car was outside, and besides, that was unworthy of both her and Jake.

When she opened the door, he was standing there with that stupid smile that always made her heart skip. But today it didn't—it made her heart clench with guilt or fear, she wasn't really sure which. Whatever it was, she didn't like the feel of it at all. She stayed in the doorway.

'Hi, Jake.'

'Hi. I saw you escaping the post office. Is everything all right?'

'Yes. I had to hurry back for a Zoom meeting. In fact, I have another one in a few minutes.' She wasn't comfortable with the lie. But then Ollie gave up being patient and barked to attract her attention. With relief, she bent to hug him, burying her face in his fur so that Jake wouldn't see her eyes.

'I'm just heading out for the day, but I wanted to talk for a few minutes.'

'Sorry, Jake, I really can't. Not now.' Aware that she was being incredibly rude, Lou straightened, still avoiding his eyes, and glanced at her watch. 'In fact, I have to go now. Catch you some other time. Bye.'

'But it's import—'

She stepped back and shut the door. She stared at it, completely aware that he was still standing on the other side. She could so easily picture the shock and hurt on his face. The temptation to open the door, apologise and confront her fears was strong, but she couldn't do it. It wasn't just her own family relationships at stake. It was Jake's family's too.

She sighed with relief when she heard his footsteps going down the stairs.

CHAPTER 29

'Hey, son. Good to see you.' Russ Barnes gave his son a welcoming slap on the back before bending over to scratch Ollie's head. 'You're a bit early. Your mother's not home from work yet.'

Jake knew that. His mother's timetable on a Thursday always involved her staying late at the school where she combined teaching maths with choir mistress duties. His father's late day was Monday, when he worked with the debating team. They'd always joked about how this gave them private time away from each other. For the first time, Jake wondered how that time had been used.

He and Lou had barely spoken on the drive back from Gwabegar. She'd asked why he hadn't told her that his father and Luca knew each other, and he'd truthfully answered that he hadn't known. After that, she'd fallen silent. Jake assumed she was thinking about whatever the letter had contained. The implications of that photo were immense; even now he could barely even begin to think about it. He could only hope the same thoughts weren't running through her head. When Lou had closed the door in his face yesterday, he was ashamed at the moment of relief he'd felt at avoiding that confrontation. Now, at least, he might learn the truth first.

He followed his father through to the kitchen, wondering if he would be able to meet Russ's eyes when he asked the question that he did not want to ask. Because if the answer was yes, then his whole world would fall apart. Everything from his belief and respect for his parents, to the way he felt about Lou and any hopes he had for the future.

'I actually wanted to talk to you, Dad, before she gets home.'

His father's grin faded. 'Sure. Is something wrong? How can I help?'

Jake didn't take his usual seat at the table. He leaned against the bench while Ollie found his mat by the back door.

Russ didn't comment as he headed for the fridge. 'Fancy a beer?'

'No thanks, Dad.'

His father stopped and took a seat at the table. 'What's wrong?'

It took just a moment for Jake to call up the photo he was looking for on his phone. A photo of a photo. 'I saw this the other day. That's you, isn't it?' He handed over the phone and stepped back.

His father looked at the screen for a few seconds, his brow creased. Then, slowly, he smiled.

'Yes, it is. Well. This was a long time ago. It was taken after a dance. I'm not sure where … maybe Tamworth?'

'Why did you never tell me you knew Luca? I talked about her a lot when I was driving the library for her. You didn't say anything.'

'Luca? I don't know …' Russ's brow creased again as he enlarged the photo. 'Wait—that's the woman with the blonde hair?'

'Yes.'

'The one who had the library? She died a few months ago?'

Jake nodded, his eyes fixed on his father's face.

'I remember now. Mick—that's him with the dark hair—dated her for a while. It was a long time ago. To be honest, I wouldn't have remembered her name if you hadn't told me. Fancy her being your library lady. It really is a small world.'

'I told you her daughter, Lou, had come to the Ridge. That I was helping her with the library. She found that photo in a box where Luca kept things that were important to her. You know, Lou is maybe a year or two younger than me.' Jake hesitated. He couldn't accuse his father of anything, but the idea that had formed in his brain, as unthinkable as it was, would not let go of him. 'When was this taken?'

'When was what taken?' His mother entered the kitchen and dropped her things on the table. She kissed Russ's cheek then hugged Jake before peering at the phone lying in the middle of the table, the image still zoomed. Jake's heart sank as she reached for it. He'd hoped to resolve this without his mother ever knowing his fears.

She frowned. 'Where did this come from?'

'Jake's friend Lou.'

'The librarian's daughter?' Wendy picked the phone up and reduced the size of the image so she could see the whole photo. 'Oh yes, that's Mick and you. And Mick's girlfriend. What was her name?'

'Luca. Her name was Luca.' Jake could hear the tension in his own voice.

'Luca. Oh, I get it now. Your librarian friend? Well, fancy that. I'd forgotten her name. If only we'd realised, perhaps we could have spent some time with her before she passed.'

Jake took back his phone. 'Do you know when this was taken?' he asked again. Did neither of his parents understand the dangers here?

'Of course I do. Who do you think took it?'

'You were there?'

'Yes. I was very pregnant with you at the time. I didn't want to be in the photo, so I took it. On her camera. I think Mick joined the army shortly after this. We drifted apart and he settled down in Tassie. You were born not long after this and I don't think we saw her again. I don't know where she went. Do you?' She raised an eyebrow at Russ.

'No. Strange that she should end up at Wagtail Ridge and get to know Jake.'

Jake watched his father's face. There was no deception there. He was not Lou's father. To hide his relief, Jake went to the fridge and helped himself to a beer.

'I'll have one of those too, please, son.'

Their eyes met as Jake handed over the cold can. Russ's look said that he knew what Jake had been thinking. His nod said everything was all right.

'How is she doing? Your friend Lou?' His mother had put something in the oven and joined her two men at the table.

'It's hard for her. This all began with her trying to find out more about her mother. Now she's started to wonder about who her father was. Sometimes, I think she's torn between wanting to know and wanting to forget it all and get on with her life.'

His mother lifted that eyebrow again. She was far too perceptive. Always had been.

'And yes, I do like her,' he said. 'I like her a lot. But ...'

'You need to leave her alone to figure this out.' Wendy completed the sentence for him.

'Not quite alone. But, yeah, I don't want to pressure her.'

'Good.'

'And also, I promised Luca I would help Lou find her way, but wouldn't tell her anything. It started to feel like I was manipulating her. That's almost over … but not quite. There is one more thing Luca wanted me to make sure Lou did. I hope she'll do it without any prompting from me. If not, I have to tell her what Luca wanted. But this time I'll be honest with her and tell her right from the start.'

'Also good.'

'How is she going about looking for her father?' Russ spoke gently.

'This photo is about her only lead. But now it seems that's a dead end too.'

'Well, this was the only time we met her,' Russ said. 'And depending on how old the daughter is, I doubt Mick is the one.'

'So do I. The timing doesn't fit.'

'Do you have any other clues?' asked Wendy. 'There were a few of us who used to meet up all the time at the B&S balls. Maybe we can still help.'

'The only clue, if that's what it is, is a necklace Luca left for Lou.'

'What sort of necklace?'

'It's quite unusual. It's some sort of rock crystal mounted in silver and strung on a silver chain. It doesn't look like the sort of thing you'd buy at a jeweller's. It looks more … I don't know. Artistic?'

Wendy reached for her phone and started scrolling through the photos. At last she found what she was looking for and zoomed in. 'A bit like this?' The image she showed him was of someone wearing a necklace.

'Yes. I mean. Not exactly the same. And the crystal is purple, not green. But that sort of thing.'

'That one belongs to a friend. Hang on.' She got up and left the room. A few moments later they heard her talking to someone.

'You didn't think …?' Russ said quietly.

'No, not really.' As he said it, Jake realised it was true. 'I know you wouldn't do that to Mum.'

'Good. Because it's true.'

'Yeah. You guys are great together.'

'When you find the right one, son, you know. And you'll never do anything to risk that.'

Before Jake could ask how you knew when you met the one, Wendy was back.

'I think this might help. She says she got hers from a place in Cessnock, when they went there on a winery tour. There's a shop in town and it sells things made by local craftsmen. One of them makes this sort of jewellery. Maybe he made the necklace Lou has. He might be able to tell you who he sold it to. That's if you're really certain you want to do this.'

'I'm pretty certain she wants to. Maybe "needs" to is a better way of putting it. But …'

'You're afraid that if she does find out, she'll go back to Sydney and you'll never see her again?'

'Mum!'

'Be honest with yourself, Jake.'

'I'm afraid she'll go back to Sydney and I'll have to go too, because I don't want to let her go. Not without giving us a chance.'

CHAPTER 30

After spending the night at his parents' place, Jake was up early to load Ollie into the car. As always, the dog was eager to join the outing. Jake wondered if he would be so keen if he knew where they were going and why.

'I wish you could have said goodbye to Lou,' Jake told the dog as they drove through the quiet Lithgow streets towards the highway. Ollie wagged his tail at the mention of Lou's name. 'But she didn't want to see us. Well, specifically, she didn't want to see me. She adores you, but I'm not so popular right now. I think it's because I didn't really talk to her at all after I saw that photo of Dad. She probably thinks I'm lying to her again, or keeping secrets. I'm not. I didn't really believe Dad was the one … but I had to talk to him before I said anything more to Lou. For everybody's sake. I'm sure we'll sort it out. The thing is, she's going to be even angrier when she finds out about today.'

When they arrived at the guide dog centre, Ollie's tail was again at its happiest. He was grinning and confident as he walked into the compound next to Jake. He'd always enjoyed their visits here and his puppy classes. So had Jake, but he suspected neither of them was going to enjoy this visit.

One of the trainers was walking another dog through the grounds. 'Hey, Jake. How's Ollie?'

'He's great. Ready to start training.'

'That's good. This girl will be heading to her new home soon, so I'll have plenty of time to take Ollie.'

Ollie woofed and wagged in apparent agreement.

Jake was unexpectedly sad as he led Ollie through into the main building and he didn't understand why. Ollie wasn't the first guide dog puppy he'd raised and he wouldn't be the last. He was a lovely dog, but they all were. What made Ollie different? Perhaps it was the hours he and Ollie had spent with Lou on the road together, going for walks. They'd shared some happy times.

'Hello, Jake. Ollie,' the receptionist greeted them, and Jake steeled himself for what he knew would be a pretty tough half-hour. He hung around while the vet gave Ollie a check-up.

'He's in great shape,' the vet told him. 'And well behaved. You've done a good job with him.'

'Thanks.'

Jake walked Ollie back to the kennels, where one of the staff was waiting for him. Jake crouched down and ruffled the dog's ears. 'This is goodbye, mate.'

Ollie must have heard the sadness in his tone. He cocked his head to one side to listen.

'You be a good dog. You've got an important job ahead of you. Someone needs your help, and in return, they will love you and care for you, and share their life with you. I think that's a pretty good deal. What do you think?'

Ollie gave a small bark and licked Jake's hand.

'Thanks, mate. And good luck to you too.' Jake handed over the lead and, without any hesitation, turned and walked away. Ollie barked once and Jake felt very close to tears, but he kept walking. Ollie would be fine. Sometimes trainee dogs failed to meet the needs of the job, and in some cases, the puppy walkers who raised them were given the opportunity to take them home as pets. It didn't happen often, and Jake was pretty certain it wouldn't happen with Ollie. The dog was far too smart for that. He would soon be making someone's life better and safer. Jake should be pleased about that, but as he headed out of the city, taking his favourite route through the national park, he felt very much alone.

As he approached the turnoff leading to Lithgow, he thought about his mother's words. *A place in Cessnock ... a shop in town and it sells things made by local craftsmen.*

He drove straight past the turnoff and kept driving towards Cessnock. He parked in the main street, telling himself not to get too hopeful. This was likely to be a waste of time. Even if this man had made Luca's necklace, it must have been years ago. There wasn't much chance he would remember who he'd sold it to. Maybe he should simply grab a cup of coffee and keep going. He still had to tell Lou about Ollie and that was going to be hard enough.

The artists' collective was almost next to the coffee shop. One of the older shops in the street, the window featured an assortment of pottery, paintings both good and not so good, and various craft related items such as hand-spun wools. There was also jewellery. Silver jewellery set with rock crystal. Jake stayed outside, finishing his coffee. He looked at the items in the window, telling himself he could be looking for a gift for his mother's birthday. But that was a lie and he knew it. He was looking for purple amethyst set in silver.

When the coffee was done, and he had no further excuse to wait, he tossed the cup into a rubbish bin and entered the shop. At first he thought it was empty, then he spotted a woman on a stool behind the counter, knitting.

'Hi there.' Her fingers did not falter as she spoke. 'Take all the time you want to look around. Or are you looking for something in particular? I'm happy to help if I can.'

'Thanks.' Jake walked to a glass display cabinet where silver jewellery glinted under a bright light. 'Is all this stuff made by local artists?'

'Yes. We run the shop as a co-op. All of the profits go back to the artists themselves.'

'That's good.' The second jewellery cabinet looked more promising, containing some of the silver and crystal items, including earrings and necklaces quite similar to the one Luca had left for Lou. But nothing with that purple stone. 'These are nice. Who makes them?'

'Those are by someone who lives just outside town. He is very good, isn't he? I have a couple more here.' The woman put down her knitting and retrieved a small box from under the main counter. She took a piece of folded black velvet out of the box and spread it on the glass counter, then laid out some more items. They were similar in style to those on display, and even Jake's untrained eyes could see they were of excellent quality. But still no purple amethyst.

'Are you looking for something in particular? He does custom work.'

'Maybe. How would I get in contact with him?'

'We take turns looking after the shop. He'll be here all of next week if you want to drop in and talk to him.' The woman started packing the items back in the box. 'Let me give you his card.'

'Thanks.'

Jake slipped the card in his pocket without really looking at it, and thanking the woman for her time, he left the shop. When he got back to his car, he pulled out the card. Adam Lassiter Jewellery. The card gave a website. He brought it up on his phone. The service was a bit slow, but finally the website began to fill his small screen. And there it was. The purple amethyst necklace he'd seen so often around Luca's neck, and more recently around Lou's. It obviously had special meaning to its maker if he'd put it as the featured image on his site. Maybe he was the one who had given it to Luca. Which would mean he might be Lou's father.

That seemed a bit far-fetched. More likely the jeweller had sold the necklace, and simply used it on his website because it was such a nice piece.

There was one way to find out. Jake could bring Lou and the necklace to the shop next week and see if they could solve the mystery. Maybe that would make up for taking Ollie away without giving her a chance to say goodbye.

CHAPTER 31

Wagtail Ridge was a hard place to live if you wanted to avoid someone. Lou was in the kitchen banging pots and pans about as she tried to make dinner. She would really prefer to go to the pub, but Jake would probably be there. More than anything else in the world, she wanted to avoid seeing him while the terrible fear that he might be her half-brother still haunted her every thought. If she knew the answer to that question, she could make decisions. Stay. Go.

If he wasn't her half-brother, did she want to let her feelings grow?

If he was, she had found her father. For the first time in her life, she'd have blood relatives. That sounded like something she would want to explore. Or would she? Her appearance would totally disrupt Jake's family. If Lou's father had been a married man, that might easily explain why Luca had remained alone all these years.

And what if Lou never found out one way or the other?

That was easy. If she never found out, she'd have to go away. She couldn't stay here, plagued by uncertainty. She would have to leave Jake because she would never feel free to be with him the way she wanted to.

She was tempted to drive back to Sydney, get away from this confusing mess and maybe seek some advice from her mum and dad. But she couldn't do that either. The possibility of her birth family appearing in her life affected them too. She didn't want them hurt, or afraid they would lose her. They never would, of course, they were her mum and dad, but fear didn't respond to logic.

This was so unfair. At her age, she should be starting a career, dating young men, dancing and travelling. This was too much to put on her shoulders. But not as much as being a single mother and being diagnosed with a crippling illness. Luca had faced all that when she was in her twenties. Could her daughter find the same strength now to deal with the fallout? She had to. This was about who she was—and she really didn't know the answer to that any more.

She opened the fridge and reached for one of the cans of beer that had been there since Jake's last visit. There was also the not exactly tiny issue of what she would say to Jake next time she saw him. Should she tell him what she feared? His reaction to seeing the photo had been … what? She wasn't sure. It probably hadn't even occurred to him that his father might have had an affair with Luca. That said a great deal about him and his relationship with his parents. She had no right to do anything to harm that.

She pulled the top off the can of beer and stood there looking at it. What was she doing? She didn't want a beer. The problem was, she didn't know what she wanted. She put the beer back in the fridge, knowing it would sit there in the can for a day or two, go flat and be poured down the sink. She could pour it down the sink now, but even that decision required more focus than she had to give.

When she heard the car outside, she knew who it was without even looking out the window. After all, he was the only one who had ever visited her in this house. Well, maybe it was a good thing. They needed to talk. Now was as good a time as any.

She waited for the knock on the door, left the beer on the sink and went to answer it.

Jake greeted her with a tentative smile. 'Hi.'

'Hi.' She waited for the patter of paws on the steps. There was none. 'Where's Ollie?'

'Ah. Yes. Well …' Jake looked down at his feet and Lou's heart clenched.

'Is he all right? Has something happened to him?'

'No. No. He's fine. I took him down to Sydney yesterday. It was time for him to go back to the guide dogs association.'

'What? You took him back? And you didn't tell me or even give me a chance to say goodbye?'

'I did try. But you …'

Weeks of mixed feelings and fears burst forth as outrage and anger. 'You sent him away! Just like that. How could you? Poor Ollie. He must be confused. And frightened, in a strange place. He probably thinks we don't care for him any more. What a horrible thing to do!'

'But … he was always going to go back. That's—'

'And look at you. I bet you didn't shed a tear, did you? You didn't care at all. So now what? You get another one. Keep it for as long as you want and get rid of that one too?'

'Lou?' Jake's voice dropped to little more than a whisper. 'You're overreacting. What's really wrong?'

'Go away and leave me alone.' She ducked back into the cottage, slamming the door behind her. She knew she was overreacting, but she couldn't help herself. She let the tears stream down her face, feeling as if her life had lost focus and purpose. She hadn't done anything with her degree. She'd allowed herself to become caught up in a search for a birth mother she had never wanted to know, but now couldn't let go of. To make matters worse, she also needed to find her biological father, because if she didn't, she'd have to forget all about Jake. And Ollie was gone. Lovely, friendly, happy Ollie. She was never going to see him again.

She was being silly. She shouldn't feel like this over a dog she'd only known for a couple of months; a dog she didn't even own. But her heart wasn't listening. It had endured too much and there was no room left for this added hurt.

She staggered into the living room and sank down onto the carpet. The copy of *The Thorn Birds* she had been reading was sitting on the coffee table, next to the flowering primrose in its comical china pot. She had planned to take that to her mother in Sydney, but there it sat, next to the photo of Lou with Luca.

'I was happy, before all this,' she told the woman in the photo. 'I knew who I was and where I was going and what I was going to do with my life. Why did you have to change that? Now I can't go back. But I can't move on either.'

She dropped the book onto the carpet and buried her face in her hands as she sobbed.

Jake sat behind the wheel of his car, looking at the cottage and wondering what the hell he should do. He didn't blame Lou at all for yelling at him. It was pretty clear that she'd been upset before he knocked on her door. He wished now that he'd arranged a delay in returning Ollie, even for a day or two. But he knew how many people were waiting for guide dogs and the centre had asked for his return. Lou was wrong when she said he didn't care. Of course he missed Ollie. The seat next to him seemed very empty. But this was what Ollie had been bred to do. More importantly, Jake missed Lou. He missed her smile and her quick wit. He missed the way her lovely brown eyes sparkled in the sunshine, and how she hummed when she was thinking, probably without even knowing she did it.

And he wanted to kiss her again. And again. He wanted to give them a chance at … something. Whatever this thing was. It was unlikely to work. He was a country guy and she was a girl from the city … Although, when you thought about it, he was almost a city guy who had moved to the country, while she was a country girl who had been taken to the city. Perhaps there really was some way this could work. He only knew he wanted to try.

Which brought him back to the reason he was sitting outside her house, wanting nothing more than to wrap his arms around her and make her feel better.

The one thing he couldn't do. Not now. Not when he was so close to perhaps discovering who her real father was. He wasn't exactly doing it behind her back. He'd come here to tell her what he'd discovered. He would have told her if she hadn't slammed the door in his face.

He started the engine and pulled away from the cottage. He was due at the pub to cook the evening meals, and for once his heart wasn't in it. He'd do it because Deb was relying on him, although he didn't really want to face her right now either. He wouldn't tell her what he had discovered. He would say nothing until he had a better idea if he was right or wrong.

There was only one way to fix things with Lou.

He was going to go back to Cessnock. He was going to talk to this Adam Lassiter to see if he could shed any light on Lou's father. And then he was going to tell Lou everything. He only hoped she would listen to him this time.

CHAPTER 32

Lou woke on Monday morning with one thought on her mind: she would get this thing done and then get on with her life. Luca's plan, the one that Jake had followed without telling Lou about it, ended with one final stop. Wagtail Ridge. It was time for Lou to open the library doors in this town and accept whatever ending this chapter of her story had.

She picked up the phone and rang the one person who could do what she needed.

'Oh, hello, dear.' Val sounded excited to hear from her. 'What can I do for you?'

'Val, how do I let the town know the library will be opening its doors this afternoon? Here, in the Ridge.'

'Oh, how marvellous. It will be great to have it back. I am so sick of going into Scone when I run out of books.'

'Thank you.' She wasn't going to tell Val this this was a one-off. 'Where did Luca park it?'

'Why, right here. Outside the post office.'

'Really?' The road outside the post office was no wider than anywhere else. It seemed to Lou that the library would need a bit more space, if the people coming and going were to be safe.

'Well, not exactly outside. Just down a bit. And on the other side of the road. In the car park next to the hall.'

That made a lot more sense, although she wasn't surprised by Val's attempt to assert some kind of ownership over the library.

'Val, I don't know how to get word to everyone that the library is going to open.'

'Oh, leave that to me, dear. I can fix that for you.'

Of course she could. 'Great. Thank you. I'll have it there about four o'clock this afternoon. Do you think that will work?'

'Yes. We'll be ready for you.'

And she was ready for them too. Or she would be.

After ending the call, not an easy thing to do with Val, Lou made herself a cup of tea and headed for the shed. She had not been inside the library since Gwabegar, when Jake had said those words that still haunted her.

That's my father.

The library was a bit dusty and a bit messy. She had never reshelved the books returned on that last stop. Nor had she done anything to restock the shelves and fill the gaps left behind by eager readers. She'd start by sorting out the returns. The first book she picked up had a torn cover that needed fixing. She remembered seeing some extra plastic covers and tape in the desk drawer. It didn't take long to repair the book, and she felt surprisingly satisfied as she slid it back into its proper place. Before she continued, she pulled her phone from her pocket and put some music on.

Time passed quickly, and when she'd tidied all the shelves, Lou saw there were some gaps. It seemed only right that, if this was to be the very last opening of the library, she fill those gaps. She went back into the house to raid the bookshelves there. As she searched, she put aside titles she had always wanted to read but had never found the time. She hung onto a few classics and some by favourite authors. She'd take those back to Sydney with her. She would read them all eventually, and she was sure her mother would like some of them too.

There was another pile of books on the coffee table. She knew them by heart. *The Shiralee. Seven Little Australians. Picnic at Hanging Rock* … Not only did she know the titles, she knew the order they had been thrust into her consciousness, along with the letters they contained. Half of her wanted to get rid of them too, but she wouldn't, not yet. There might still be something they had to tell her. There were plenty of other books to fill the library shelves.

By the time she had collected what she needed, there were too many books in the pile for her to carry, so she looked around for some sort of box or basket. Nothing sprang to view. Nor was there anything in the kitchen. Then she remembered the suitcase under the bed. She hadn't looked at it since the day she found it.

It took just a moment to drag it out and she hefted it up onto the bed and opened it. That same delicate blue shawl lay on top of the neatly folded clothes. It was such a pretty thing. She carefully put it to one side to take home. Not for sentimental reasons, of course, but because it really was beautiful. The item below it was a hand-knitted jumper. She picked it up and squeezed it, revelling in the softness of the wool. Did Luca knit this? Lou lifted it and rubbed her cheek against the creamy texture. As she did, she thought she caught a whiff of scent. It was the same jasmine fragrance she had noticed the first time she opened the suitcase.

That scent was still vaguely familiar, but she couldn't put her finger on why. Surely she wasn't remembering a simple scent from a time when she had no visual memories? Whatever it was, it wasn't going to help in her current task. She upended the suitcase. She'd leave the contents on the bed while she ferried the books to the library, then pack the clothes up to take to a second-hand shop when she went back to Sydney.

The last item from the suitcase landed on top of the pile of clothes. It was small, carefully wrapped in tissue and enclosed in a plastic bag for protection. Curious, Lou picked it up. That same scent wafted past her nostrils as she opened the bag and began unwrapping the tissue paper. Her hands started to shake a little as she realised what it contained. The booties were pale yellow, the wool so soft it felt like the down of a baby chick had been spun to create it. Like the cream jumper, the booties had been knitted by a skilful hand. Luca's? Had they been knitted with as much love as skill? A second item from the very bottom of the case now lay on top of the pile of clothes. It was a small black velvet bag with a drawstring, very like the one she had found the amethyst necklace in. She picked up the bag, but whatever was in this one, it wasn't metal or gemstones. It was soft to the touch and very light. She opened the bag and reached inside to withdraw a lock of hair, a golden curl from the head of a small child. Lou knew it was her own hair in that velvet bag as surely as she knew it was her own hair on her head. Luca had kept these booties and this lock of hair for more than twenty years.

A single tear fell onto the velvet bag as Lou carefully placed the lock of hair back inside and drew the string tight. With the same care, she placed the velvet bag and the booties on the bedside table. Then she turned to the pile of clothes on the bed. If this was where Luca had kept something that precious, surely the answer would be here. She started unfolding the clothes, shaking them out in the hope that a letter or another photograph would be revealed. Anything to solve the mystery that was tearing her apart. With each passing moment, her frustration and anger grew, until she literally flung the last few items against the far wall of the bedroom.

There was nothing more. Just clothes.

She slumped to the floor beside the bed, eyes closed, exhausted. She saw the booties, the hair and Luca's face as clearly as if she was staring at her. It was not a memory of her childhood, just a photo that was burned into her brain.

'Why are you doing this?' she asked the silent room. 'Why are you tormenting me? Why didn't you simply leave me a single letter, telling me what I need to know? Why are you dragging everything out like this?'

She listened to the sound of her own ragged breathing.

'I hate you.'

CHAPTER 33

Jake was supposed to be doing lunches at the pub today. Dinner too. And he was also supposed to be building a new chute down at the stockyards. What he wasn't supposed to be doing was driving to Cessnock again on a wild goose chase. But that was exactly what he was doing. He'd thought about telling Lou what he was doing or inviting her to join him, but in the end he'd decided against it. She'd made it clear she didn't want to talk to him. And he didn't know what the outcome of today's journey would be. This Lassiter might know who Lou's father was. He might even be Lou's father. If he was, maybe he didn't want anything to do with his daughter. Or maybe he didn't even know she existed. It wouldn't be right to expose Lou to the emotional trauma until Jake had at least tried to find out what was going on. He didn't like keeping secrets from her, but she could hardly be angrier at him than she was right now over Ollie. Over everything, really. If this came to nothing, then he'd done his best and there was no harm done. If this trip revealed something … Well, he'd figure out the best way to deal with that when it happened.

He turned the radio up to cover the emptiness left behind by the lack of Ollie, and even more so by the lack of Lou. He'd so much enjoyed their hours on the road together. He didn't want to believe they were over.

The artists' collective was still shut when he arrived. It appeared Monday was late opening day. He had an hour to kill.

The coffee shop was open and had a free table, but all the reading matter on display seemed to be aimed at women. Jake thought about going to a bookshop, but instead pulled out his phone. It was the work of a minute to find the ebook of *The Harp in the South*. He downloaded it to his phone and started to read.

Two cups of coffee, a pumpkin scone and several chapters later, the collective had been open for half an hour and it was time for Jake to do what he had come here to do. He walked down the street and paused as if looking in the window. He could see three figures standing near the counter. He didn't want to go in while there were other customers, so he perused the window a little longer. A few minutes later the couple left, chatting happily about a painting one of them carried. Jake took a deep breath and slipped into the building.

'I'll be right with you,' a voice called from the back of the shop.

'I'm in no rush.' He wasn't either. He felt, not exactly nervous, but uncomfortable. Half of him wanted to drive back to the Ridge and tell Lou everything he knew. But it was too late to back out now. Out of the corner of his eye, he saw a man emerge from the back of the shop, his face almost hidden by the large painting he was carrying. He made his way to the wall of the shop and hung the painting in the space no doubt vacated by the couple's purchase. Then he stood back to look at it. As he did, he tilted his head slightly to one side, a movement that caused Jake to catch his breath. It was too familiar.

The man turned around. 'What do you think?'

The light pouring through the big glass window lit the man's face, and Jake knew he had found what he—what Lou was looking for.

If Lou's face looked like Luca's, she had inherited her eyes from her father. They were the same shade of brown with the same gold flecks, the same shape and held the same spark of intelligence and humour. The same joy in existence. There was even the same hint of sadness.

'The artist is a local woman, and quite popular.' Adam Lassiter seemed to think Jake's silence was a comment on the painting. 'But she's not to everyone's taste. Can I help you with anything in particular?'

'Ah. Yes. Jewellery. Rock crystal jewellery.'

'You've come on the right day. I am the man who makes it.' There was quiet pride in his voice as he led Jake to the glass cabinet.

The contents had not changed noticeably since Jake's previous visit. He remained silent, just nodding while Lassiter talked about his work. All the time, Jake's mind was racing. This was Lou's father! He was sure of it. But he had no proof. And if he did, what was he to do with it? He was telling the truth the day he told Lou he didn't know who her father was. But now he did. It wasn't his secret to tell, but at the same time, if he didn't tell Lou, he would now be lying by omission. And he'd be breaking his promise to tell her everything.

'Is there any particular piece that interests you?'

'Oh. Sorry.' Jake gathered his scattered wits. 'Actually there is. The purple amethyst necklace on your website is particularly lovely. Do you still have that?'

The flicker of some strong emotion crossed the man's face and was gone in just a second. 'No. I'm sorry. I only ever made that one piece, and I no longer have it.'

'Oh.' Jake feigned disappointment. 'Someone I care about is really taken with that one piece. I wanted to find it for her. Do you know who has it now?'

Lassiter frowned. 'No. I'm sorry. I can't give you any information about my customers.' The friendliness in his voice had vanished, replaced by suspicion.

Jake may have imagined the slight hesitation before the last word, but he didn't think so. 'Of course not. My apologies.'

'Not at all. Perhaps you'd like to bring this person in to look? I'll be in the shop all week and I have a few more pieces at home in my workshop. I'll bring those in too if you like. I assume this person is a young lady?'

'Yes.'

'Then I have a couple of things I've almost finished that she might like. Or perhaps I can make a custom piece for her. It might be a bit more expensive than some of the other items, but I guess she must be worth it to make you so eager to find the piece she wants.'

'She is worth it.' Jake meant every word.

When he left the shop, Jake let go of his iron control. He was facing a dilemma and needed time to sort it out. Should he simply tell Lou everything? If he didn't, it would be exactly the same as lying to her, and he didn't want to do that. But at the same time, if this man had rejected both Luca and Lou, he didn't want to add to Lou's already heavy burden. Then there was his promise to Luca. He'd done what she asked, but now he was beginning to wonder if Luca had wanted Lou to make this discovery. In which case, the woman he thought was his friend had been lying to him all along.

There was also the issue of Luca not telling him that she had once known his father. Their encounters had been a long time ago, but Luca and he had talked about his family many times. She must have made the connection.

There was so much to think through. Jake knew he couldn't go back to the Ridge until he had. He didn't want to face Lou until he had sorted out his own conflicted emotions.

His phone buzzed and he looked at the screen. A message from Val. His finger hovered over the phone, and then he switched it off. He didn't want to read a message from Val.

He glanced at his watch. It was almost lunchtime. He'd pop into the pub for a beer and a burger while he decided what he should do. Then he'd head back to the Ridge to do dinner at the pub. He wasn't worried about seeing Lou there. The way she felt about him at the moment, he doubted she would come anywhere near the place where he worked.

CHAPTER 34

Lou grunted with effort as she heaved the heavy double doors of the shed open. They were starting to sag on their hinges and drag on the ground. Despite Jake's best efforts, the shed was sorely in need of more maintenance. Not that it mattered to her. She would be out of here in a day or two. She'd sell the place and then it would be somebody else's problem.

She stood in the open doorway, hands on hips, and glared at the library. She was expected in town in thirty minutes, but she didn't have a driver. She certainly wasn't going to call Jake and ask for his help. She was still mad at him about Ollie. Although, if she really was honest with herself, he had tried to tell her and she'd sent him away. But the reason she'd done that was just one more reason she couldn't ask Jake to drive this truck for her. How could she sit next to him in that cab, where they'd spent so much time together? Where she'd allowed herself to think about ... No. Don't go there. She had to stay clear of him until she knew the truth.

And if she never discovered the truth? Well, she wasn't staying in Wagtail Ridge anyway, so that didn't matter.

Getting the library into the centre of town, however, did. It was too late to back down. Val's grapevine was far too efficient and the whole town would know by now that the library was scheduled to call. She couldn't not do it. She thought of the kids who had eagerly climbed into the library in other locations. Of the people who didn't have a way to get to Scone to visit the library. Wagtail Ridge had made her welcome. Even Val had been welcoming, if annoying at times. The least she could do was pay them back with this one small thing before she left.

One driving lesson with Jake hadn't been enough to get her licence, but she could drive the truck a few blocks to the hall, couldn't she?

She turned around and almost marched to the gate with its familiar curls. She opened it as wide as it would go, but the gap still seemed very tight for the library truck. With a deep, determined breath, she walked back to the shed.

Once behind the wheel, she inserted the key into the ignition and sat for a moment, thinking about everything Jake had told her. That lesson had been a while ago but she could remember every word of it, in the same way as she could remember the way Jake's eyes twinkled when he was joking. And the way his lip curved when he smiled. And the way he looked, walking away from her wearing those tight jeans.

No. Thinking like that was getting her nowhere—and was just a little bit creepy. She had a job to do and would focus on that.

She checked the truck was in neutral and turned the key. The engine roared to life. That was Jake's doing too. Everything in her life seemed to keep leading her back to Jake. Carefully, she put the truck into gear and released the clutch. The truck leaped forward a few inches and stalled. No. She could do better than that. She had to. On the second try, the truck obligingly moved forward at a slow but steady rate. She watched in the side mirrors until the whole vehicle had safely cleared the shed doors, and then turned her attention to her next obstacle … the gate and the road beyond.

'That gate *is* wide enough.' Perhaps saying it out loud would make it true.

The library passed between the gate posts easily enough, but as she started to turn onto the road, Lou realised she was cutting the corner. She straightened the wheel, but it was too late. There was no way she could back up to straighten the truck, so she gritted her teeth and kept going. In a series of stops and starts, the truck cleared the gate, leaving the gate post still standing, even if the mailbox on top of it looked a bit bent. Then she was on the road, but still moving at the ridiculously slow speed which she had no intention of increasing. From here it was a straight line to the other end of town, and then she had to turn the corner towards the post office and the hall. That corner might be a bit tricky. And she didn't even want to think about how she was going to park the truck when she reached her destination. She also didn't want to think about the fact that she was breaking the law by driving on a public road without a licence.

She would do this. She had to do this. She wasn't going to fail in this final task. All she could do was mentally cross her fingers and hope everyone stayed well out of her way.

She managed to negotiate the street and even the corner without dire consequences, but her foot slammed down on the brake when she saw the crowd gathered outside the hall. It was as if the whole of Wagtail Ridge was waiting for the library. There were kids and dogs running around, tables and chairs and no open space that looked even vaguely big enough to safely park the library. That might be fine with Jake in control of the big vehicle, but with her behind the wheel, the whole scenario screamed disaster. She honked the air horn to catch the crowd's attention. Instead of making them step back for her approach, the horn only made matters worse, as some of the kids and dogs started running towards her. She reached for the ignition key. The library truck might still be sitting in the middle of the road, but there was no way she was going to move it one more inch unless it was safe.

Before she could turn the engine off, she heard a loud shout from the middle of the crowd. The running kids and their dogs stopped and turned around. The crowd at the hall was moving back to clear a path for the truck and Lou lifted her foot from the brake pedal. The engine growled a little as she pulled forward ever so slowly. The crowd parted, guiding her onto a clear area of grass in front of the hall. Obviously everyone apart from Lou knew the way this worked. She edged the truck in and turned the engine off with a sigh of relief. She gripped the steering wheel hard for a few more seconds to give her hands time to stop shaking, then almost had to prise them away from the sweaty plastic. She was hit by the terrifying truth that to get the truck back home, she was going to have to reverse out.

No. No, she wasn't. The truck could stay here forever. She didn't care. She wasn't going to do something that stupid again.

From her raised position in the cab, she searched the crowd for Jake. She couldn't see him. Fine! She'd just blame him for the mess.

She climbed down from the cab, ignoring the strange angle at which the library was parked.

Deb was waiting for her. 'Um, do you …?'

'No. But it's here now. Someone else can drive it back.'

'Jake's not here. He called to say he would be back in time to do the dinners. I guess he can do it at some point.'

'Jake's not the only person in town with a truck licence, is he?'

'Well, no, but …'

'This all looks great.' Eager to move the conversation away from Jake, Lou waved a hand at the people gathered around picnic tables laden with food.

'We always did this when your mother drove the library, turned her visit into something of a town event. It's fun, especially for the kids.'

'But I only decided to do this a few hours ago.'

'And you also did the only thing that could possibly have triggered this—you told Val to spread the word. About the only thing Val likes more than that sort of invitation is organising a town picnic.' There was a layer of fondness in Deb's exasperated tone, such that when Val appeared a moment later, Lou was able to give her a genuine smile.

'You did all this?'

'Yes, I did.'

'Wow. Thank you. I love the party atmosphere.' For that's what it was. There were even some balloons around a table where the youngsters were playing a game. 'I guess I should open up shop.'

As soon as she started lowering the steps to the library door, there were cheers from the younger members of the assemblage, who raced each other to get into the library. In their exuberance, they almost ran over the top of one little girl.

'Hey. Slow down.' Lou hastily grabbed the girl and set her back on her feet. 'There's no need to push. There are plenty of books for everyone.'

'Sorry!' was the chorus and the kids waited until the girl was safely inside before following.

Lou hurried up the stairs and took her accustomed place at her desk, humming to herself as she handed out books and recommendations. At some point, Val slipped inside and left a slice of cake and a glass of something cold and fruity on her desk. Lou tasted the drink cautiously; the last thing she needed was alcohol. She was pleased to find it was juice and lemonade. She drank the glass eagerly. The cake was good too. Obviously not of Val's making.

Once the kids were back at the party outside, the adults all seemed to want to talk about Luca as they selected their books.

'She would be so proud.'

'Luca suggested this book. She was so right. I loved it.'

'Luca got this book in for me. She was so kind.'

'I remember Luca bringing you here as a baby. It was such a shame, what happened.'

This time, their words did not fill her with anger, but rather with a kind of gentle melancholy that left her able to do no more than just listen.

'This was one of my favourite books when I was young. I'm sure that was Luca's influence too,' she told one customer. 'Did Luca ever tell you why she loved this particular book?' she asked another.

The time passed swiftly, and the sun was starting to go down when at last the library was empty of people and the picnic outside was done. The shelves looked a bit bare. Lou sighed and opened the tin. Only one empty book sleeve remained and no-one had returned the book it belonged to. She shut the tin, fighting her disappointment. This had been the last chance. Lou still had unanswered questions about Luca and even more about the man who had fathered the child who was now temporary custodian of Luca's life work. But there was nothing left for her here. It was time to go. That thought should have been a relief, but instead it prompted an unexpected sadness.

'Excuse me, Miss Taylor?' A small face appeared in the doorway.

'Hello, Vicki.'

'I didn't get a book. I had to wait for my daddy to bring me down.' A second figure appeared in the doorway.

'Hello, Matt.' The real estate agent nodded and smiled. Lou held out her hand to the little girl. 'Well then, Vicki, come on in and let's find you a good book.'

The little girl almost bounced into the truck, then turned to see if her father was still there.

'Now, honey, remember I have to go to the shop before it closes, so don't take too long.'

The girl's face fell.

'What if we let your daddy go to the shop while you and I look for books?' The girl's eyes widened and Lou could see the fear starting to fill her. 'You can stay here in the library with me and look at books until he gets back. What do you think?'

'It will be all right, honey. I'll only be gone a few minutes.'

Vicki frowned as she thought about that, then nodded. 'Promise you'll come back soon, Daddy.'

'I promise, honey. You have a nice time with Miss Taylor.'

'Okay, let's look at some books.' Vicki already knew where the children's books were. Lou sat on the floor and crossed her legs as careful consideration was given to several titles. When she had made her selection, Vicki came and sat on the floor next to her.

'Will you read with me until Daddy comes back?'

'Of course I will. What a good choice you've made. I'm sure you'll enjoy them.' Lou set *The Muddle-Headed Wombat* on her knee, but before she could start reading, Vicki spoke.

'Oh. That's pretty. I remember the other lady wearing that.' She was looking at the crystal necklace that was no longer hidden inside Lou's T-shirt.

'That's right. It was hers.'

'I miss the other lady. She was nice.'

'I'm sure she was.'

'I'm always the last to get my books. She helped me. Sometimes she would cry. I asked her why she was sad and she said I reminded her of someone she loved. That person wasn't here any more.' A pair of innocent brown eyes looked up at Lou. 'Was that you the other lady talked about?'

Lou's eyes were filling. 'Yes. That was me. The other lady was my mother.'

'She was a nice lady.'

'I know she was.'

'I don't have a mummy any more.' The little girl's face fell. 'Daddy says she went to live with God.'

'I'm sorry, honey. You must miss her a lot.'

'Sometimes I cry. Then Daddy picks me up and everything is better.'

'What a lucky girl you are to have such a loving daddy.'

'Do you have a daddy?'

'I do, sweetheart. In fact I have a daddy and a mummy living in the city.'

'You have two mummies?'

'I do. I am very, very lucky.'

'Do you have two daddies too?'

'I do, sweetheart, but I only know one of them.'

'Why don't you know your second daddy? Doesn't he love you?'

'I'm sure he does. All fathers love their daughters.' That wasn't true, but it was what Vicki needed to hear. 'I just never had the chance to know him.'

She was interrupted by the sound of footsteps on the library stairs. Deb appeared in the doorway. 'Vicki, your daddy is back. He's waiting for you. Off you go now.'

'All right. Goodbye, Miss Taylor. I'll come back when I've read the book.'

'Bye-bye, Vicki.'

Matt appeared in the doorway and Vicki took his hand as she left.

Lou remained sitting on the floor, legs out in front of her.

Deb sat down opposite her, taking up the same pose. 'I have something for you.'

She held out a book. Of course the last book would be with Deb. And of course it would be *Dot and the Kangaroo*. Lou took the book and opened it. There was the envelope—the same as all the others. She looked at it.

'Your mother was my best friend for more than twenty years,' Deb said. 'I mourned her when she died. I still do. I know it must be hard for you to understand why she did what she did. Like all of us, she had her own scars. Growing up without a father. The loss of her own mother. She loved you so much and she wanted to give you better than she had.'

'You could have given this to me weeks ago when I asked if you had one and saved me a lot of heartache.'

'I didn't lie when you asked me. I said Luca wanted you to find the letters in your own time. I'm sorry I misled you. I haven't read this letter, and I don't know if getting it any earlier would have saved you any heartache. All I know is that she had her reasons and I had to respect her wishes. Jake did too. Please don't punish him for it.'

Lou didn't say anything. She could hardly explain the real reason she was avoiding Jake.

Deb nodded slowly. 'Don't judge him too harshly. Or Luca either. If you want to talk some more after you've read the letter, just come and find me.'

She got up and left the library. The door was open, but there was no noise. The crowd had gone, and Lou was alone with the last letter from Luca.

My Darling Daughter,

This is my final letter. I'm finding everything more difficult now. I struggle to remember what day it is, but I can still recall events from many years ago. I can barely make a cup of tea. And when I do, I can't drink it. I only hope I can finish this. These letters have been so important to me, as I hope they have been to you.

Jake, lovely helpful Jake, has put the library in the shed. He will look after it until you come home, and I really hope you will. If you don't, you'll never hear all the things I needed to say. You'll never understand why I did what I did. How much I suffered and how much I regret.

I'm sorry I made it so hard for you to find these letters. Please forgive me. And forgive Jake for his part in all this. He was just doing what I made him promise to do. I wanted you to understand the life I lived. I wanted you to see the places that meant so much to me. I hoped it might bring back some memories for you of the short time we had together. Even now, I remember every second of that time. Those memories have been my comfort and my joy. I'll never know if you share any of those memories. I only hope you do recall something of me, or the love I have for you.

And yes, I hoped it would make you want to stay. To adopt the life you would have had with me. It makes me happy to think you might choose that, but I will understand if you don't. The world has changed so much and there is so much more for you to be and do and have. More than I could ever have imagined.

And I guess that brings me to the question that is probably forefront in your mind now. Your father.

Where do I start?

I loved your father. Very much. And he loved me. I think it's important for you to know that you were conceived with love and joy.

I was working at the library in Scone, and had saved enough money for a short holiday. I went to Byron Bay. I even treated myself to a reasonably nice hotel. Not one of the expensive ones, but nice. It was my first trip away since that last trip to the Northern Territory. I wanted it to be special.

And it was, because on the first day, I met your father. He was on holiday alone too.

I fell in love in a heartbeat. It wasn't just that he was handsome, although he was. So very very handsome. He was tall with wavy hair in the most wonderful shade of reddish gold. His brown eyes were flecked with gold too—those eyes seemed to see deep inside me. He saw my fears and my weaknesses, and he loved me anyway. Just as I saw his and loved him with every fibre of my soul. Not despite his weaknesses, but in part because of them.

We didn't plan to fall in love. It just happened. There was a deep sadness in him that spoke to the sadness in me. We were both struggling with loss and together we found a way of coping. We weren't together long, but we never could be. He was married.

Before you judge him, you need to know that he never lied to me or misled me. He said right at the start that he would never leave his wife. She'd been severely injured in an accident about two years before we met. He had to look after her. He would not banish her to some care home and just leave her there, even though for much of the time she didn't know who he was. I never argued with that.

We took consolation in each other and then we parted.

He never knew about you. I knew where he was, and I could have told him. I wanted to. He would have been so happy. He wanted children, but his circumstances meant he never would. But how could I tell him? He would never have been able to be a full-time father to you, and being anything else would have tormented him.

So I never told him. I decided I could raise you alone—but then I had to give you away.

I messed up. I am so sorry. Perhaps there was some way we could all have been together, but try as I did, I couldn't find that path. I thought about telling him about you, so he could raise you. But it was all he could do to care for his wife. And I didn't want you to grow up in a household under the shadow of such sadness as he faced every day.

And now I am messing everything up again. I am so sorry.

I set out to write this thinking I could tell you who he was … but now I find I can't. It's not my secret to tell. You deserve to know, but after all these years, I somehow just can't let it go. It's as if by doing that, I will lose the last part of him that I have left—and as I write this, barely able to sit up any more, I want to keep something for myself. As I get closer to leaving this world, I find it's easier to see his face. Hear his voice. He gives me strength I so desperately need. I am afraid that if I give up my secret now, I'll lose that.

I am so afraid of dying and I cannot face it without him.

You are in my heart and he is there too. I will never lose either of you. You are together there. Can you be content with that?

Can you forgive me?

There is so much more I want to say to you. And so much I wish I could ask you, if only you were here. I want to hear all about your life and your plans for the future. Whatever you decide to do with your life, you should know that I will always be proud of you, because I always have been.

I don't want this letter to end, because when I stop writing, it's over. But I have no strength left. I have so much to say, and nothing more to say. I hope you understand. I hope you have forgiven me, and I hope that maybe somewhere deep inside you, there is just a small flicker left of the love you had for me when you were a child. Because you did love me. I knew it then, and I shall take the small hope that you still do with me as I leave this world.

Your loving mother,

Luca.

CHAPTER 35

She read the letter again. And again. She sat there on the floor of the library that had meant so much to Luca, and stared at the words until it was too dark to see them any more. Not that it mattered. She already knew every word by heart.

The pages of the letter fell to the floor as she slowly stood up, her muscles protesting every movement. But the pain in her body was nothing to the other pain that was overwhelming her. She felt stifled—not by the airless space the library had become after hours parked in the sun, but by the memories and emotions that seemed to be crowding into this tiny space with her. She could almost feel Luca, here, touching the books. Sitting at that desk. Smiling down at her and humming. She had to get out.

All the townsfolk were long gone and there was no-one to see as Lou almost fell down the stairs and walked to the nearby picnic table, where she slumped onto the wooden bench. It was over. She would never find out who her father was. It was clear that no-one, not even Deb, could solve that mystery for her. Only her mother had known and she hadn't told anyone. It took a strange sort of strength to do that. To hold something that important in a place where no-one else could see it. How often had Luca wanted to talk to her friend about the man she had loved? Lou remembered all the times she had turned to Fiona or Richard when she needed comfort. Or to her grandparents or friends. Luca had turned to no-one.

How lonely had those years been without her lover and her child? The nights must have seemed endless and without joy.

In the distance, Lou heard a dog bark. It was a lonely sound, but it dragged her back to the here and now. She saw headlights pass along the highway at the end of the street. The pub wasn't far away. She could go and find Jake. She needed to get the library back home, but she wasn't going to drive it again. That would be foolish.

Jake! The relief that swept through her was like a wave of water, washing away the debris of fear. Jake's father was not her father. She might not know who her father was, but Jake was not her half-brother. Those feelings, those kisses—she could allow herself to feel again what she had felt when Jake was near her. She would have to tell him, of course. What would he think of her? Would he be angry that she could even suspect his father of such a thing? Maybe they could laugh about it together one day—if indeed there was a future ahead for them.

Another car flashed past on the main road. She had to do something or else she would sit here all night. She had to find Jake, and not just to ask him to drive the library home.

When she had safely locked the library, she pocketed the keys and set off to walk to the pub. The bright lights shining in the windows were inviting. She could hear a hubbub inside. Deb and Shane were having a good night and Jake might be too busy to help Lou. Well, she could always leave the library where it was until the pub shut.

Shane was behind the bar, moving swiftly between customers to try to keep their glasses full. 'Hi, Lou,' he said as he rushed to the other end of the bar.

'Hi. Is Jake here?'

'No.'

That was unexpected.

'Deb's in the kitchen, if you want to go through.' Shane passed, heading in the other direction with his hands full of empty glasses.

Lou ducked behind the bar and opened the door to chaos. Deb was stirring something on the stove with one hand and the other was stretching towards the handle on the door of the big walk-in fridge.

Lou darted for the fridge. 'Let me help. What do you need?'

'Thanks. I need butter. If I stop stirring, this will burn. It will also burn if I don't get more butter into the pan.'

'I've got it.' Lou opened the fridge door and grabbed the butter from its place on the top shelf. She put it down next to Deb and pulled off the top.

'Can you throw a slab of that in with the steaks?'

Lou did as she was asked. The butter sizzled immediately, sending a burst of steam that was sucked into the kitchen fan.

'Great. Those two plates over there—'

'With the corn and the baked potatoes?'

'Yep.'

Lou fetched the plates and with a skilful flick of her spatula, Deb dropped a steak on each.

'I don't suppose you could take these out for me? They're for the Davidsons. Ella and Pete. They're sitting over near the pool table.'

'They're the couple who came to the library earlier?'

'Yes. She has long brown hair.'

'No worries.'

Lou carried the plates out, deftly weaving between the tables. This she could do. All those weeks waitressing in her uni holidays had paid off in more than just wages.

'Thanks,' Ella said as she reached for her meal. 'And thanks for having the library out again. We've really missed it. Luca would be so happy to see it being cared for again.'

Lou nodded and headed back to the kitchen and Deb. 'Where's Jake?'

Deb opened the oven and pulled out a steaming dish of pasta. 'He went to Cessnock today for something. His car broke down and he's stuck. He's probably going to have to stay until the garage opens tomorrow.'

'That's left you shorthanded?'

'We always have a busy night on library days.'

'Jake probably didn't know it was a library day. We didn't discuss it.'

Deb paused for a moment in her whirlwind cooking. 'Is the truck still parked at the hall?'

'Yep.'

'It should be all right there. Shane can drive it back for you after the pub shuts, if you like.'

'That would be great. Thanks.' Lou hesitated. She should leave now and let Deb get on with her busy night. Or … 'Do you need a hand? I know about as much about pub cookery as I do about driving a truck, but I can deliver plates and wash up, at the very least.'

'Would you? That would be so helpful. Thank you.' Deb had both hands full so she nodded in the direction of a deep drawer under the counter. 'The burger rolls are in there. Could you pull out a couple and add the trimmings?'

'Sure.' Lou found the rolls and a knife and within a minute or two was happily adding lettuce, tomato and beetroot to the burgers.

'Thanks, Lou,' Shane said as she walked past him on her way to deliver the burgers. 'You are an angel.'

'No problem.'

And it wasn't. Lou was so busy, she didn't have time to worry about whether the pub patrons would raise the subject of Luca. She paused briefly to tie a bar towel around her waist as an apron, and then started darting between the kitchen and the bar and lounge, delivering meals and occasionally drinks. Her appearance with laden plates was usually greeted with a chorus of thank yous. As she cleared the empty plates away, people commented on the quality of the food. Some of her library customers talked about how good it was to have new books without driving all the way to Scone.

'Thanks for the recommendation. I've already started reading it and I love it.'

'Lou, can you tell Deb that her pie's even better than Jake's?'

'Are you working here now? Jake better be careful. He'll be out of a job, the way this lasagne tastes.'

'Well, it's actually one he prepared yesterday. But let's not tell him that.' The chat came easily to her now and she realised that the people in this pub, the people in this town, were no longer strangers to her. She might even call some of them friends.

Towards the end of the evening, when things had slowed down and everyone else had been fed, Deb filled two plates with fish and chips, and she and Lou sat down to eat.

'I can't thank you enough for your help,' Deb said between mouthfuls. 'It's made me realise how much we've come to rely on Jake.'

'I suppose it wasn't his fault his car broke down.'

'No. He's very reliable.'

'Well, I'm glad I was here to help.' Lou was about to tell Deb to call her any time, but she realised with shock that today she had run out of reasons to stay in Wagtail Ridge. There were no more letters. She had no clues that led to her father. It was time to move on with her life. She had never wanted to come to Wagtail Ridge, and now she was reluctant to leave it. She had enjoyed this evening so much. She had friends here and was beginning to feel settled in Luca's home. And there was Jake.

Those days on the road with Jake had been fun. And that dance. But even though she could now relax about their relationship, it wasn't enough to keep her here. She wasn't sure he would even care if she stayed, not after the tension of the past few days. And if she explained her suspicions about his father, he certainly wouldn't want her to stay. But she did have to tell him. She couldn't accuse him of lying to her by omission, then do the same to him.

Despite the emotional roller coaster of her quest, she had enjoyed her stay in Wagtail Ridge very much. She had always enjoyed living in the city, but was beginning to understand that those bits of the city she loved the most were the parts least like a city: the parks and the headlands overlooking the water. It seemed she might just be a country girl after all. She was beginning to feel totally at home here at Wagtail Ridge. Could love of place be inherited, like blonde hair or a truck filled with books?

Lou offered to stay to help clean up, or to watch the bar while Shane got something to eat, but Deb wouldn't hear of it.

'You get off home now. You've done more than enough. Why don't you come in later in the week when it's quiet and have dinner on me? Or maybe on Jake.'

As she walked out of the pub, Lou caught a glimpse of a ute parked behind the pub. Jake's ute. He'd obviously fixed it and driven the rest of the way home. Strange that he hadn't let Deb and Shane know he was here. Maybe he'd just arrived. She was about to turn around and go back, but changed her mind. The things she had to say to Jake should be said in private. She needed to apologise to him and tell him her search was over. Tomorrow would be soon enough for that.

She walked back to the hall where the library was parked. She had forgotten to leave the keys for Shane to drive it to the cottage. That's if Deb even remembered her offer. They'd had such a busy night. It was late and there were no other cars or even people in sight. Maybe she could get the library home? She wouldn't even try to park it in the shed, but it would be better outside her house than parked at a strange angle near the hall.

She unlocked the door and was reaching up to open it, when someone spoke behind her.

'You're not thinking of driving that, are you?'

She dropped back to the ground and turned around. The small spark of hope that it might be Jake was dashed. She'd seen this man before, but she wasn't sure exactly when.

'I'm not going to leave it here overnight.'

'You don't have a licence to drive it home, though, do you?'

He was right, but she was starting to feel a bit anxious. Who was he to question her?

Her concern must have shown in her face because he held up one hand in a reassuring manner. 'It's all right. I don't know if you remember me. We met briefly at the hall the other weekend. I'm Ken Matthews. Sergeant Ken Matthews?'

Relief coursed through her. 'You're the local policeman.'

'I am and I'm afraid if you try to drive that home, I might have to arrest you. So why don't I do it for you? That way not only is the library safe, but the town is as well.'

'You saw me drive up, didn't you?'

He nodded and pointed to a building almost directly opposite the hall. There was a rectangular blue and white sign out front.

Lou winced. 'Sorry. I was … um.'

'Don't say anything incriminating.' Sergeant Matthews grinned. 'Let's just say I'm doing my job by preventing an illegal act. Come on. Hand over those keys.'

She did and climbed up into the cab next to him. It took a few minutes for Sergeant Matthews to turn the truck and drive it to Lou's house, where he manoeuvred it into the shed with an ease that made her very glad she hadn't been tasked with doing it. He locked the truck and helped her pull the shed doors closed.

He handed her the keys. 'There you go. Now please don't ever do that again.'

'I won't. I promise. Thanks, sergeant.'

'Ken. I'm off duty. Good thing for you, too.' His smile took the sting out of the words.

'Can I drop you back home? In the car.'

'No thanks, Lou. I'll walk and enjoy the fresh air. Goodnight.'

'Goodnight. And thank you again … Ken.'

CHAPTER 36

Jake didn't want to answer his phone. Lou was calling him, and he wasn't ready to talk to her yet. He didn't know what to do with the knowledge he had. To tell her would be to break faith with Luca's wishes. To not tell her was tantamount to lying, and he'd promised himself—more importantly, he had promised Lou—he would never lie to her about this.

He let the call go through to voicemail.

He'd barely had time to take another mouthful of coffee when his phone rang again. He glanced at the number. This call he did take. He listened as he ate the last bit of toast. 'Yeah. Sure. I can leave in about fifteen minutes.'

He finished the call and his coffee at the same time and, as he washed his mug, began to plan his day. This unexpected request would take several hours, and he wanted to be sure he'd be back in time to work his shift at the pub tonight. His first stop would be the garage. He was confident there wouldn't be a repeat of yesterday's breakdown, but he needed petrol if he was going to drive all the way to Sydney. His apology to Deb last night had been waved off by both Shane and Deb. They'd managed with Lou's help, so everything was fine. He wondered what Deb would have said if she'd realised that he'd arrived home in time to work the tail end of the shift. He'd gone to the pub ready to do his job, but then he'd seen Lou through the windows. She seemed so happy, laughing with Deb as she washed dishes. That said a lot about her kindness and generosity of spirit. And it said a lot about his cowardice that he just couldn't face her. In fact, his decision to accept that second call arose from the same desire to avoid her. He still didn't know what he would say or do when he did see her. He had never been good at hiding his feelings. And he had no chance to hide anything from Lou. The connection between them was special. He felt it every time she looked at him. He understood it every time they kissed. With such a strong connection, she'd know the moment she saw him that something was wrong. She would know he was breaking his word to her, and this time she would be right.

Avoiding her was the coward's way out, but it was the best thing to do until he knew what to say. There'd be plenty of time to figure it out while he was on the road.

When he reached the garage, he pulled up to the bowser and began pumping petrol into his tank. Then he glanced up and his heart clenched. Lou was walking towards him. She was wearing jeans and some sort of top that clung to her body in all the right places. Her blonde hair shone so much in the early morning light it was almost blinding. As always, he felt that special pull that had been there since the day they'd met. But this time, for the first time, he didn't welcome it. He felt as if the world was hovering on the brink. If he did the wrong thing now, he would lose everything.

Lou raised her hand in greeting. It may have been chance that placed them in this unlikely place at the same time, but it was clear she wanted to make the most of it. He glanced at the petrol nozzle in his hand, wishing he'd filled the car last night in Cessnock. His world was spinning a little out of his control. Maybe now he was beginning to understand what Luca had felt. What Lou had felt too, and probably still was feeling. He was the man everyone came to when anything needed fixing—from a broken window in the hall to rails in the stockyards—yet he had no idea of how to fix these other things that he cared so much about.

He pressed harder on the handle of the nozzle, but nothing was going to make the petrol come out any faster.

'Hi, Jake.'

'Hi, Lou.'

'Glad you made it back. Deb told me you had car trouble yesterday, so I helped out last night at the pub.'

'Yeah. I know. I talked to Deb.'

'Did she tell you I had the library out yesterday—here in the Ridge?'

That was a surprise. 'No. Who—you didn't drive it, did you?'

'Yep.' She sounded almost proud of herself.

'You're lucky Ken Matthews didn't see you. He's the—'

'Local sergeant. I know. He did see me. But he kindly let me off with a warning and drove the truck home for me.'

'He's a good man.' That would have to be enough petrol. So far he'd escaped this conversation lightly but he had to get away before things got more complex.

'Deb had a letter from Luca.'

Too late.

He replaced the pump on the bowser. 'Sorry, I have to go pay for this.' He left Lou open-mouthed as he darted into the garage. If he'd hoped she would leave, he was wrong. She was leaning against his ute when he came back out again. Frowning.

'Jake, did you know Deb had a letter from Luca? All this time? A letter about my father.'

Jake froze. His problem was either about to be solved or get a whole lot worse. 'I thought she might, but it was only a guess because they were friends. Neither ever said anything to me.' He waited, hand on the door of his car. 'Did it tell you what you wanted to know? About your father?' If the answer was yes, his plans for the day would have to change drastically.

'No. Luca said she wanted me to know, but couldn't bring herself to tell me. Part of me hates her for that. I was happy when I didn't know about either of my biological parents. But now … now I want to know so much.' Lou's eyes started to mist up and Jake was lost. He wanted to take her in his arms and comfort her. He wanted to tell her everything. But it still felt like a betrayal.

'Lou. I'm sorry. So sorry …'

'I don't know where else to turn. I'll never know now.'

'I'm sorry, Lou. I really am. But … I have to go.' The wrong words, words that would change everything, were hovering on his lips and he had to get out of there before he spoke them.

He opened the door and got into the ute. 'I have to go to Sydney and I'm running late. I'll talk to you tomorrow. I promise.' He turned the ignition and pushed the accelerator to the floor. The ute moved away from the bowser at a dangerously high speed.

But staying would have been even more dangerous.

Lou took a step back, not because of the gravel flicked up by the spinning wheels of Jake's ute, but taken aback by his abrupt exit. She watched the car vanish down the road, heading south, and felt as if the ground under her was shaking. Why was he behaving like that? Now that his promise to his friend Luca was fulfilled, he obviously wanted nothing more to do with Lou. She had thought they had a connection, but she'd been wrong. She'd been wrong about so many things since she'd seen that solicitors' letter lying on the table of her parents' kitchen. How she wished she had never opened it.

Well, she'd had enough. She didn't give one hoot for Wagtail Ridge or anyone in it. She especially didn't give a hoot for Jake. As for Luca … well, she had never been a mother to her daughter, and nothing was going to happen now to change that. Lou was done.

She resisted the urge to raise her hand in a rude gesture at the tail-lights of Jake's ute, and instead walked in the direction of the real estate office. A couple of people greeted her, wanting to thank her for getting the library back in service. As she passed the store, Kelly appeared in the doorway.

'Good morning, Lou.'

'Hi.' She wasn't in the mood for casual chatter.

'It was lovely to see the library back and to have another town picnic like that. I've missed them.'

Lou smiled but kept walking.

'You know, your mother would have been so happy to see you do that. And even happier to see how much you were enjoying it. I'm so glad you've caught the Wagtail spirit.'

That stopped her. 'What do you mean, the Wagtail spirit?'

'It's a thing we say. That the town has a spirit all of its own, and once you've caught it, it never really lets you go. Isn't that right, Val?'

Lou hadn't noticed the postmistress arriving.

Val nodded vigorously. 'It sure is. Always has been. Your mother had it. I think that's why she stayed here all those years. Because she loved and needed this community just as much as we all loved and needed her.'

'That's nice.' It was a totally meaningless comment, but it was enough to offer Lou the chance to escape. She gave them a half wave and moved on, leaving the two women staring after her.

By the time she'd reached the real estate office, her temper had cooled, but not her resolve. She found Matt Ambrose already talking to a client. She nodded her understanding as he waved her to a waiting area at the side of the room. She wasn't the only one there. Vicki was curled up in one of the armchairs, her nose buried in the book she'd collected at the library the day before.

'Hello, Vicki.'

'Hello.'

'Are you enjoying the book?'

'Yes.'

'I'm glad. It's one of my favourite books too.'

'Did you read it when you were small?'

'I did, and guess what? It's at home waiting for me to read it again.'

'But you're grown up. This book is for kids.'

'Books like that are for everyone.' Across the office, the couple were taking their leave. Lou resisted the urge to hug the motherless little girl as she got to her feet.

'Thank you for your kindness to Vicki,' Matt said. 'It's been hard for her, for both of us, since we lost her mum.'

'I imagine it has been. I was very glad to help.'

'Having the library back in town has really made a difference. And not just to Vicki. Everyone is saying how much of a lift they got from the picnic. When are you doing it again? I don't know about anyone else, but Vicki reads fast. She never missed a visit when your mother did her weekly opening. Anyway, enough of that. How can I help you this morning?'

Lou cringed internally, knowing her words were going to spoil his day, and more importantly, Vicki's joy. 'I wanted to talk to you about selling the house.'

CHAPTER 37

The letters were the last thing to pack. They were lying on the kitchen table, neatly spread out to be read in order. And she had read them. Over and over again. As she did, she fingered the amethyst necklace she was wearing. There was nothing new on those pages. By now she knew every word of every one by heart, but she kept reading them in the hope that a word here, a phrase there, would trigger some memory. At last, she gave up and carefully folded them into a single envelope. Her first thought was that there was no point keeping them; there was nothing left for her to discover. She should throw them away because they would bring her nothing but more of the same heartache they had already caused. But she couldn't bring herself to do that. She placed the envelope into the suitcase of books she was planning to take back to Sydney. Her collection of Luca's photos was there too. It sat there next to the folder containing the solicitors' papers. The books stared up at her. *Blinky Bill. The Silver Brumby. The Thorn Birds.* Titles that chronicled both her past and her failure.

She glanced at the phone that remained steadfastly silent on the table. She hadn't heard a word from Jake since their encounter at the petrol station yesterday. That told her everything she needed to know. She'd spent the whole day packing and cleaning the house ready to lock it behind her when she walked out the door. The case of books was the last thing to go in the car. When she carried it out, it slotted neatly into the space she'd left for it on the back seat. Her little car was pretty well laden now. As well as the clothes she'd brought with her and the box of books, she had selected a few things from the house to keep. One of those was the beautiful blue shawl. Another was the little parcel with the baby booties and a lock of her hair. She really wasn't sure about those, but throwing them away seemed so final. Intellectually, she knew this voyage of discovery was over, but emotionally, she wasn't quite ready to let go of everything. Luca. The hope of finding her biological father. Jake.

Carefully lodged between other bits and pieces was the primrose she'd bought at the market. At last she would do what she had intended with that. She'd take it back to Sydney and give it to her mother. The quilt too. It was her way of letting Fiona know she was sorry for the uncertainty of the past few weeks, and that she was home for good.

Lou took one last look around the house. She hesitated in the living room. Her car keys lay on the coffee table. She had added the cottage keys with the cheap souvenir pineapple to the car keys ages ago. She had become used to that aged pineapple. She might keep that even when the house was sold. In the kitchen, she opened a cupboard and collected a couple of small enamel dishes. They would come in handy, particularly when she was camping. As she packed them, she remembered using them to cook dinner for Jake. Was there anything else she should keep?

No. She would not allow there to be anything else, because if there was, she'd stay another minute, and another hour and then another day. If she admitted to herself how much this little cottage had come to feel like home, how fond she had grown of this small town, then she might never leave. And she had to leave. There was nothing for her here.

She locked the door carefully behind her. After placing the last few items into her car, she walked down the side of the house, just as she had done on that first day. The big old shed was waiting for her, the library safe inside. But this time there was no puppy to greet her with a happy smile and a wagging tail. And there was no Jake.

She backed the loaded car out of the driveway, and paused long enough to firmly shut the gate with its fake wrought iron decorations. It was so familiar now, she wasn't sure if it was a memory from her childhood, or from the recent past. Not that it mattered any more.

She drove slowly through the town. She had left spare keys with the real estate agent, so there was no need to stop there. She should say goodbye to Deb, but calling later to explain would have to do. Deb would understand. She was Luca's friend. Maybe now she was Lou's friend too. The road leading to Jake's house didn't warrant so much as a glance, despite every fibre of her being telling her to turn and drive down there. She could at least try to patch things up before she left. But what difference would that make now she was leaving for good? She was so focussed on the thought, she didn't see the white wooden church until she was level with it. Her foot dropped on the brake and she pulled over next to the fence that surrounded the small cemetery.

This was one place she had never visited. She'd thought about it. Thought about Luca buried here, perhaps close to her own mother,

Christina. The graves of her family, whether she acknowledged them or not. She should at least visit them once before she left town. It would be a fitting end to her search.

Lou got out of the car, taking her shoulder bag and keys with her. She didn't lock the car, reminding herself that was one habit she'd have to get back into in Sydney.

The graveyard was incredibly peaceful. Someone obviously cared for it. The grass was neatly mowed and the fences painted. She wondered if Jake was responsible for that. It was the sort of thing he would do. Apart from a couple of angels carved from white stone, the graves were plain. Just simple headstones with dates and expressions of love. *Beloved wife … Much loved brother … Always remembered.*

She found them in the far corner, where a slight rise in the ground gave a view over the cemetery and the church to the town beyond. Both headstones were pale grey granite, although one was showing signs of age. She looked at that one first. *Christina, beloved mother of Luca.* Lou felt a gentle sadness for the grandmother she had never met. Another life unfairly cut short.

At last she found the courage to turn her attention to the next grave, and a headstone that had not been placed there by a loving daughter.

Luca Bonnet

Who loved one thing beyond all else.

Lou dropped to her knees and studied the headstone. She brushed away a couple of dried leaves that had fallen on it. There were no flowers, as there were on some of the other graves. No sign that anyone had ever placed flowers here for Luca, although surely Deb must have.

'I do wish I could remember you. Anything at all, really. Something to make you seem real to me.' She stroked the amethyst necklace that hung around her neck.

Her only answer was the rustle of the breeze in the gums that sheltered the small cemetery.

Surprisingly reluctant to leave, Lou settled into a comfortable position by the headstone and pulled a book from her bag. It was old, but had been treated with love. She opened it to the inscription.

To my darling daughter, with all my love. Mum.

She recognised the handwriting now. Luca had written those words to her daughter many, many years ago, before her heart had been broken. She turned the page, running her fingers gently and with much love down the illustration of the girl and her companion. Then she turned to the first words.

'Chapter 1,' she read softly out loud. 'Little Dot had lost her way in the bush. She knew it, and was very frightened …'

She paused for a moment, closed her eyes and listened. Surely now she would remember something. She would feel her mother's presence, or hear her voice.

But all she heard was the silence.

CHAPTER 38

Lou's car was gone. Jake didn't have to knock on the door, he could feel the warmth had left the cottage. He was too late. He started his car and drove to the pub. Ignoring his passenger, he raced into the bar.

'Deb. Do you know where Lou is?'

'No.' Deb emerged from behind the bar. 'Why? What's wrong?'

'I've made a mistake. I need to find her.'

'She's gone,' said a customer eating a burger at the bar. 'I was walking past Matt's place earlier and he was putting a new sign up in his window. That cottage Luca left to her. It's up for sale.'

The words almost ripped the ground out from underneath Jake.

'No. That can't be right.'

The man shrugged and returned to his burger.

Jake left the bar. He got back into his car, wondering how long ago Lou had left. Could he still catch her? His phone lay in the centre console, but that wasn't good enough. The things he needed to say had to be said face to face. And Lou had no reason to trust him, or do him any favours. Not after his behaviour at the service station. Not after the way he had manipulated her from the moment she arrived in town. Sure, he had reasons for his behaviour. But reasons did not excuse him. He would drive all the way to Sydney if he had to.

He kept driving along the road heading out of town. Then he saw Lou's car parked near the church. With a sigh of relief, he pulled up next to it. This time, he did stop long enough to collect his passenger.

The two of them walked through the gate and he instantly saw Lou. She was sitting by Luca's grave, her head in a book. He thought he could hear her voice in the stillness of the place. His companion definitely could. The pup pricked her ears and bounded away, her golden coat shining in the sunlight.

He watched as the retriever bounced up to Lou.

'Well, hello. Who might you be and what are you doing here?'

When she looked around and saw Jake, she smiled and his heart lifted.

He dropped to the grass beside her. 'I see you've met Hazel.'

'Is she another guide dog puppy?'

'Yes. She was supposed to go to someone else, but there was a problem, so they asked me to take her. That's where I was going yesterday.'

Lou ruffled the pup's ears. 'I'm sorry I said all those awful things to you when you took Ollie back.'

'Don't worry. I understand. When I was a kid and my parents gave back their first puppy, I said horrible things to them too. I saw Ollie when I went to pick Hazel up. He has a new owner, a teenage girl, and they're starting their training together.'

'That's nice to know. There's something—'

'No, wait. Please. I have spent the last twenty-four hours rehearsing what I'm about to say. Please … I need to get this right.'

She tilted her head to the side and nodded. 'All right.'

'You were right when you said I was doing all this because your mother asked me to. Luca was my friend, a woman I liked and admired. I wanted to keep my word to her.'

'I understand that.'

'I should have told you. Right from the start I should have been honest with you. I was manipulating you on her behalf. It seemed a reasonable request when she asked me to help you, but I didn't know then what I know now. I didn't know you. And … well, I'm sorry. I know you had a lot to deal with and I made it harder, not easier.'

'I'm not really sure if you did. It was never going to be easy.'

'I know, but it shouldn't have been that hard. I almost hate Luca for doing that to you.'

'I did for a while too, but I got past that. You will too. I know now that she truly loved me.'

'There's one more thing.'

'I'm listening.'

'When I saw that photo of Luca and my father, I had this terrible thought that maybe he and Luca … But I was wrong. My father didn't. He wouldn't. I feel ashamed for even thinking it. But for a while there …'

'You thought we were half-brother and sister?'

'Yes.'

'So did I. But I know now we're not. That is such a relief.'

She glanced up at him, and the joy in him almost exploded. He put a hand on her shoulder and pulled her towards him. He touched his lips to hers and kissed her, a long, slow kiss full of love and longing and promise.

'I'm so glad I don't have to think of you as my sister,' he said at last.

'Me too.'

'And I have a promise to keep to you too.'

'A promise?'

'I promised I would never lie to you. Or not tell you something you need to know. Especially about your father.'

'It's no good, Jake. I've read her last letter. She didn't tell me who my father is. I can't think of anything else I can do to find him. That's why I was leaving.'

'Was?' A little hope flared deep inside him.

'Was. I came here hoping I might remember Luca. Any small memory. But I don't think I ever will. I can accept that now. I can let go of the anger I felt when that letter arrived from the lawyers, thrusting her back into my life. I know that she just wanted me to know who she was. I'm starting to know her now, and I want to know more. I'm going to stay here and run the library, at least for a while. I'm finally beginning to feel more at home here and I want to give that feeling a chance to grow. And I'm getting to know the part of me that is Luca's daughter better too. I think she could—I could—be happy here.'

He saw the tears shining in her eyes. 'I'm happy for you. And for me too. I hated the thought of you leaving.' As his fingers intertwined with hers, he knew what he had to do.

'I may not have the memories, but in some way, I have got her back, Jake. The house. The library. Wagtail Ridge and all the people. You. Even Val. You have all given my mother back to me and that is the greatest gift. My mum, Fiona, told me that my birth mother had asked for a clean break. I thought I was okay with that, but I'm so much happier now I know her.'

'So tell me, if you could find out who your father was, would you want to know?'

'Yes.' There was not a moment's hesitation. 'My father? Do you know?'

He nodded as hope lit her face. 'Yes. That's why I couldn't face you at the petrol station. I'd only found out the day before, and I didn't know how to handle it, because I was not going to lie to you—ever again. And I didn't know if you would want to meet him.'

'Meet him? I could meet him?'

Jake nodded.

'And you're sure he's my father?'

'I'm not completely sure, but I think so. I haven't talked to him about you or Luca. It wasn't my place to do that.'

'When can we see him?'

'How about now?'

She leaped to her feet and gathered her things. Hazel came running back from wherever she had been exploring, and barked her eagerness to get underway.

Before they left, Jake looked down on Luca's grave. 'I'm doing the right thing,' he told his friend. 'I'm sorry you and Lou never got to know each other properly and I won't let that happen to her again. She deserves to know him.'

There was no answer, just the rustling of the breeze in the gums, but deep inside, Jake knew that if she could, Luca would give her blessing to the journey ahead.

They didn't talk much as they drove, but that didn't matter. Hazel sat between them in the front of the ute, just as Ollie had done. Lou had left her car at her house. She wasn't going to need it today. Or possibly even tomorrow. She was excited and a little afraid of what waited for her at Cessnock, but whatever happened, she wasn't driving back to Sydney any time soon. Or rather, she was, but only to tell her parents what had happened, and to pack what she needed for a more permanent stay at Wagtail Ridge.

It was late morning by the time Jake pulled up opposite the artists' collective.

'His name is Adam Lassiter. I know he made that necklace you're wearing and I think he gave it to Luca. He told me he would be at the shop all week. Are you sure you want to do this?'

She nodded.

'Okay. Hazel and I will wait for you in that coffee shop, unless you want me to come with you.'

'Thanks. This is something I have to do alone, but it helps to know you're near.' Lou curled her fingers around his hand and squeezed, taking comfort in the strength she felt in him.

She got out of the car and walked across the road. Standing outside the shop, and pretending to look at the displays in the window, her heart thumped so loudly she was sure everyone for ten miles would hear it. As she took deep breaths, seeking a modicum of calm, she spotted a black velvet case. It contained a necklace and earrings. The necklace was green jade, but the silver work around it reminded her of the pendant she was wearing. Then she saw a shape inside the shop, moving towards the door.

She pulled the collar of her shirt closed to cover the necklace as the door opened and a man came out.

She guessed he was in his fifties. He was taller than her, with sandy hair. He was carrying an advertising stand, which he placed on the footpath. When he looked at her, it was like looking into her own brown eyes. Lou could barely breathe.

'Can I help you?'

'Hello. I was just—' She stopped. What could she say? *I think you are my father?* How do you tell a total stranger that you are his daughter? She shuffled her feet and as she did, the neck of her shirt fell open. Instinctively she raised a hand to cover the necklace, but he'd already seen it. She could see the shock in his eyes.

'That necklace?'

'Yes. I wanted to ask, did you make it?' She wasn't sure if it was the right question to ask, but she couldn't just stand there staring at him.

'Yes. I did. It was a long time ago.' His voice sounded wistful.

'Did you sell it to someone?'

'No.' He studied her face, closely. Then his eyes met hers and she thought she could read the question there. 'I gave it to someone. Someone I … cared for very much.'

'You gave it to Luca Bonnet?'

'Yes. When I first saw you I was shocked, because you look a lot like her. You're probably about the same age she was when we knew each other.'

There would never be a better opportunity to say what she had come to say. 'There's a reason for that. I'm Luca's daughter.'

He froze, and when he finally spoke, she could hear the effort he was making to keep his voice calm. 'Oh. Does she live around here? I lost touch with her a long time ago. It would be nice to see her again.'

She saw the emotion flickering in his eyes. If she had doubted his love for her mother, she wouldn't again. She dreaded the words she was about to say. 'I'm sorry. My mother died a few months ago.'

His eyes closed and he took a long breath as if trying to bring his emotions under control. When he opened his eyes again, she could see his genuine grief. 'I'm so sorry to hear that. My condolences. Luca was a special person.'

'Yes. She was. She always thought of others before herself. She gave me up for adoption when I was very small, because she didn't think she would be able to give me the life she wanted for me.'

His face changed. She wasn't sure if what she saw there was simple understanding or hope. 'Your father …'

'She never told my father about me. They spent such a short time together. He was married and his wife was suffering and needed him. She understood that he would never leave his wife, and she didn't want to add to his burden.' The tears Lou felt on her cheeks reflected the ones in her father's eyes.

'My name is Adam Lassiter. My wife is gone now. I'm alone.'

'My name is Lou Taylor, and you are not alone. Neither of us is.'

'Have you got time to come inside? Would you like to talk?'

Lou nodded. 'Yes. Very much.'

He stood back and held the door open for her to go in.

Across the road, Jake saw the closed sign go up on the shop window. He smiled and looked down at Hazel.

'I think we'll be here for a while. Let's go for a walk, shall we?' He attached a lead to the dog's collar and they got out of the car.

Hazel jumped up and down a couple of times and started to strain against the lead but Jake held it firmly.

'Not like that, Hazel.' The pup turned her head and grinned at him. 'That's a good dog. The first thing you need to understand is patience. We all need patience. Some things we need to wait for, but they're worth it in the end.'

EPILOGUE

Three Months Later

Something of a party atmosphere hung over the old corrugated iron hall and the open area next to it. Almost the entire population of Wagtail Ridge was there, as well as a goodly gathering of people from the nearby properties. Jake was busy tying streamers and bunting to the trees around the picnic tables. Hazel was watching over the kids on the new equipment that had been installed in what was now known as Luca's playground. Adam Lassiter was responsible for that, and at this moment, he was helping set up the barbecue near the picnic tables. Shane and Deb Fraser were unpacking food and drinks from their car and adding them to the already laden tables.

A car appeared at the end of the street, moving slowly towards the activities as if the driver wasn't entirely sure where they were going. Jake left the rest of the bunting to others and waved to the driver, guiding them into a parking place under the shade of a tree.

'Hi, nice to see you again.' He held out his hand as Richard Taylor got out of the car.

Richard shook Jake's hand, but Fiona didn't hesitate to throw her arms around Jake when she reached his side of the car. 'It's so good to see you again too.'

Jake hugged her right back. They'd only met twice, once when he'd helped Lou move more of her things from her parents' house to the cottage in Wagtail Ridge, and once more when they'd visited for a weekend.

'She's not here yet?'

'No. She texted to say she was on her way back. It shouldn't be too long now.'

'We brought these.' Fiona opened the back door of their car to reveal boxes of food and a bunch of balloons.

'Are your family here yet?' Richard asked. 'I'm looking forward to meeting them.'

Jake spotted another car approaching. 'Here they are. Right on cue.'

Jake's parents had also come bearing gifts.

'We did a bit of a book drive at school,' Wendy said. 'There are a couple of boxes in the back. Textbooks. Some sheet music and about twenty copies of *Summer of the Seventeenth Doll.* Our school did a production of it last year and the kids really enjoyed it. I thought they might be useful to one of your schools.'

'Thanks, Mum. If you come with me, I'll introduce you to Lou's mum and dad.'

Wendy and Russ had already met Adam, but this was their first time meeting Lou's adoptive parents. Jake left them to it after a couple of minutes. It was clear the four of them were going to get on just fine.

Adam had finished his decorating and was now pacing a little nervously. 'Jake, are you sure she doesn't know?'

'I'm sure. When she left this morning, she was so excited about doing her first solo run she wasn't thinking about anything else.'

Adam nodded, and checked his watch again.

'My folks have just arrived. You should go and say hi while you wait,' Jake said.

'I will. Who's that they're talking to?'

'Richard and Fiona Taylor. Lou's adoptive parents.'

Adam stopped in his tracks.

'They're good people, Adam. And they're looking forward to meeting you.' Jake could almost feel the man beside him gathering his courage as they approached the small group still chatting by the cars.

'Richard. Fiona,' Jake said gently. 'I'd like you to meet Adam Lassiter.'

Jake saw the understanding flash into Fiona's eyes. She stepped forward and kissed Adam on the cheek.

'I have been looking forward to meeting you,' she said. 'Lou has told us so much about you, we feel like we know you already.'

Adam held out his hand to Richard, and when he spoke, his voice quivered. 'I want to say thank you. Lou is the most wonderful young woman, and that's all due to the two of you. You gave her such a good home, and taught her … well, everything I couldn't.'

'I'm sorry you missed so much of her life. I hope you know that we would have welcomed you, had we known.'

Adam nodded, too full of emotion to speak.

'And now we are all part of Lou's family. That's the important thing.' Fiona's eyes shone with tears. 'And that means you too, Jake. We owe all this to you.' The look she cast him made Jake blush. Luckily, he was saved by the somewhat boisterous arrival of Hazel, a small girl in hot pursuit.

'Hazel. Settle down, girl.' Jake clicked his fingers and the dog trotted to his side and sat, staring up at him with big brown eyes, her tongue lolling happily from the side of her mouth.

'When is she going to be here, Uncle Jake?' the little girl asked.

'Soon, Vicki. Now, you just be a bit careful when you play with Hazel. We don't want her running out in the road, do we? She might get hurt.'

Vicki's brown creased as she considered that. 'All right.'

'After all the running around, Hazel might be thirsty. Do you know where the tap is at the back of the hall? The one with the tub for the dogs to drink out of?'

Vicki nodded.

'Why don't you take Hazel there and see if she wants a drink?'

'Okay. Come on, Hazel.' Vicki tugged the dog's collar. Hazel glanced up at Jake, who gave a tiny wave with one hand, after which she stood up and followed her friend.

'That dog's learning fast,' his father commented. 'She'll be a good one.'

Jake agreed, but his attention was focussed on the road—surely it wouldn't be long now?

The music following the library truck along the road was a bit of classic John Denver with an overlay of a moderately in-tune female voice—one that only missed one of the high notes in 'Take Me Home, Country Roads'. Behind the wheel, Lou was smiling as she sang. The seat beside her was empty and she kinda missed Jake after so many weeks of driving with him, but she'd loved every minute of this first solo trip. It had been a big step.

Today she had visited a new town and met a new group of people. She hadn't had a lot of customers, but what they lacked in numbers they had more than made up for in enthusiasm. One young mother with a new baby in a pram was almost in tears as she thanked Lou for coming. The library books, she said, would be a lifeline in the long, sleepless nights with a restless baby. Lou had also delivered a box of scraps of material collected in the other towns for a quilting project at the town's single-teacher school. And, as at every stop, more books appeared. Pre-loved books that were ready to take a place on the library shelf.

She sometimes felt overwhelmed by the generosity of the people in her towns, for that's how she thought of them now. Her towns. She was following the same route Luca—her mother—had always followed. And there were other communities out there that she had contacted about adding to her route. If she was passing by, there was no reason at all not to pull over, let down the steps and open the doors for more people to explore the world waiting on the library's shelves.

There had been no letter from her mother waiting to be collected today, but she no longer expected those. She knew everything her mother had wanted to say, and those nine letters were sitting inside a box on the bookshelves of the cottage in Wagtail Ridge that was now Lou's home.

Her singing got just a little bit louder as Wagtail Ridge came into sight. She eased back on the accelerator as she approached the church and its small cemetery. As always, she gave a mental wave to the women buried there.

'Thank you,' she whispered as she drove on past and the pub came into sight. She blinked twice as she read the words on the banner that was swaying gently outside the pub.

Wagtail Ridge Mobile Library—this way. The arrow was big and purple and pretty hard to miss.

What was going on?

She slowed even more as she drew level with the banner. It was bright and cheerful and she loved it. She assumed it had been made for her—or rather for the library. It was a great idea and would come in useful as she expanded the library's route. It was the sort of thing Jake would do. Her heart gave a little skip. Jake wasn't the reason she'd decided to stay in the Ridge and run her mother's library, but he was a contributing factor. Him and his lovely smile and his broad shoulders and his kindness.

The arrow on the banner pointed down the street to her left and as she looked she saw a flurry of activity near the hall. Lots of people and—were those balloons? There was nothing for it but to investigate. Even though there were no other vehicles on the road, she flicked her indicator on. Her driving teacher had been tough and the habit was totally ingrained in her.

As she approached the hall, people started assembling near the library's usual parking spot. A few kids even left the swings in her mother's playground to wave and cheer as she parked the library. She turned the engine off and pulled on the handbrake. When she opened the door, the first face that greeted her was Jake's. His smile was matched by that of Vicki Ambrose, balanced on his shoulders. The haunted look was almost gone from the little girl's eyes now. She no longer clung to her father, who Lou saw some distance away, tending to a barbecue. The library had changed Vicki's life almost as much as it had changed Lou's. Close behind Jake, Lou saw her parents standing next to her father. She hadn't exactly been delaying their meeting, but uncertainty had not encouraged her to push for it. Now it was done, and from the looks on their faces, done well.

She jumped down from the cab of the truck and lifted her face for Jake's kiss. Her friends and family cheered.

'Was the party your idea?' she whispered.

'No. Deb is the mastermind here.'

She would thank Deb first chance she got, but there was business to attend to. She turned to the library, flung the door open and lowered the steps into place.

'The library is now open!'

There was another cheer as customers started gathering at the bottom of the stairs.

The library visit was as enjoyable as ever, if perhaps a little more boisterous because of the party. When the last visitor had left, books in hand, a small face appeared once more in the doorway.

'Hello, Vicki. Did you want another book? You can't have read that one already.'

Vicki shook her head. 'Can we read together?'

Lou nodded. 'I'd love to read with you. Why don't you wait there, and I'll be with you as soon as I've tidied everything up here?'

With a nod, Vicki vanished.

A few minutes later, Lou emerged from the library to find Vicki happily settled on the bottom step, her book on her knees.

Lou dropped down beside her. 'Where are you up to?'

'Dot has just eaten the berries, so she can talk to the animals now.'

'Of course. I remember that bit. Why don't you read it to me, while I just sit here and listen?'

'All right.'

Lou closed her eyes. In the background, she could hear people talking around the picnic tables, and kids squealing and laughing in Luca's playground. The noise seemed to fade, leaving only her and the little girl by her side.

As Vicki read, Lou could almost hear, somewhere in the distance, a woman softly speaking the same words, in a voice so very like her own. Tears pricked her eyes, and as she opened them, she looked up. For a moment she thought she saw a figure silhouetted against the setting sun. A woman smaller than Lou herself, and older, but with the same blonde hair and the same way of tilting her head to one side. She was wearing a colourful shirt under a pair of dungarees and an amethyst pendant glinted at her neck. She looked happy. The woman smiled and her lips moved.

A tiny zephyr teased Lou's face like a butterfly kiss, bringing with it the scent of a familiar yet unknown flower, and Lou heard her mother whisper her name.

ACKNOWLEDGEMENTS

I remember how excited I used to get on the day the Mobile Library pulled up opposite the tiny group of shops near where I lived. That library and the librarians who ran it sent me on so many journeys full of wonder. Libraries are a treasure, and I urge everyone to do what they can to support them before they are lost to us forever.

I loved writing Lou's story. Her world was a joyful place to be when much of the world was struggling. At a time when we were not able to meet in person, online chats with the wonderful women of the Naughty Kitchen and the equally wonderful Quayistas kept me going. Thank you all.

I write the stories—but this beautiful book you hold in your hands is the work of the incredibly dedicated and talented editorial team and HarperCollins. Thank you all—particularly Christine Armstrong who put the Willy Wagtail on the W on the cover. I still smile when I see it. I may have to write more Wagtail Ridge books just to get him back again.

As always, thank you to my agent Julia Silk, who looks after most of the real publishing world while I live in the worlds I create.

I never quite know what to say about the amazing support I get from my husband John—I guess 'I love you' will have to do.

And dear readers—I love you all too. For without you these stories of mine would have no purpose.

Janet

PROLOGUE

Nyringa, New South Wales
Spring, 1956

Alice gave a twirl as she closed the wooden gate behind her and turned towards the centre of town. Her grandmother's welcome cake had been safely delivered to the new teacher and now she was free for the rest of this special day. The circus was coming to town for the first time ever and she didn't want to miss any of the excitement. She started walking more quickly. Wayne was going to be there too, and they'd watch the parade together. Afterwards they might slip down to that spot by the creek. That thought was enough to send a little tingle through her. Granny didn't hold with fifteen-year-old girls having boyfriends, but Alice was almost sixteen, and Wayne *was* her boyfriend. They'd been going steady now for nearly three months. Yesterday he'd slipped his hand under her blouse while they were making out down by the creek. She'd told him off of course, because she didn't want to seem easy or a tramp like that Suzie at school—Suzie went with anyone and girls like that never got married. But next time Wayne was with her down by the creek, Alice would let him touch her breasts. Maybe even today. After the parade, though. She'd never seen a circus before.

Alice was determined to find a place at the front so she could see the parade up close. According to Granny, Nyringa was going to be more crowded today than ever before in the town's history, and Granny would know because she was ancient and had lived in this boring little town forever. Then tomorrow, the circus was going to do a show. She'd go with Wayne and wear the new yellow dress her mum had made for her. She'd talked her mother into taking the hem up another couple of inches, and she wanted to see what Wayne did when he saw her in it.

Alice heard a low rumble of noise coming from the main street, and then a cheer went up. The circus must be here already. She was late. She broke into a run and sprinted along the last row of houses, past the car park at the back of the store and into the crowd lining the main street, where the highway passed straight through the centre of town. Her mouth dropped open and she skidded to a stop.

Elephants! There were elephants in Nyringa.

They were big and grey and slow, swinging their trunks as they walked. Their skin looked like old leather, and their eyes seemed too small for such a big animal. Their feet though … their feet were huge. Imagine if one of them stood on you! All four creatures were adorned with brightly coloured headpieces and a man sat on each one, waving to the crowd. Alice waved back as she pushed her way forward. Her friend Martha had been to the cinema once in Newcastle. She'd seen a film with elephants in it and bragged about it for weeks. But this was better. These elephants were real! And they were so big! Alice felt a tiny frisson of fear that was exciting in its own way.

'Alice!' Wayne appeared next to her and grabbed her hand. He looked down at her, his whole face alive with excitement. 'Aren't they great?'

She nodded, too tongue-tied by everything to speak.

'Look, Alice. Look at the jugglers.'

Men wearing embroidered white shirts moved along the edge of the crowd, tossing small balls into the air with speed and precision and never dropping a single one.

'I could do that.'

The nearest juggler heard Wayne's words.

'Here you go, kid.' The man threw him a ball. 'Now try two. Like this.' The juggler tossed two balls into the air and kept them aloft with just one hand. He wasn't even really looking as he did it.

'Sure.' Wayne threw a ball in the air. Then a second. He caught one but the other bounced at his feet. The juggler swooped in to catch it with one hand and added it to his one-handed display.

'Good try, kid.' The juggler took the second ball from Wayne's hand and moved on.

'I would have done it next time,' Wayne muttered.

'Of course you would.' Alice took hold of his hand again and squeezed it. Wayne laced his fingers through hers and smiled down at her. For a moment Alice forgot the elephants and saw a future in which she and Wayne left Nyringa behind for good, and went out into the world. They would marry and have children one day, of course, but not before they had explored the whole world.

'Look, here come the horses!'

Alice followed Wayne's pointing finger. She loved horses. Most of the other girls in her class lived on farms and had their own ponies and horses. Living in town, Alice didn't have a pony. Every year since she was small she'd asked her parents for one for her birthday and for Christmas, but they never listened. The horses coming towards her were more beautiful than any she'd seen on the farms around Nyringa. They were all grey, with soft white manes and tails. Their harness glinted with silver as they tossed their heads. They didn't seem at all disturbed by the cheering people lining the street.

Then Alice saw the girl sitting sideways on the back of the lead horse. She was dressed in a tight pink costume like a bikini and a tiny skirt covered in sequins. She was wearing white ballet slippers and tights. There were jewels in her wavy blonde hair and dark mascara and shadow on her eyes, making her look very exotic. Granny would not have approved. As Alice watched, the girl stood on her horse's back and opened her arms to the crowd, who cheered loudly. Beside Alice, Wayne was cheering loudest of all. His eyes were shining and his attention was now entirely on the girl. He was ignoring everything else around him, including Alice. His fingers loosened in hers and their hands fell apart as he moved to get a better look at the girl on the horse, who suddenly leaped into the air in a graceful move that was almost like ballet, landing again on the horse without so much as a stumble. All around Alice, the crowd gasped and cheered even louder.

'The parade is nearly over.' Alice grabbed Wayne's hand and tugged at it. 'I have to get back soon. Why don't we go down to the creek and sit for a while?' She opened her eyes really wide and looked up at him through her eyelashes, because that's what the actresses did in the films, and everyone thought they were so sexy. Right now, Alice wanted to be sexy more than anything else in the world.

'I want to follow the parade,' Wayne said. 'I'll see you later.'

Never taking his eyes off the girl on the white horse, Wayne again pulled his hand away from hers and began to follow the parade.

Alice looked down at her empty hand. How could Wayne just leave her like that?

She felt a strange pain in her chest, like nothing she had ever felt before. It felt as if her heart was breaking.

CHAPTER 1

'The classroom layout is very different, as you can see, Miss Walker. It works better this way with the age range.'

Meg nodded. Everything about this school was different from the places she'd taught in Sydney. The desks were arranged in small squares, there wasn't a computer to be seen and the view outside the windows was just the dry yellow grass of a big oval surrounded by tall gum trees. The whole school was a single wooden building containing three classrooms, only two of which were being used for classes; the third was a combination store room and staff room. There was no library, gym or assembly hall. There were no lockers for the students, nor was there a lockable cabinet for the teacher. The gate she'd passed through when this tour began was only waist height and there were no security cameras. She wasn't sure if that was a good sign or a cause for concern. This place was about as far as she could get from the inner-city schools she'd previously taught at. The schools where she had discovered her love of teaching—and then lost it again.

'Each group of tables represents a class year. You have grades seven to twelve. A lot of the older kids go off to boarding school, if their parents can afford it, so the groups are quite small,' Meg's tour guide said. 'I have quite a few more kids in the primary classroom.'

Meg nodded again. Her new colleague Anna was doing everything she could to make her feel at home. But she no longer felt at home in the classroom and wondered if she ever would again. This two-teacher school was very different to anywhere she'd taught before, but that wasn't what she was struggling with. She tugged the right sleeve of her blouse down over her wrist as she told herself everything would be different this time. The Nyringa school had about forty pupils split between primary and secondary classes. As she was taking the senior classes, she was, in effect, the headmistress of this tiny institution. She wasn't sure if she wanted the title, but she did want the job.

'We're so lucky you could join us for this term on such short notice, Miss Walker.' Anna beamed. 'Your predecessor left quite suddenly. Family matters.'

'Please, call me Meg. Tell me about the kids.'

'You must call me Anna. Some of our kids are from here in town but most are from nearby properties. There's a bus run every morning and afternoon that brings those kids in and takes them home. Attendance is good—there's not exactly much to tempt the kids to play truant around here.'

'I guess not.' Meg hadn't seen much of the town yet, she'd only arrived an hour ago. She had a couple of days to settle in and, on Monday, she would be standing in front of students again. She took another glance around the room, and it occurred to her that, as she moved between the desks, her back would be turned to one group while she attended to another. She felt her stomach churn and fought down her reaction. It would be fine. She could make it work. She had to. Because if she couldn't teach here, she would never teach anywhere, ever again. And if she couldn't teach, she didn't know what she would do.

'Perhaps we should go to the cottage now,' Meg said quickly. She'd come back to the classroom tomorrow and spend some time here alone. She could maybe change a few things or add some personal touches to make it seem like she belonged. To make it feel as though this was a safe place. But right now she needed to be somewhere else, where the screams in her head were not so loud and she could breathe again.

'Yes, of course.' The other teacher waved her hands around. 'How stupid of me. You must be tired and you'll want to settle in. All this could have waited until tomorrow.'

'It's fine, honestly. It's good to get a feel for the school.'

'Come on. I have the keys to the cottage.'

The school teacher's cottage was tucked away in a corner of the school grounds, set well back from the classrooms. It was one of those small wooden houses so common in towns like this. Set on stumps, it had the tiniest veranda and a peaked iron roof. It didn't have a garden worth the name, just a few native bushes and a sparse area of what might be called lawn in a better year, if one was being generous. One narrow gate led to the schoolyard and a second larger gate to the road. Meg's car, packed with cardboard boxes and suitcases, was parked in the driveway. Meg followed Anna up the short flight of stairs to the solid-looking front door.

'This lock is a bit tough,' Anna said. 'We probably should get someone to come and take a look at it. To be honest, around here a lot of people don't both too much about locking their doors.' She was so busy fighting with the lock, she didn't notice the way Meg tensed at her words.

At last, the door swung open. Meg stepped into a large, pleasant room. One window looked towards the school, the other towards a line of trees that Meg guessed was the creek shown on the town map she'd printed from Google. The room was furnished with a large sofa, bookshelves and a coffee table. There was even a television. In the middle of the ceiling, a fan awaited the start of the really hot weather. On the other side of the room was a small kitchen with a breakfast bar. It looked quite modern. Through the open door at the back of the room she could see a small hallway. That would lead to the bedroom, bathroom and laundry.

'I hope this will be all right for you,' Anna said hesitantly. 'I guess compared to what you had in the city, it's a bit …'

'No. No. It's fine. Thank you,' Meg assured her. And it really was fine. The last thing she wanted was a place that in any way reminded her of the city and what had happened there. 'Thank you so much. I guess I should start getting settled in.'

'Yes. Of course. It's just so nice to have a new person to talk to. You know where the shop is, right? You must have seen it as you drove in. But if you find yourself stuck, we live just a couple of streets away. You have my number. If there's anything I can do …'

'Thank you. That's very kind of you.' Meg held out her hand for the keys.

'Yes. Well …' Anna handed over the keys and, with many more offers of help, left.

Meg closed the door behind her with a sigh. She leaned against it for a few seconds, then spun and turned the key in the lock. Then she checked the rest of the house. The windows all had old but functioning locks. So did the back door. Like the kitchen, the bathroom appeared to have been recently refurbished. She looked at the double bed in the bedroom and told herself things would be different here. She would sleep well in that big, comfortable-looking bed.

She heard the distant cry of a crow and glanced at the window. It was already late afternoon. She needed to bring her things inside and then she'd have to do some shopping at the store. If she got to work now, she should have it all done before dark. She could ring her parents back home in Sydney, and unpack her boxes and suitcases after that—when she was safely inside and the doors were locked.

talk about it

Let's talk about books.

Join the conversation:

facebook.com/harlequinaustralia

@harlequinaus

@harlequinaus

harpercollins.com.au/hq

If you love reading and want to know about our authors and titles, then let's talk about it.